## PRAISE FOR JAMES PATRICK KELLY AND
### *LOOK INTO THE SUN*

"In LOOK INTO THE SUN, James Patrick Kelly stalks science fiction's grandest game, the intelligent alien."
                                —*New York Times Book Review*

"A vivid and moving tale of betrayal, transformation and transcendence. I loved it."

                                —Kim Stanley Robinson,
                                author of THE GOLD COAST

"Jim Kelly has been a well-kept secret in this field for too long. LOOK INTO THE SUN delivers everything a science fiction book is supposed to deliver: engrossing characters, well-wrought speculation, mystery, surprises, strangeness. You should read it."

                                —John Kessel

"Reads like a classic Heinlein novel that's been ripped apart, juggled, and slammed back together by a smart architect's powerful cyber-design program. Very strange indeed, and weirdly effective."

                                —Bruce Sterling

LOOK INTO THE SUN is a brilliant novel which recalls the wonder of Ursula K. Le Guin's THE LEFT HAND OF DARKNESS, and may well take a place beside it.

# LOOK INTO THE SUN

## JAMES PATRICK KELLY

A TOM DOHERTY ASSOCIATES BOOK
NEW YORK

LOOK INTO THE SUN

Copyright © 1989 by James Patrick Kelly

A TOR Book
Published by Tom Doherty Associates, Inc.
49 West 24 Street
New York, NY 10010

Cover art by Royo

ISBN: 0-812-54293-2     Can. ISBN: 0-812-54294-0

Library of Congress Catalog Card Number: 88-34683

First edition: April 1989
First mass market edition: February 1990

Printed in the United States of America

0  9  8  7  6  5  4  3  2  1

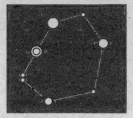

**T**he goddess screamed.

Harumen twitched upright in bed. There was a moment of icy silence; the darkness itself seemed to throb as she strained to hear. Then Teaqua screamed again. Although the heavy door to the sanctum muffled the sound, the others in bed with Harumen roused, uncoiling from uneasy sleep. She could smell their fear—and her own: a copper tang crawled up the back of her throat. Someone clutched at her. It was unnerving to hear the ruler of the world crying out in the night like some frightened animal.

Harumen was Teaqua's favorite, so she climbed over bodies and slipped from the common bed. It was not the first time the goddess had woken them like this. Harumen listened for a moment at the door, then rapped a knuckle against the wood.

"Teaqua?"

Something was wrong. "*No*. Tired." The goddess spoke in a frantic singsong. "Too *long*." She did not think Teaqua was talking to her.

Harumen lifted one bare foot and then the other off the cold stone floor. She could not decide what to do. In her opinion the goddess should not be sleeping alone; she should be out here in bed with her lovers. And not only was she sleeping alone, she had not shared pleasure with any of them in months. It was unnatural. No wonder she had strange dreams. Harumen gathered her courage and opened the door.

Teaqua was wrestling with the darkness. She writhed on her pallet like someone being crushed by a great weight.

"Teaqua?"

She was getting old. The old heard their whispers more often and sometimes saw things that did not exist. Soon it would be time for Teaqua to be reborn.

Harumen crouched beside her. "*Teaqua*." She wished she could be anywhere else but here, watching Teaqua suffer. As the goddess pitched forward, Harumen caught her by the shoulders. Teaqua moaned, tried to tear free and then slumped back as if she had been released from a stranglehold. "You were dreaming," Harumen said softly. She stroked the down on Teaqua's face. "Now wake up." A silver thread of spittle dangled from the corner of her mouth. Harumen daubed at it with her finger.

"It's dark." Teaqua said nothing for a moment as she came to herself. "Chan spoke to me again."

"A dream." Harumen was embarrassed. She knew the others were listening. There was no way to hush this up. It hurt her to hear Teaqua babbling about Chan. As if a star could talk.

"The sun spoke. The room was full of light."

Teaqua had been sleeping badly of late but had never seemed quite this crazy before. She used to say that her divinity was a metaphor for power. She had long since stopped taking it literally and so had her bedmates. At night they had mocked the credulous priests and discussed the truths as if they were bad poetry. Of course, Teaqua had explained, it was still necessary to play god for the masses. The people's belief in the sun and their goddess held the thearchy together; it could only be dismantled over time and with care. Teaqua's hints of sweeping changes had drawn them all into an irresistible conspiracy. She had been the smartest, the sanest, by far the strongest person Harumen knew. Now she was crumbling.

Teaqua wrinkled her snout. "I could smell his breath." She flagged terror, her head thrashing against the pillow.

Harumen could imagine what the messengers would think. They would look down at this backward little world from their starships and they would laugh. It was absurd. Teaqua herself depended on messenger technology to reach the people; Teaqua was the one who had encouraged Harumen to learn from them. The whispers of the god were hallucinations; there was proof. Chan was unscientific.

"You're upset." She tried to smooth the erect hair along Teaqua's shoulders. "Come back to bed with us." Harumen could never worship the sun. Not anymore. She might as well bow down to the wind or pray to the glaciers.

"He showed me a terrible truth." Teaqua gripped Harumen's wrist. "I won't be reborn. The god has chosen a different path for me."

In the next room someone chittered nervously; Harumen wanted to slap the idiot. Luckily the others rushed to quiet him. Harumen stared at Teaqua, her feelings in a whirlwind. She loved Teaqua, pitied her suffering, but Harumen was angry too. Teaqua had promised her a revolution. If this madness continued, she would destroy everything. Teaqua had to be reborn or else whispers would drag her—and perhaps the whole world—back into superstition. The goddess had to be reborn or she would die.

"We'll have to tell them. All of them, everyone. Chan has showed me my death."

Harumen did not know what to say, how to react. This was disaster of historic proportions. The realization twisted her perspective. She felt removed from herself, as if it were someone else who shivered in the night and watched helplessly as an era came to an end. She looked down at her hand on Teaqua's shoulder as if from a great distance. The hand seemed to move of its own volition as it groomed Teaqua's fur. Harumen wondered if it would not be better for all of them if that odd disembodied hand were to close around Teaqua's neck. She watched as it brushed across the ridge of Teaqua's breastbone, ruffling the tight fur. She was horrified and fascinated as it slid higher, the fingers curling. Then Teaqua swallowed and Harumen could feel the goddess's throat move in her grip and she jerked back as if she had been burned. She could not do such a thing. "Teaqua, *no*." Not yet.

"I'll need the messenger's help." Teaqua did not seem to notice. She was looking at something which Harumen could not see, that she hoped never to see. "Tell Ndavu that Chan has spoken to me and that we must obey him. I will die in his light." Teaqua sounded afraid, as if she might scream again. "There is to be a shrine."

Harumen could hear someone keening softly in the next room. Then others joined in. She did not know whether to mourn for Teaqua or herself.

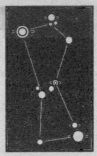

hillip Wing was not a religious man, so he was surprised when he found out what his wife had been doing with her Wednesday afternoons. He did not understand; he had thought Daisy was too busy to take time off. They both tended to overwork but that was because each of them loved what they were doing. In love with their careers, in love with each other; even strangers admired their marriage.

"You've joined what?"

"A friend invited me to sit in on a study group at the mission." Daisy refilled her glass from a decanter. "I've been twice, that's all. I haven't joined anything."

"What are you studying?"

"Sitting in, Phil—it's not like I intend to convert. I'm just browsing." She sipped her wine and waited for

Wing to settle down. "They haven't said a word about immortality yet. Mostly they talk about history."

"History? History? The messengers haven't been here long enough to know anything about history."

"Seven years. First contact was seven years ago." She sighed and suddenly she was lecturing. "Cultural evolution follows predictable patterns. There are interesting correlations between humanity and some of the other civilizations that the messengers have contacted."

Wing shook his head. "I don't get it. We've been together what? Since '51? Five years and all that mattered was the inn. They nuke Geneva, so what? Revolution in Mexico, who cares?"

"I care about you," she said.

That stopped him for a moment. Absently, he filled his glass from the decanter and took a gulp before he realized that it was the synthetic riesling that she was trying out as a house wine. He swallowed it with difficulty. "Who's the friend?"

"What?"

"The friend who asked you to the mission. Who is he?" Wing was just guessing that it was a man. It was a good guess.

"A regular." Daisy glanced away from him and nodded at the glow sculpture on the wall. "You know Jim McCauley."

All he knew was that McCauley was a local artist who had made a name for himself in fancy light bulbs. Wing watched the play of pastel light across her face, trying to see her as this regular might see her. Daisy was not beautiful, although she could be pretty when she paid attention to detail. She did not comb her hair every time the wind caught it nor did she much care about the wrinkles at the corners of her eyes. Hers was an intelligent, hard-edged, New Hampshire Yankee face. She was a cool woman; perhaps she did not show her emotions often enough. But she looked like someone who would know about things that mattered, not like some suburban vidqueen whose brain had been fried by telelink. Wing had good reasons for loving her. He slid across the couch and nuzzled under her ear.

"Don't tickle." She laughed. "You're invited, you know." She pulled back, but not too far. "The new messenger, Ndavu, is interested in art. He's mentioned the Glass Cloud several times. You really ought to go. You might learn something." Having made her pitch, she kissed him.


Wing watched the roadbuster below him eating the section of NH Route 302 that passed through Crawford Notch. Its teeth flayed the ice-slicked asphalt into chunks. Then a wide-bladed Caterpillar scooped the bituminous rubble up and into trucks bound for the recycling plant in Concord. Once the old highway had been stripped down to its foundation course of gravel, crews would come to lay the Glass Cloud's underground track. After spring thaw a paver the size of a brachiosaurus would regurgitate asphalt to cover the track. Route 302 through Crawford Notch was the last phase of the ninety-seven-kilometer track which followed existing roads through the heart of the White Mountain National Forest.

"Won't be long now," said the hover pilot. "They're talking a power-up test in ten weeks. Three months tops."

Wing said nothing. Ten weeks. Unless another preservationist judge could be convinced to meddle or the Seven Wonders Foundation decided it had spent enough and sued him for the overruns. The project was two years late already and had long since gobbled up a generous contingency budget. Wing knew he had made mistakes, although he admitted them only to himself. Sometimes he even worried that he had wasted his chance.

The hover was the property of Gemini Fabricators, the lead company in the consortium that had won the contract to build the Cloud and its track. Wing knew that the pilot had instructions to keep him in the air as long as possible. Every minute he spent inspecting track was one minute less he would have to go over the checklist for the newly completed docking platform with Laporte and Alz. Laporte, the Canadian whom Seven Wonders had hired as project manager, made no secret of his dismay at having to waste valuable time with Wing. Laporte had made it clear that he believed Wing was largely to blame for the project's misfortunes. Both men recognized that at this late stage of construction there was no positive contribution that Wing could make. All he could do was notice the differences between what they had built and what he had imagined.

Wing had spent five years at Yale grinding out a practitioner's degree but when he graduated he was certain that he had made a mistake. He was offered several jobs but not one that he wanted. He had studied architecture with the impossibly naive hope that someday, someone would let him design a building as large as his ambitions. He wanted to build landmarks, not program factories to fabricate this year's model go-tubes for the masses too poor to afford real housing. Instead of working he decided to spend the summer after graduation hiking the Appalachian Trail. Alone.

As he climbed Webster Cliff in Crawford Notch, he played a poetry game against his fatigue. *A zephyr massages the arthritic tree.* It was only a few kilometers to the Appalachian Mountain Club's Mispah Spring Hut where he would spend the night. *Plodding promiscuously into tangerine heaven.* Wing made it a game because he did not really believe in poetry. *Stone teeth bite solipsistic toes*. A low cloud was sweeping through the Notch just as the late afternoon sun dipped out of the overcast into a jagged band of blue sky on the horizon. Something strange happened to the light then and for an instant the cloud was transformed. *A cloud of glass*.

"A glass cloud," he murmured. There was no one to hear him. He stopped, watching the cloud but not seeing it, experiencing instead an overpowering inner vision. A glass cloud. The image swelled like a bubble; he could see himself floating with it, free of care, fulfilled. For the first time he understood what people meant when they talked about inspiration. He kept thinking of the glass cloud all the way to the hut, all that night. He was still thinking of it weeks later when he reached the summit of Katahdin, the northern terminus of the trail, and thought of it on the hover to Connecticut. He did some research and made sketches, taking a strange satisfaction from the enormous uselessness of it. That fall Seven Wonders announced the opening of the North American design competition. Phillip Wing, an unregistered, unemployed, uncertain architect of twenty-seven committed the single inspiration of his life to disk and entered the competition because he had nothing better to do.

Now as he looked down out of the hover at Crawford Notch, Wing could not help but envy that young man stalking through the forest, seething with ambition and, at the same time, desperately afraid he was second-rate. At age twenty-seven Wing could not imagine the trouble a thirty-two-year-old could get into. Schedules and meetings, compromises and contracts. That eager young man had not realized what it would mean to capture the glittering prize at the start of a career, so that everything that came after seemed lackluster. That fierce young man had never been truly in love or watched helplessly as time abraded true love. Wing motioned to the pilot, who banked the hover and headed for North Conway where the docking platform was ready for final inspection.

The hover settled onto its landing struts like an old man easing into a hot bath. Wing waited for the dirty snow and swirls of litter to subside. The job site was strewn with coffee cups, squashed beer bulbs and enough vitabulk wrap to cover Mount Washington.

Wing popped the hatch and was greeted by a knife-edged wind; there was no welcoming committee. He grabbed his workslate and crossed the frozen landing zone toward the field offices, a group of linked commercial go-tubes that looked like a chain of plastic sausages some careless giant had dropped. The Seven Wonders tube was empty and the telelink was ringing. Wing would have answered it except that was exactly the kind of thing that made Laporte mad. So instead he went next door to Gemini looking for Fred Alz. Wing suspected that some of the project's problems arose from the collusion between Laporte and Alz, Gemini's field super; they did not have much use for architects. A woman Wing did not recognize sat at a CAD screen eating a vitabulk donut and staring dully at details of the ferroplastic structural grid.

"Where is everybody?" said Wing.

"They went to town to see him off."

"Him?"

"I think it's a him. A messenger: No-doubt or some such."

"What was he doing here?"

"Maybe he was looking for converts. With immortality we might actually have a chance of finishing this one." She took a bite of donut and looked at him for the first time. "Who the hell are you anyway?"

"The architect."

"Yeah?" She did not seem impressed. "Where's your hard hat?"

Wing knew what they all said about him: that he was an arrogant son of a bitch with a chip on his shoulder the size of Cheops's Pyramid. He now spent some time living up to his reputation. The engineer did not stay for the entire tirade; she stalked out, leaving Wing to stew over the waste of an afternoon. Shortly afterward, Alz and Laporte breezed in, laughing. Probably at him.

"Sorry to keep you waiting, Phil—" Laporte held up both hands in mock surrender—"but there's good news."

"It's two thirty-eight! This plugging project is twenty-one months late and you're giving tours to aliens?"

"Phil." Alz put a hand on his shoulder. "Phil, listen to me for a minute, will you?"

Wing wanted to knock it away. Laporte brushed a finger against his moustache, not quite hiding a contemptuous smile.

"Mentor Ndavu has made a generous offer on behalf of the commonwealth of messengers." Alz spoke quickly, as if he expected Wing to explode if he stopped. "We're talking major funding, a special grant that could carry us right through to completion. He says the messengers want to recognize outstanding achievement in the arts, hard cash and lots of it—you ought to be proud is what you ought to be. We get it and chances are we can float the Cloud out of here by Memorial Day. Ten weeks, Phil."

Wing looked from Alz to Laporte. There was something going on, something peculiar and scary. People did not just hand out open-ended grants to rescue troubled projects for no reason—especially not the messengers, who had never shown more than a polite interest in any of the works of humanity. Three years of autotherapy

**11**

had taught Wing that he had a tendency to make conspiracy out of coincidence. But this was real. First Daisy, now the Cloud; the aliens were getting close. "Could we do it without them?"

Alz laughed.

"They're not monsters, Phil," said Laporte.

Wing wished there was a way to be sure of that.


A tear dribbled down Wing's cheek. His eyes always watered when he sniffed too much Focus. The two-meter CAD screen that filled one wall of his studio displayed the south elevation of the proposed headquarters for SEE-Coast, the local telelink utility. There was something wrong with the row of window dormers set into the new hip roof. He blinked and the computer replaced the sketch with a menu. A doubleblink changed the cursor on the screen from draw to erase mode. His eyes darted; the windows disappeared.

He ought to have known that the SEE-Coast project would be more trouble than it was worth. Jack Congemi was trying to cram too much building onto too small a site, a sliver of riverfront wedged between an eighteenth-century chandlery and a nineteenth-century hotel. If he could have gotten a variance to build higher than five stories, there would have been no problem. But SEE-Coast was buying into Portsmouth's exclusive historic district, where the zoning regulations were carved in granite. Wing knew; he had helped rewrite them.

It was a decent commission and the cost-plus fee contract meant he would make good money, but like everything he had done since the Cloud, Wing was bored with it. The building was pure kitsch: a tech bunker hiding behind a Georgian facade. It was like all the rest of his recent projects: clients buying a safe name brand and to hell with the vision. Of course they expected him to deliver stick-built at a price competitive with Korean robot factories. Never mind that half the local trades were incompetent and the other half were booked.

At last he could no longer bear to look at the monster. "Save it." He closed his eyes for a moment and still saw those ugly windows burned on the insides of his lids.

"Saved," said the computer.

He sat, too weary to move, and let his mind soak in the blackness of the empty screen. He knew he had spent too much time recently worrying about the Cloud and the messengers. It was perverse since everything was going so well. All the checklists were now complete, preflight start-up tests were under way and Seven Wonders had scheduled dedication ceremonies for Memorial Day.

Solon Petropolus, erratic scion of the Greek transportation conglomerate, had endowed the Seven Wonders Foundation with an immense fortune. The foundation was Petropolus's megalomaniacal gift to the ages. It commissioned constructions—some called them art—on a monumental scale. The Seven Wonders Foundation did not seek the spare and elite craft of the postgraduate schools but technological expressions of the popular culture. It was the vulgar purpose of the Wonders to attract crowds. They were to be places where a French *secrétaire* or a Peruvian *campesino* or even an Algerian *mullah* might come to contemplate the enduring spirit of Solon Petropolus, the man who embalmed himself in money.

The opening of the Second Wonder of the Modern World would have been reason enough for a news orgy, but now the messengers' involvement was overshadowing Wing's masterpiece. Telelink reporters kept calling him from places like Bangkok and Kinshasa and Montevideo to ask him about the aliens. Why were they supporting the Cloud? When would they invite humanity to join their commonwealth and share in immortality? What were they really like?

He had no answers. Up until now he had done his best to avoid meeting any of the aliens. Like many people, Wing had been bitterly disappointed by the messengers. Their arrival had changed nothing: there were still too many crazy people with nukes; the war in Mexico dragged on. Although they had been excruciatingly diplomatic, it seemed that human civilization impressed them not at all. They kept their secrets to themselves—had never invited anyone to tour their starships or demonstrated the technique for preserving minds after death. The messengers claimed that they had come to Earth for raw materials and to spread some as-yet vague message of galactic culture. Wing assumed that they held humanity in roughly the same esteem with which the conquistadors had held the Aztecs. But he could hardly admit that to reporters.

"Something else?" The computer disturbed his reverie; it was set to prompt him for new commands after twenty minutes of inactivity.

He leaned back in his chair and stretched, accidentally knocking his print of da Vinci's *St. John the Baptist* askew. "What the hell time is it, anyway?"

"One-fourteen-thirty-five A.M., 19 February 2056."

He decided that he was too tired to get up and fix the picture.

"Here you are." Daisy appeared in the doorway. "Do you know what time it is?"

"One-fourteen-forty-two A.M., 19 February 2056," said the computer.

She straightened the Baptist and then came up behind his chair. "Something wrong?"

"SEE-Coast."

She began to massage his shoulders and he leaned his

head back against her belly. "Can't it wait until the morning?"

The skin was itchy where the tear had dried. Wing rubbed it, considering.

"Would you like to come to bed?" She bent over to kiss him and he could see that she was naked beneath her dressing gown. "All work and no play . . ."

The stink of doubt that he had tried so hard to perfume with concentration enhancers still clung to him. "But what if I wake up tomorrow and can't work on this crap? What if I don't believe in what I'm doing anymore? I can't live off the Glass Cloud forever."

"Then you'll find something else." She sifted his hair through her fingers.

He plastered a smile on his face and slipped a hand inside her gown—more from habit than passion. "I love you."

She pulled him from his chair. "It's better in bed."

"Daisy, I . . ."

She put a finger to his lips. "Just you keep quiet and follow Mother Goodwin, young man. She'll take the wrinkles out of your brow."

He stumbled as he came into her arms but she caught his weight easily. When she hugged him he wondered what she had been doing all evening.

"I've been thinking," he said softly, "about this party. I give in: go ahead if you want and invite Ndavu. I promise to be polite—but that's all." He wanted to pull back and see her reaction but she would not let him go. "That's what you want, isn't it?"

"That's one of the things I want," she said. Her cheek was hot against his neck.

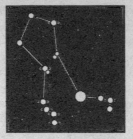

**P**iscataqua House had been built by Dr. Nathaniel Goodwin in 1763. A handsome building of water-struck brick and granite, it was said to have offered the finest lodging in the bustling colonial city of Portsmouth, New Hampshire. Nearly three hundred years later it was still an inn and Daisy Goodwin was its keeper.

Wing had always been intrigued by the way Daisy's pedigree had affected her personality. It was not so much the old money she had inherited, most of which was tied up in the inn. It was the way she could bicycle around town and point out the elementary school she had attended, the Congregational Church where her grandparents had married, the huge black oak in Prescott Park that Great-great-great-uncle Josiah had planted during the Garfield administration. She lived with the easy grace of someone who knew exactly who she was, who was doing exactly what she had always intended to do.

Wing had never really been sure of anything until he met Daisy. He had been born in Taipei but had fled to the States with his Taiwanese father after his American mother had been killed in the bloody reunification riots of 2026. His father, a software engineer, had spent the rest of a bitter life searching in vain for what he had left on Taiwan. Phillip Wing had gone to elementary schools in Cupertino, California; Waltham, Massachusetts; and Norcross, Georgia. He knew very little about either side of his family. "When you are old enough to understand," his father would always say. "Someday we will talk. But not now." Young Phillip learned quickly to stop asking; too many questions could drive his father into one of his binges. He would dose himself to the brink of insensibility with memory sweeteners and stay up half the night weeping and babbling in the Taiwanese dialect of Fukien. His father had died when Wing was a junior at Yale. The old man had never met Daisy, whom Wing had first dated just before graduation. Wing had fallen in love with her and the Cloud at approximately the same time. He liked to think that his father would have approved.

Wing tried hard to fit into Daisy's world, to be the man she wanted him to be. He had gutted the Counting House, a hundred-and-ninety-five-year-old business annex built by the merchant Goodwins, and converted it into his offices. He was polite to the guests despite their annoying ignorance about the Cloud; most people thought it had been designed by Solon Petropolus. He helped out when Daisy was shorthanded, joined the Congregational Church despite a complete lack of religiosity and served a term on the City's Planning Board. He endured the dreaded black-tie fund-raisers of the National Society of Colonial Dames for Daisy's sake and took her to the opera in Boston at least twice a year even though it gave him a headache. Now she was asking him to play host to an alien.

An intimate party of twenty-three had gathered in the Hawthorne parlor for a buffet in Ndavu's honor. Laporte had flown down from North Conway with his wife, Jolene. Among the locals were the Hathaways, who were still bragging about their vacation on Orbital Three, Magda Rudowski, artistic director of the New Theater-by-the-Sea, Reverend Smoot, the reformalist minister, the new city manager, whose name Wing could never remember, her husband, who never had anything to say, and the Congemis, who owned SEE-Coast. There were also a handful of Ndavu's hangers-on, among them the glow sculptor Jim McCauley.

Wing hated these kinds of parties. He had about as much chat in him as a Trappist monk. To help ease his awkwardness, Daisy sent him out into the room with their best cut-glass appetizer to help the guests get hungry. He wandered through other people's conversations, feeling lost.

"Oh, but we love it upcountry," Jolene Laporte was saying. "It's so peaceful and the air is so clean and the mountains—"

"—are tall." Laporte finished her sentence and winked as he reached for the appetizer. "But it's plugging cold—Jesus!" Magda Rudowski laughed nervously. Laporte looked twisted; he had the classic hollow stare, as if his eyes had just been fished out of a jar of formaldehyde. Maybe he had been working too hard.

"Don't make fun, Leon," Jolene said, pouting. "You love it too. Why, just the other day he was saying how nice it would be to stay on after the Cloud opened. I think he'd like to bask in his glory for a while." She sprayed a test dose from the appetizer onto her wrist and took a tentative sniff. "How legal is this?"

"Just some olfactory precursors," Wing said, "and maybe twenty ppm of Bliss."

"Maybe I'm not the only one who deserves credit. Maybe Phillip here wants a slice of the glory too."

Laporte's voice seemed to boom because he was the only one in the room talking. Wing turned away just in time to see Daisy wheel Ndavu through the door.

"Phillip, I'd like you to meet Mentor Ndavu."

The alien was wearing a loose, black pinstripe suit. He might have been a corporate vice-president with his slicked-back gray hair and long, ruddy face except that he looked to be over two meters tall. He had to slump to fit into his wheelchair and his knees stuck out like bumpers. The chair whined as it rolled; Ndavu leaned forward extending his hand. Wing found himself counting the fingers. Of course there were five. The messengers were nothing if not thorough.

"I have been wanting to meet you, Phillip."

Wing shook hands but could not think of a reply. Ndavu's grip was firm and oddly sticky, like plastic wrap.

The messenger smiled. "I am very much interested in your work."

"As we all are interested in yours." Reverend Smoot brushed past Wing. "I, for one, would like to know—"

"Reverend"—Ndavu spoke softly so that only those closest to him could hear—"must we always argue?"

"—would like to know, Mentor," continued Smoot in his pulpit voice, "how your people intend to respond to the advisory voted yesterday by the Council of Churches."

"Perhaps we should discuss business later, Reverend." Ndavu shot a porcelain smile at Laporte. "Leon, this must be your wife, Jolene."

Daisy got Wing's attention by standing utterly still. Between them passed an unspoken message which she punctuated by a barely perceptible tilt of the head.

Wing's inclination was to let Smoot and Ndavu go at each other but he took firm hold of the reverend's arm. "Would you like to see the greenhouse, Magda?" he said, turning the minister toward the actress. "The freesias are just coming into bloom; the place smells like the Garden of Eden. How about you, Reverend?" Glowering, Smoot allowed himself to be led away.

A few of the other guests had drifted out into what had once been the stables. Daisy's parents had replaced the old roof with sheets of clear optical plastic during the Farm Crusade, converting the entire wing into a greenhouse. In those days the inn might have closed without a reliable source of fresh produce. Magda Rudowski paused to admire a planter filled with tuberous begonias.

"Lovely," she said, cupping a softball-sized flower in her hand. "I'm so jealous. I can never get anything to bloom this early."

Reverend Smoot squinted through the krylac roof at the stars, as if seeking heavenly guidance. "I just have to wonder," he said, "who the joke is on."

Wing and Magda exchanged glances.

"How can you talk about flowers when that alien is undermining the foundations of our Judeo-Christian heritage?"

Magda touched Smoot's sleeve. "It's a party, Reverend."

"If they don't believe in a God, how the hell can they apply for tax-exempt status? 'Look into the sun,' what kind of message is that? A year ago they wouldn't say a word to you unless you were from some government or conglomerate. Then they buy up some abandoned churches and suddenly they're preaching to anyone who'll listen. Look into the sun, my ass." He took two stiff-legged steps toward the hydroponic benches and then spun toward Wing and Magda Rudowski. "You look into the sun too long and you go blind." He stalked off.

"I don't know what Daisy was thinking of when she invited him," Magda said.

"He married us," said Wing.

She sighed, as if that had been an even bigger mistake. "Shall I keep an eye on him for you?"

"Thanks." Wing thought then to offer her the appetizer. She inhaled a polite dose and Wing took a whiff himself, thinking he might as well make the best of what threatened to be bad business. The Bliss loosened the knot in his stomach; he could feel his senses snapping to attention. They looked at each other and giggled. "Hell with him," he said, surprising them both. He headed back to the parlor.

Jack Congemi was arguing in the hall with Laporte. "Here's just the man to settle this," he said.

"It's not about architectural fees, I hope." Wing offered the appetizer to his client.

"Jack here thinks telelink is maybe going to put the trades out of business." Laporte spoke as though his brain were parked in lunar orbit and he were hearing his own words with a time delay. "Tell him you can't fuse plasteel gun emplacements in Tijuana sitting at a console in Greeley, Colorado. Makes no plugging difference how good your robotics are. You got to be there."

"The Indians did it. They had sixty percent completion on Orbital Three before a human being ever set foot on it."

"Robots don't have a union," said Laporte. "The fusers do."

"Before telelink, none of us could have afforded to do business from a beautiful little nowhere like Portsmouth." Congemi liked to see himself as the local prophet of telelink; Wing had heard this sermon before.

"We would have all been jammed into some urb hard by the jump port and container terminals and transitways and maglev trunks. Now no one has to go anywhere."

"But without tourists," said Wing, "inns close."

Congemi held his hands out like an archbishop blessing a crowd. "Of course, people will always travel for pleasure. And we at SEE-Coast will continue to encourage people to tour our beautiful Granite State. But we are also citizens of a new state, a state which is being born at this very moment. The world information state."

"Don't care where they come from." Laporte's voice slurred. "Don't care whether they're citizens of the plugging commonwealth of messengers, just so long as they line up to see my Cloud." He poked a finger into Wing's shoulder as if daring him to object.

It was not the first time he had heard Laporte claim the Cloud as his. Wing considered throwing the man out and manners be damned. Instead he said, "We'll be eating soon," and went into the parlor.

For a time he was adrift on the tides of the party, smiling too much and excusing himself as he nudged past people on his way to nowhere. He was annoyed but the problem was that he was not exactly sure why. He told himself that it was all Daisy's fault. Her party. He aimed the appetizer at his face and squeezed off a piggish dose. But he had lost his appetite altogether.

"Phillip. Please, do you have a moment?" Ndavu gave him a toothy grin. There was something strange about his teeth: they were too white, too perfect. He was talking to Mr. and Mrs. Hatcher Poole III, who were standing up against the wall like a matched set of silver lamps.

"Mentor Ndavu."

"Mentor is a title my students have given me. I am your guest and we are friends, are we not? You must call me Ndavu."

"Ndavu." Wing bowed slightly.

"May I?" The messenger turned his wheelchair to Wing and held out his hand for the appetizer. "I had hoped for the chance to observe your mind-altering behavior this evening." He turned the appetizer over in his long spiderlike hands and then abruptly sprayed it into his face. The entire room fell silent and then the messenger sneezed. No one had ever heard of such a thing, a messenger sneezing. The Pooles looked horrified, as if the alien might explode next. Someone across the room laughed and conversation resumed.

"It seems to stimulate the chemical senses." Ndavu wrinkled his nose. "It acts to lower the threshold of certain olfactory and taste receptors. There are also trace elements of another substance—some kind of indole hallucinogen?"

"I'm an architect, not a drug artist."

Ndavu passed the appetizer on to Mrs. Poole. "Why do you ingest these substances?" The alien's skin was perfect too; he had no moles, no freckles, not even a wrinkle.

"Well," she said, still fluttering from his sneeze, "they *are* nonfattening."

Her husband laughed nervously. "I take it, Ndavu, that you have never eaten vitabulk."

"Vitabulk? No." The messenger leaned forward in his wheelchair. "We serve it at the mission."

"I once owned a bulkery in Nashua," said Hatcher Poole. "The ideal product, in many ways: cheap to produce, nutritionally complete, an almost indefinite shelf life. Without it, hundreds of millions would starve—"

"You see," said Wing, "it tastes like insulation."

"Depends on the genetics of your starter batch," said Poole. "They're doing wonders these days with texturization."

"Bread flavor isn't that far off." Mrs. Poole had squeezed off a dose that they could probably smell in

Maine. "And everything tastes better after a nice appetizer."

"Of course, we're serving natural food tonight," said Wing. "Daisy has had Cook prepare a traditional meal in your honor, Ndavu." He wished she were here chatting and he was in the kitchen supervising final preparations. "However, some people prefer to use appetizers no matter what the menu."

"Prefer?" said Poole, who had passed the appetizer without using it. "A damned addiction, if you ask me."

Two white-coated busboys carried a platter into the room, its contents hidden beneath a silver lid. They set it on the mahogany sideboard beneath a portrait of Nathaniel Hawthorne brooding. "Dinner is served!" The guests lined up quickly.

"Plates and utensils here, condiments on the tea table." Daisy's face was flushed with excitement. She was wearing that luminous blue dress he had bought for her in Boston, the one that had cost too much. "Cook will help you find what you want. Enjoy." Bechet, resplendent in his white chef's hat, placed a huge chafing dish beside the silver tray. With a flourish, Peter the busboy removed the lid from the silver tray. The guests buzzed happily and crowded around the sideboard, blocking Wing's view. He did not have to see the food, however; his hypersensitized olfactories were drenched in its aroma.

As he approached the sideboard, he could hear Bechet murmuring. "Wieners, sir. Hot dogs."

"Oh my god, Hal, potato salad—mayonnaise!"

"Did he say *dog*?"

"Nothing that amazing about relish. I put up three quarts myself last summer. But mustard!"

"No, no, I'll just have to live with my guilt."

"Corn dog or on a bun, Mr. Wing?" Bechet was beaming.

"On a bun please, Bechet." Wing held out his plate. "They seem to like it."

"I hope so, sir."

The guests were in various stages of gustatory ecstasy. The fare was not at all unusual for the wealthy; they ate at least one natural meal a day and meat or fish once a week. For others, forty-five grams of USDA guaranteed pure beef frankfurter was an extravagance: Christmas dinner, birthday treat. One of the strangers from the mission was the first to go for thirds. Ndavu had the good manners not to eat at all. Perhaps he had orders not to alarm the natives with his diet.

The party fragmented after dinner; most guests seemed eager to put distance between themselves and the messenger. It was a strain being in the same room with Ndavu; Wing could certainly feel it. Daisy led a group of gardeners to the greenhouse. Others gathered to watch the latest episode of *Jesus on First*. The religious spectacle of the hard-hitting Jesus had made it one of the most popular scripted sports events on telelink. The more boisterous guests went to the inn's cellar bar. Wing alone remained trapped in the Hawthorne parlor with the guest of honor.

"It has been a successful evening," said Ndavu, "so far."

"You have an agenda?" Wing saw Peter the busboy gawking at the alien as he gathered up dirty plates.

Ndavu smiled. "Indeed I do. You are a hard man to meet, Phillip. I am not sure why that is, but I hope now that things will be different. Will you visit me at the mission?"

Wing shrugged. "Maybe sometime." He was thinking to himself that he had the day after the heat death of the universe free.

"May I consider that a commitment?"

Wing stooped to pick up a pickle slice before someone—probably Peter—squashed it into the Kashgar rug. "I'm glad your evening has been a success," he said, depositing the pickle on Peter's tray as he went by.

"Before people accept the message, they must first accept the messenger." He said it like a slogan. "You will forgive me if I observe that yours is a classically xenophobic species. The work has just begun; it will take years."

"Why do you do it? I mean you, personally."

"My motives are various—even I find it difficult to keep track of all of them." The messenger shifted in the wheelchair and his knee brushed Wing's leg. "In that I suspect we may be alike, Phillip. The fact is, however, that my immediate concern is not spreading the message. It is getting your complete attention."

The alien was very close. "My attention?" Rumor had it that beneath their perfect exteriors lurked vile creatures, unspeakably grotesque. Evolutionary biologists maintained that it was impossible that the messengers were humanoid.

"You should know that you are being considered for a most prestigious commission. I can say no more at this time but if you will visit me, I think we may discuss—"

Wing had stopped listening to Ndavu—saved by an argument out in the foyer. An angry man was shouting. A woman pleaded. Daisy. "Excuse me," he said, turning away from Ndavu.

The angry man was the glow sculptor, McCauley. "No, I won't go without you." He was about Wing's age, maybe a few years older. There was gray in McCauley's starchy brush of brown hair. He might have been taken for handsome in a blunt way except that his blue and silver stretchsuit was five years out of date and he was sweating.

"For God's sake, Jimmy, would you stop it?" Daisy

was holding out a coat and seemed to be trying to coax him into it. "Go home. Please. This isn't the time."

"You tell me when. I won't keep putting it off."

"Something the matter?" Wing went up on the balls of his feet. If it came to a fight, he thought he could hold his own for the few seconds it would take reinforcements to arrive. But it was ridiculous, really; people in Portsmouth did not fight anymore. He could hear someone running toward the foyer from the kitchen. A knot of people clustered at the bottom of the stairs. He would be all right, he thought. "Daisy?" Still, it was a damned nuisance.

He was shocked by her reaction. She recoiled from him as if he were a vision out of her worst nightmare and then sank down onto the sidechair and said "Oh, Jimmy." Something in the way she had said his name had paralyzed Wing. She looked like she wanted to cry.

"I'm sorry," said McCauley. He took the coat from her nerveless hands and kissed her quickly on the cheek. Wing wanted to throw him to the floor but found he could not move. Nobody in the room moved but the stranger his wife had called Jimmy. All night long he had sensed a tension at the party but, like a fool, he had completely misinterpreted it. Everyone knew; if he moved they might all start laughing.

"Shouldn't have . . ." McCauley was murmuring something; his hand was on the door. "Sorry."

"You don't walk out now, do you?" Wing was proud of how steady his voice was. Daisy's shoulders were shaking but her eyes were dry. Her sculptor did not have an answer; he did not even stop to put on his coat. As the door closed behind him Wing had the peculiar urge to call Congemi out of the crowd and make him take responsibility for this citizen of the world information state. His brave new world was filled with people who had no idea of how to act in public.

"Daisy?"

She would not look at him. Although he felt as if he were standing stark naked in the middle of the foyer of the historic Piscataqua House, he realized no one was looking at him.

Except Ndavu.

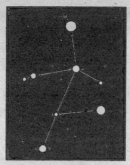

**T**he prophet enjoyed performing miracles. So he did not really mind hearing from the villagers first, even though this time it meant skipping a meal. Country people asked so little of the goddess, which was one reason why her prophet Ammagon loved them so much. A debt was too long overdue, a severed thumb was slow to regrow, two neighbors bickered constantly. Here was a farmer, trembling with age, who begged permission to go to Mateag to be shriven. A young potter sought Teaqua's blessing for a move to the city. Ammagon perched on the edge of the golden cart, legs dangling above the corduroy of log pavers, and listened carefully. Very few of these people had problems requiring divine intervention; all they really needed was a little advice backed up by Teaqua's good name. This Ammagon was glad to give. As for the rest, he had to decide not only who he could help, but also who most deserved his help. It was no small thing to grant a miracle. All around the village square, meanwhile, the priests were busy calibrating their scopes and taking directions from control.

Ammagon's stomach rumbled as the audiences stretched into the third hour. "I wonder if there's anything to eat?" he said absently.

The shepherd had been complaining about the weather. He flagged surprise.

"You know, food?" Ammagon bit at the air. "I'm sorry—been a long morning. Go on, then."

They brought him half a loaf and a mug of wine. He broke the bread; the crust was thick and as hard as if it had been fired in the potter's kiln. Dunking it in the local vintage softened it enough so that he could choke it down, lump by lump. At least the wine was drinkable. Ammagon beckoned the next villager to approach him. The line was getting shorter.

Sometimes he envied them their simplicity. Although they worked hard, at least villagers could see the results of their labor. They knew when they would eat, even if the fare was plain. They slept with friends, had homes and furniture—pillows of their own! Above all, they enjoyed the comfort of certainty. They would never think to question the goddess or doubt their whispers. For Ammagon, this simple and unquestioning faith in the truths was what made them beautiful, despite the mud and the shaggy fur and the homespun coats. He knew that spiritual beauty was as real as anything in the world. If it was subtle, it was also unmistakable. You had only to open yourself to it, like the music of moving water, the fragrance of newly split wood.

It was the faith Ammagon found in the villages that made it all worthwhile: the bone-shaking trips over bad roads, the heaping platters of hardscrabble food, the open mockery of Teaqua's cronies. Ammagon knew how they made fun of him; he had long since smelled them out. Harumen, Ipposkenick—that crowd. The scholars. They wanted to shake the faith, disrupt the peace of the villages. In Ammagon's opinion they were sad, dry, godless people, thin as paper. Yet Teaqua encouraged them.

It was something Ammagon often prayed about.

"She doesn't love me anymore."

Ammagon rubbed his snout. It was the oldest, the saddest story of all. "How do you know?"

"We've been together for years. She kept saying nothing had changed. But she lied."

Ammagon studied the farmer silently, trying to gauge the strength of his faith, his susceptibility to the whispers.

"She never told me she was unhappy."

"You visit the common bed?" said Ammagon. "You share yourselves with your friends?"

"It isn't pleasure. Pleasure has nothing to do with it. She's a potter. The best in the highlands. Her pots"—the farmer flagged his confusion—"she puts such shapes to them—there is no need for such pots! They are so beautiful, these pots. Too beautiful for oil or dried beans. You hate to put things in them, you know? She says she wants to go to the city."

"I see."

"I don't want to lose her."

"Did you tell her?" said Ammagon.

"We don't talk like we used to. I don't understand her."

"You have to give her a reason for wanting you. What would that reason be?"

"I'm a farmer; I work hard." The farmer put his head in his hands. "There's no farm work in the city."

"Maybe she should go."

"Maybe. Maybe I'll never be happy again."

"What do your whispers say?"

"Nothing." The farmer slumped. "I wish they would speak. I need the god's help."

Ammagon grasped him by the shoulders. "You'll get it. Today, I promise." He gave the farmer a bracing shake. "When I call you to the stage, Teaqua will help you hear your whispers."

The farmer bowed; he seemed satisfied. Ammagon felt certain that the farmer would accept whatever decision his whispers led him to. His would be a miracle of faith, one which would carry him through the pain.

After he had heard the last of them, Ammagon stuck his head into the control tent to tell the director he was done.

"How many this time?" she said impatiently. The director was sitting in the dark, her board lit up with five views of the golden cart which Ammagon used for a stage. On the screens three burly priests were wrestling Teaqua's throne into place. She fidgeted with the board and two of the images shifted.

"The usual," said Ammagon. "Half an hour should do it."

"I'll make the link then." She did not glance away from her work. "Ready on the scopes." She was not talking to him.

"Look into the sun," said Ammagon politely. The director was too busy to make the proper reply. Ammagon snorted and let the tent flap slide back into place, then shooed the knot of curious onlookers away. "We'll be starting soon." He whisked his hands through the air like brooms. "Go on, go on, if you want a spot up front." He did not want them peeking into the tent; it did no one any good to see how the ghosts were projected. It was bad enough that Teaqua used messenger technology to do the work of the god; Ammagon had no intention of giving tours. He ducked into the dresser's tent.

"You ate?" Chiskat had laid out Ammagon's second-best jacket, the yellow one with light blue piping.

"A snack, yes." He raised his arms, let Chiskat lift off his tunic and then settled onto a stool. It was time for Ammagon himself to open himself to the god in preparation for the thanksgiving. It was not as easy for Ammagon as it was for the villagers; he knew too much. And now he found that he was not in the mood; the director's rudeness had annoyed him. He had seen it before: how many times had he warned Teaqua? Machines deadened the spirit.

Chiskat rubbed a light oil onto Ammagon's chest and then brushed it out. His fur gleamed in the lamplight.

It had been different when only scholars had opened the links and produced the thanksgiving ceremonies. They were lost anyway, poor souls. But now Teaqua had priests doing the work. No priest—certainly not Ammagon—could hear the god when he was squinting at a control board or aiming scopes. Teaqua liked to say that the links had forged villages across the world together into a great chain of faith. She had a weakness for metaphor, the goddess did. But a chain was a thing without life, cold. The faith was alive and the people had to burn with the fire of the sun.

"Five minutes," said Chiskat.

Ammagon grouched. "And if I'm not ready?"

"They're out there." Of course, Chiskat had her orders too. "You don't want to let them down." Get the prophet on stage and working the crowd at the appointed hour. It did not matter whether or not Ammagon felt inspired; there was a schedule. The machines were in control. Chiskat picked up the blue jacket and held it open.

Flagging disapproval, Ammagon slipped into it. As Chiskat tugged at the sleeves and smoothed wrinkles, the air to their left seemed to shiver. A window appeared.

The ghost of the goddess frowned at them. "Ammagon, we have to talk." Teaqua was wearing the ceremonial regalia: golden robe, cut-glass helmet. She was ready for the thanksgiving. "Go away, you." She dismissed Chiskat and the young dresser scurried from the dressing tent.

Ammagon sank onto his stool. "Something's happened." She never used her link to visit him. He could not remember when she had last spoken to him in private.

"You'll have to cut the tour short. I want you to come back to the city after today's thanksgiving."

"People will be disappointed."

"We'll be giving them something else to think about. I need your help, Ammagon. Chan has spoken to me; he has plans for us. There must be a change."

Ammagon felt a momentary rush of dread. Change was a scholars' word. Chan did not change; the sun was eternal. Of course, they would call it the god's will. "Teaqua, I . . ." He stiffened; he was not going to preside over the destruction of the faith. "If this is Harumen's work, I want no part of it." It was a brave thing to say; Ammagon was surprised at himself.

He expected outrage. Instead Teaqua dropped to her knees. "I've come to ask your forgiveness."

Ammagon pushed off his stool in shock and it tipped backward. *"Teaqua."* It was unnatural. How could the goddess make supplication to her own prophet? He was so flustered that he tried to lift her up before anyone saw her there. His hands passed right through the projected image.

"There's no need to pretend. We both know what has happened." Teaqua's ghost smeared where he had touched it but she paid no attention. "I lost the way, Chan's way. The messengers distracted me. You knew I had strayed but you were patient. You waited for me.

Now Chan has brought me back. I ask again for your forgiveness. Will you give it?"

"Yes, of course—please, just get *up*."

The hands of offwindow servants hauled the goddess up by the armpits. So there had been witnesses. A public repentance. Ammagon was torn between embarrassment and joy. Unless this was some scholars' trick, his prayers had finally been answered.

"I hear whispers again, Ammagon. Do you know how long it's been?"

He closed his eyes and looked into the sun. He could see it clearly. A luminous blue spot filled his head and pressed gently against his ears. The blue of truth. His whispers told him to believe.

"And Chan has come to me in dreams," she said. "He's showed me the future; everything will be different. I need you to make it happen."

"Something's wrong," said the director as she pushed through the flap of the dresser's tent. "The board shows I've got a window open . . ." She saw the goddess. "Oh." She bowed. "Oh."

"Let's go then." Teaqua straightened her glass helmet. "It's past time, isn't it? We don't want to keep them waiting."

The procession was only a few minutes late. The villagers called out thanks to Chan. They shouted for Teaqua. The priests panned the crowd with their scopes, projecting cheering ghosts all over the world. Wherever there was a link, people settled in for the midday thanksgiving. It was a chance to visit with their goddess and watch her prophet perform miracles in her name.

Ammagon knew a secret: the greatest miracle of all had already happened. Things were going to be different.

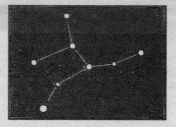

 said you've had
enough." The dealer pushed Wing's twenty back across
the bar. "There's such a thing as an overdose, you know.
And I'd be liable."

Wing stared at the twenty, as if Andy Jackson might
offer him some helpful advice.

"Why don't you go home?"

Wing glanced up without comprehension, trying to
bring the man into focus.

"I said go home."

Wing could not concentrate; he kept thinking of
Daisy's vid. She was sitting in shadow, her face a low-res
blur. She sounded like she had a cold. "It's not fair, what
you're doing. You can't just throw everything away
without giving me a chance to explain. I know I waited
too long but I didn't want to hurt you . . . Maybe you

36

won't believe this but I still love you. I don't know what to say . . . it can't be like it was before but maybe . . ." A long silence. "Call me," she said and the screen went blank.

"What's the matter?" said the dolly. "Not hungry?"

He had lost time somewhere. He could not remember picking up the dolly. He squinted at her but all he could see was plastic: the glossy yellow plastic of the table that separated them, the orange plastic bench she sat on, the long row of garish booths set against the orange-and-yellow striped plastic walls and the plastic oak-parquet floor. Empty wrap was scattered on the tabletop in front of her. A bulb full of chili-flavored vitabulk cooled untouched before him.

"Bet you're a natural, right?" The dolly's lipstick glowed when she spoke, its phosphors reacting to the warmth of her breath. "You have the look."

He pushed the bulb away. "I like real food, yes."

"Is decadent, Freddy. Slaughter animals with immortal souls just to fill your gut? Exploitation karma."

It was lust which had burned through the fog in his mind. She talked too much but she looked clean. At least she did not smell. "My name is Phillip."

"Maybe you got artsy taste buds or something, Philly. Me, I've eaten raw batch more than once. Used to shack with a New Shaker, liked to keep things simple, you know. You going to eat that chili or what?" She dipped a plastic spoon into the bowl. "You saying you never eat bulk?"

"Pancake flavor." Wing did not know why he was telling her. "With honey from the hives in my backyard."

"Beehives?" The dolly gave a low whistle. "Philly boy, just what are we talking about here? A one-nighter or what? 'Cause I could be talked into a series by a man with a yard."

"I live in New Hampshire." Wing shook his head. "Leaving tomorrow."

"Aren't they all?" The dolly sighed and dropped the spoon into the empty bowl. "You nearby?"

He was staying at the Stop Inn, a tube rack just off the T-way. He was on a business trip. But his business was not until morning.

There were three pedicabs parked outside the flash bar. A burly hack heaved himself off the bench by the door and lumbered over to them. "Is cold, yes?" He smiled; his teeth were decorated with Egyptian hiero-glyphs.

"Call us a car," said the dolly.

"You wait ten minutes, yes?" He stamped his feet against the icy pavement. He was wearing thin joggers and the gold sweat suit of the Stamford Cab Company.

The cold helped Wing think. "How far to the Stop Inn? Across from the terminal."

"Not." His breath curled like smoke in the frigid air. "Downhill."

"Your rig have heat?" said the dolly.

"Plenty heat, you bet yes."

They squeezed into the rear of the wedge-shaped ped-icab; the big hack slithered onto the driver's crouch and slid his feet into the toe clips. A musty locker-room smell lingered in the passenger compartment. There was no space heater but after a few minutes of the hack's furious peddling, the smell turned into a warm stink.

The pedicab clattered south toward the T-way, passing through the dark architectural graveyard which was downtown Stamford, Connecticut. Once the office tow-ers and corporate headquarters and pricey hotels had glittered at night: brilliant glass towers rising high above noon-bright boulevards. Then the city had been like a vast electrical bonfire raging out of control. Now down-town had gone out. The glass towers cost too much to heat and light. Some had been converted to warehouses; others were simply empty, presenting gap-toothed facades to the quiet streets. Their only inhabitants were watchmen, bag people, the odd weather gypsy who had overstayed the season.

As they approached the T-way, their cab was caught briefly in a traffic jam. About twenty protesters were stopping passersby in front of the messengers' mission on Washington Boulevard. A few carried electric candles; others brandished hand-lettered signs that said things like No Religion Without God and Look into the Bible. The rest circulated among the stalled bicycles and pedicars, distributing antimessenger propaganda. Wing slid down in the seat as the dolly opened her window just wide enough to accept a newsletter. "Go with Jesus," said the protester. "Sure," she said. As the pedicab rolled away, she dropped the newsletter on the seat.

"Why did you take that?" said Wing.

"Makes 'em feel good," said the dolly. "They can get mean if you ignore them."

Wing picked up the newsletter; all he could make out in the gloom were headlines: SCIENCE SAYS NO IMMORTALITY and ALABAMA BANS ALIENS and HOW THEY REALLY LOOK.

"Ever check it?" The dolly nodded back at the mission; Wing shook his head. "No worse than any other church. They feed you, give you a warm bed. But they keep trying to tell you there's no such thing as pleasure." She put a hand on his thigh. "Or pain." She squeezed. "It ain't the way life tastes to me, Philly."

They passed the Exit 7 Transit Service terminal, a squat fortress with a bush-hammered concrete facade that was supposed to discourage graffiti. Docked at the gates were a few red-white-and-blue USTS busses, mostly local carryvans but also an enormous double-decked trunk line rig. The hack cut across the lot and pulled up to the tube rack's side entrance.

Before it had been torched, the Stop Inn had been a sleek low-slung commercial office building in the joule-thief style. The fire had gutted the interior and shattered most of the thermopane but had left the structure of weathering steel and reinforced concrete intact. Its location near the T-way made it an ideal property for re-development and so it had been reborn as a rack. There were about forty fixed tubes on the top three floors and hook-ups for another forty go-tubes on the bottom three. Had he been staying longer Wing might have had his own go-tube loaded onto a semi and hauled down from Portsmouth.

The elevator was out of order so they climbed the six flights of steps. The stairwell smelled of smoke and disinfectant; the dolly complained all the way. Finally they reached his tube and Wing thumbed the lock. The hatch slid open and he was relieved to see that his bags were where he had left them. The dolly squatted to unpack her kit.

The interior of the tube was fabricated of vandal-proof plastic; all harsh colors and hard surfaces. Even so there were several places where lased graffiti had been patched over but not effaced; the window overlooking the T-way was clouded with scratches. A microwave, a sink, a mirror and a toilet were jammed into the far end of the tube; the gel mat took up most of the rest of the space. There was a monitor and keyboard mounted on a flex-arm by the headboard. The screen was flashing; he had messages.

"Phillip." Ndavu sat in an office at an enormous desk; he looked like a banker who had just realized he had made a bad loan. "I am calling to see if there's anything I can do—"

"Hey, that's one of the head beetles!" The dolly

reached past Wing to pause the vid. "I thought you didn't know anything about the messengers."

"Don't." Wing removed her finger from the key.

"—I want you to know how sorry I am about the way things have turned out. I have just seen Daisy and I must tell you she is very upset. If there is any way I can help resolve the problem, please let—"

"Sure," Wing muttered, "get the hell out of my life."

"—you did promise to stop by the mission. There is still the matter of the commission I mentioned—"

Wing stopped the message by jabbing the delete key. "How did he get this number?" The dolly did not reply. He took a deep breath before bringing up the next message in the queue.

It was from Solon Petropolus. He seemed to be in the Hall of Mirrors at Versailles as he turned from a conversation he was having with Cary Grant, Queen Victoria and Rembrandt to approach the camera. By all appearances he was a handsome man who was wearing doublet, trunk hose and canions and an extravagant wig. Probably trying to look like Louis Quatorze; the latest style was mock-baroque. Wing had never actually seen Petropolus and there were no recent pictures; however Wing thought it unlikely that he looked like this. Petropolus was at least a hundred and twenty years old.

"We regret disturbing you at this late hour," said the synthesized image, "but there is an unforeseen and unavoidable conflict which makes it necessary to reschedule your appointment. The only slot we have available for an audience is 0400 tomorrow morning." The imaginary Petropolus pulled a handkerchief from his sleeve and touched it delicately to his nose. "Recognizing that transportation might be a problem for you at that hour, we have taken the liberty of making arrangements. You will be picked up at . . ." A blank look flickered across his face and he turned to his companions. "Three-thirty, old boy," said Cary Grant, flashing a luminescent smile. "Just so," said Petropolus. "Don't be late as our time together must necessarily be brief." He looked as if he were trying to stifle a yawn and then bowed instead. Rembrandt whispered something to Victoria, who twittered. The screen went blank.

"Who stuffed that bird?" said the dolly as she pressed a microcam to the ceiling above the mat.

Wing sank onto the mat next to her. "He waves a handkerchief and I'm supposed to come running in the middle of the night?" He glanced at the monitor. "Not quite four hours."

The dolly froze. "You're not planning to pass on me, Philly? If so, say so now. I'm a working girl."

He looked at her, at the cameras she had attached to the tube walls, each cleverly positioned for the best close-ups. He did not know whether what he felt was anger or lust. It probably did not matter. "Plug him."

"Sure." She tugged at Velcro and her top whispered open. Cameras began to whirr. "But me first."

When she strapped the microcam glasses on she looked like a pink insect. Her skin was flecked with silver glitter: tiny sensors for the women and crossovers. Wing had complicated plans for this moment. He believed he could maintain his superiority to the dolly by distancing himself. He wanted to be at once spectator and participant. Even as he pulled her onto him he intended to be repelled, to wallow in disgust for the subscribers watching and sensing them on the net. Perhaps Daisy was among them; she had shocked him already with her secrets. The notion gave him a bitter sort of pleasure; it was his turn now. He had thought that as he was thrashing with the dolly he might stop and lecture them all, explain that he was only doing this because his wife had betrayed him. But the dolly was a professional, perhaps even an artist; Wing was soon shuddering with desire. Her tongue was like a flame, licking at him, burning all the plans from his mind. Soon he was nothing but another sweating body, a node on the porn net, giving and taking pleasure.

It was the dolly who made him keep the appointment. He had wanted to try it again with her because as long as he kept trying he would not have to think about what he had done. But she was finished with him.

"Come on, Philly. Show's over." She sat up in the mat and snagged her discarded isothermals with her foot. Her surgically perfected breasts dangled as she bent over and Wing felt another surge of desire. He ran a finger down her vertebrae. She reached behind her back and caught his hand in a grip that hurt. "Enough!"

He propped himself up on an elbow so that he could see her expression. If he could have seen some sign of tenderness—or better, regret—he might have been able to forgive himself. But her face was as hard as a sidewalk and he realized that she was glaring at him the way he had intended to glare at her while they were making love.

"You look like a damned puppy," she said.

He stayed on the bed while she finished dressing and repacked her kit. "I'll leave my number at the desk," she said, as she thumbed the hatch lock. "Some boys like to order copies of the vid."

Wing closed his eyes. All he wanted now was for her to go.

"You got twenty minutes before your ride shows."

Wing said nothing. He did not open his eyes again until the hatch slid shut.

Petropolus's chauffeur did not look either like Cary Grant or Queen Victoria. She was an androgynously handsome young woman who would have been totally unremarkable had she not been driving a car. Petropolus's Mercedes was the only private vehicle on the T-way at three forty-five in the morning. They passed a container train, a few trucks, some short-haul vans, and a stream of red, white and blue buses, filled with the usual cast of stolid shift workers and twisted kids. Wing envied them their flattened contentment.

They got off in Greenwich, a city masquerading as a town. By that pretense it had managed to escape the worst of the cancerous urban sprawl which had engulfed its neighbors. Although the heart of Greenwich was just as empty as that of Stamford, it was smaller and its architectural blunders had been less egregious. The Mercedes passed quickly through a neighborhood of shabby go-tube parks. The farther from the T-way they went, the more attractive the real estate, until at last they entered a section where zoning and great wealth had preserved a way of life unchanged from the era of consumption. On either side of the country road were walled estates with long driveways that led to houses built of fieldstone and brick and real wood. They turned and the chauffeur tapped recognition code. Wrought-iron gates squealed open. Wing saw two sentry spiders converging on the car out of the darkness, their ovoid bodies bristling with sensors and weaponry. He could not help but wonder what the dolly would have thought of *this* yard. Escorted by the robots, the chauffeur eased the car up the driveway toward a mansion that made Piscataqua House look like a shed.

"Go right in," said the chauffeur. "He's waiting."

The library was blood-hot. Books climbed two walls to the ceiling; a circular wrought-iron stair and two balconies provided access. Another wall was a three-story pane of optical plastic with a view of a black pond sur-

44

rounded by a shadowy formal garden. The last wall, most of the floor space and even some of the ceiling was given over to objets d'art. Wing hesitated to call it a collection; it was more a hoard. A Raphael virgin hung uneasily beside a Santiago grid; a Yoshitoshi ghoul glared at a Hopper gas station. On either side of the doorway a seated stone Buddha grinned serenely at a scowling Tlingit totem pole. A Calder mobile hung motionlessly in the stuffy air. Floating on not-quite-invisible wires in a corner was a miniature Glass Cloud.

"Mr. Petropolus?" said Wing. "Hello?"

The silence was as oppressive as the heat.

He picked his way through the clutter toward the desk. To one side was a glass case containing a scale model of Data Delphi, the first of Petropolus's Seven Wonders to be completed. On the other side of the desk was what looked like a refrigerator: an incongruous, humming, white enamel box, two meters by a meter.

"Sir?" Wing could feel sweat dribble from his armpit; his hair was already damp. "Is anyone here?" He leaned over the Delphi model and brushed his sleeve across the glass case. It came away gray with dust and he sneezed.

"You're not sick, are you?"

With a whine the refrigerator rotated toward him, revealing an ashen body plugged into its opposite side.

"Mr. Petropolus?" Wing had to sneeze again.

"You are sick!" Petropolus had the reedy voice of a twelve-year-old. "Sick."

"It's the dust."

"At least keep your mouth shut." Petropolus squirmed. "I'll be right with you. I'm filtering."

Wing found it impossible not to stare and, indeed, he quickly realized that Petropolus took a kind of perverse pleasure from the effect of his grotesque appearance. He was a little man: probably weighed less than fifty kilos. He was naked, completely hairless. His skin was the

**45**

color of spilled milk, so translucent that in places Wing could see pulsing blue and red cords beneath it. He was connected to the machine by IV collars at the neck, wrists and ankles, a bladder catheter and an array of skull plugs and sensors. He did not look like one of the world's oldest humans. He did not look human at all, but rather like a botched waxwork.

"You've been to Delphi?" said Petropolus.

Wing blinked. "No." Sweat ran into his eyes. "I've seen vids."

"Strip if you're hot." When Wing hesitated, Petropolus insisted. "Come, at least the jacket. When people faint, I lose time. You should travel more, you know. Vids lie. No substitute for being there. That's what Seven Wonders is all about. Can't believe anything you see on a screen."

Wing laid his jacket on the desk. "No."

"So what would you ask if you won the lottery at Delphi? One free query: every database in the world information net at your disposal."

Wing's shirt was drenched and he was having trouble breathing the thick air. "Why am I here?"

"Not teleology!" Petropolus's eyes rolled. "A waste of expensive computer time."

"You wanted to talk about the Glass Cloud?"

"No, no, that's over with now. Seven Wonders and all that. Obsolete. New data has come in. If I don't have to die, why build fancy tombstones?"

"What do you mean, obsolete?" The heat was making Wing dizzy. "The Cloud is finished. The dedication is in May."

"Maybe." He frowned. "Been hearing bad things from the Foundation. What's that man's name, Porter? Projections about the operating budget."

Wing wondered what would happen if he pried the old man off his life-support machine. He imagined Petropolus flopping on the hot floor like a fish. "The messengers have picked up most of the overruns."

"Messengers." Petropolus sighed. "Exactly. That's what I'd ask if I were you. Why do the messengers care about Phillip Wing?"

Wing sank into the chair behind Petropolus's desk and loosened his collar. He felt as though he might melt. "Do they?"

The old man began to talk in his odd, rambling way, as if it did not matter whether anyone was listening. "Another question: who discovered you? Eh? Did they become interested after the Foundation chose your bubble? So it would appear. But they are subtle, subtle. I've gone over the files on your selection process—not sure I understand them anymore. It was just after the messengers made first contact, everything was still a big secret. The screening committee were all professionals. Credentials long as their faces; serious, very serious and unimpeachable or there would have been hell to pay. No names on the submissions. And even so, how could they have known who you were? You were nobody. But consider: all seven are now messenger disciples. Three have actually given up their careers to live in missions. Shows a lack of imagination on your part that you know nothing of this. You! Wake up! They're interfering in your life. Don't you care?"

"No." Before the dolly, Wing might have been able to summon up the expected indignation. Now he felt nothing but a limp impatience with this strange creature, buzzing at him like some garrulous mosquito. "Your life too. You approved."

"Troubling, isn't it? Very troubling. Though I relied heavily on the selection process. I must say that I found your bubble charming in its extravagance. Not as clever, really, as Delphi. Perhaps a little silly. Still, just the sort

47

of thing to turn out the crowds. You are listening? Don't faint on me."

"I want something to drink." Wing touched his finger to the desk monitor to activate it. When nothing happened, he wrote a *D* in the dust on the screen and then smeared it. "You ought to have this room cleaned. It's disgusting."

Petropolus looked around, seemingly surprised. "Perhaps, yes, it is. It's the help, you know. I don't like having them in the room. Or anyone. Just me."

Wing was repulsed. The man was beyond mere vanity; he was using his wealth and power to create the illusion for himself that no other individual in the world existed but Solon Petropolus. Only a rich man could afford to be so utterly crazy without being locked up.

Petropolus chattered on, oblivious to the fact that Wing was not paying attention. ". . . I've been manipulated. Perhaps. But I'll twist it to my advantage, you watch. All that needs be done is to satisfy this messenger Ndavu. I do a favor for him, he owes me. Delivering you is the favor. Understand?"

Again Ndavu. "I guess I do." Wing wondered what it would take to get Ndavu to let him alone. "But I'm not interested."

"I don't believe it." Petropolus looked like a solipsist who had just heard the sound of someone breaking furniture in the next room. "You don't even know what he wants."

Wing shrugged.

"You don't realize the stakes." There was a satisfying quaver in Petropolus's voice.

Wing stood.

"Immortality!" Petropolus was crumbling before him; Wing knew from his own experience how fragile illusions could be. "They can do it. I won't be tied to this machine anymore. And I'll never die. Never."

"So what?"

"So I'll give you commissions—you can do the rest of the Wonders. Immortality too. I'll make them give it to you. I'll find a way. I promise." Petropolus's skin was pink; his chest heaved. "You want something else? What? All you have to do is visit him. He told me that's all he wants. A little chat. Tell me what you want."

"You haven't got it." Wing picked up his jacket.

"I'll junk your silly bubble." Petropolus twisted against the IV collars, trying to get Wing to look at him. "You hear? We'll sue—you'll never work again. And even if you do, no one will dare write your insurance. Wait!"

Wing paused at the door.

"I won't die, do you hear?" Petropolus's voice climbed to a screech. "Not because of you!"

"Thanks for everything." Wing brushed the grime off the Buddha's head. "I'll have to get back to you."

**T**he messengers' mission in Portsmouth sprawled over an entire block of Court Street. It was an unholy jumble of architectural afterthoughts appended to the simple neogothic chapel that had once been the Church of the Holy Spirit. There was a Victorian rectory, a squat brick-facade parochial school built in the 1950's, and an eclectic auditorium that dated from the oughts. The fortunes of the congregation had since declined and the complex had been abandoned, successfully confounding local redevelopers until the messengers bought it. The initiates of northern New England's first mission had added an underground bike lockup, washed the stained glass, repaired the rotted clapboards and planted an arborvitae screen around the auditorium and still Wing thought it was the ugliest building in Portsmouth.

In the years immediately after first contact there had been no contact at all with the masses; complex and secret negotiations continued between the messengers and various political and industrial interests. Once the deals were struck however, the aliens had moved swiftly to open missions for the propagation of the message, apparently a strange brew of technophilic materialism and zenlike self-effacement, sweetened by the promise of cybernetic immortality. The exact nature of the message was a closely held secret; the messengers would neither confirm nor deny the reports of those few initiates who left the missions.

Wing hesitated at the wide granite steps leading to the chapel; they were slick from a spring ice storm. Freshly sprinkled salt was melting holes in the ice and there was a shovel propped against one of the massive oak doors. It was five-thirty in the morning. No one inside would be expecting visitors, which was fine with Wing: he wanted to take Ndavu by surprise. But the longer he stood, the less certain he was of whether he was going in. He looked up at the eleven stone Apostles arranged across the tympanum. Tiny stylized flames danced over their heads, representing the descent of the Holy Spirit on Pentecost. He could not read the Apostles' expressions; acid rain had smudged their faces. Wing felt a little smudged himself. He reached into his back pocket for the flask. He took a swig and found new courage as a whiskey flame danced down his throat. He staggered into the church—twisted in the good old-fashioned way and too tired to run from Ndavu anymore.

As his eyes adjusted to the gloom he saw that there had been some changes made in the iconography. Behind the altar hung a huge red flag with the Buddhist Wheel of Law at its center and the words "Look into the Sun" embroidered in gold thread beneath it. A dancing Shiva filled a niche next to a statue of Christ Resurrected.

Where the Stations of the Cross had once been were now busts: Pythagoras, Plato, Lao-tzu. Others whose names he did not recognize were identified as Cabalists, Gnostics, Sufis and Theosophists—whatever they were. Wing had not known what to expect, but this was not quite it. Still, he thought he understood what the messengers were trying to do. The Romans had been quick to induct the gods of subjugated peoples into their pantheon. And what was humanity if not subjugated? That was why he had come, he thought bitterly. To acknowledge that he was beaten. Ndavu had bullied him into an interview.

A light came on in the vestry next to the altar. Footsteps echoed across the empty church. Jim McCauley stepped into the candlelight and came to the edge of the altar rail. "Is someone there?"

Wing swayed down the aisle, catching at pews to steady himself. He felt as empty as the church. As he approached the altar he saw that McCauley was wearing a loosely tied yellow bathrobe; his face was crinkled, as if he had just come from a warm bed. With Daisy? Wing told himself that it did not matter anymore, that he had to concentrate on the plan he had discovered an hour ago at the bottom of a bottle of Argentinean Scotch: hear Ndavu out and then tell him to drop dead. He saluted McCauley.

The man gathered his yellow bathrobe more tightly. "Who is it?"

Wing stepped up to the altar rail and grasped it to keep from falling. "Phillip Wing, A.I.A. Here to see the head beetle." McCauley looked blank. "That's Ndavu to you."

"He expects you, Phillip?"

Wing cackled. "I should hope not."

"I see." McCauley gestured at the gate in the center of the altar rail. "Come this way—do you need help, Phillip?"

In response Wing vaulted the rail. His trailing foot caught and he sprawled at McCauley's feet. The sculptor was wearing yellow plastic slippers to match the robe.

"Hell no." Wing picked himself up.

McCauley eyed him doubtfully and then ushered him through the vestry to a long flight of stairs. As they descended, Peter Bornsten, the busboy from Piscataqua House, scurried around the corner and sprinted up toward them, taking steps two at a time.

"Peter," said McCauley. "I thought you were shoveling the steps."

Peter froze. Wing had never seen him like this: he was wearing janitors' greens and had the lame expression of a guilty eight-year-old. "I was, James, but the ice was too hard and so I salted it and went down to the kitchen for some coffee. I was cold," he said lamely. He glared briefly at Wing as if it were his fault and then hung his head. The Peter Bornsten Wing knew was a careless young stud whose major interests were stimulants and waitresses.

"Go and finish the steps." McCauley touched Peter's forehead with his middle finger. "The essence does not experience cold, Peter."

"Yes, James." He bowed and scraped by them.

McCauley's slippers flapped as he walked slowly down the hallway that ran the length of the mission's basement. Doorways without doors opened into rooms filled with cots. It looked as if there were someone sleeping on every one. Wing smelled the yeasty aroma of curing vitabulk long before they passed a kitchen where three cooks in white were sitting at a table around four cups of coffee. At the end of the hall double doors opened onto an auditorium jammed with folding tables and chairs. A door to the right led up a short flight of stairs to a large telelink conference room and several small private offices.

McCauley went to one of the terminals at the conference table and tapped at the keyboard. Wing had a bad
angle on the screen; all he could see was the glow.
"Phillip Wing," said McCauley and the screen immediately went dark.

Wing sat down across the table from him and pulled
out his flask. "Want some?" There was no reply. "You
the welcoming committee?"

McCauley remained standing. "I spread the message,
Phillip."

Someone else might have admired the calm with
which McCauley was handling himself; Wing wanted to
see him sweat. "I thought you were supposed to be an
artist. You had shows in New York, Washington—you
had a career going."

"I did." He shrugged. "But my reasons for working
were all wrong. Too much ego, not enough essence. The
messengers showed me how trivial art is."

Wing was not going to let him get away with that.
"Maybe it's just you that's trivial. Maybe you didn't have
the stuff to make art that meant anything. Ever think of
that?"

"Yes." McCauley smiled. Daisy came into the room.

It had been twenty-eight days since he had last seen
his wife; Wing was disgusted with himself for knowing
the number exactly. After the party he had worked hard
at avoiding her. He had moved their go-tube to a cheap
local rack near the T-way and had moved in. He had
tried to stay away from the arid precincts of her Portsmouth while lowering himself into the swamp around its
edges. He had reprogrammed the door to the Counting
House to admit no one but him and had changed his
work schedule, sneaking in just often enough to keep up
appearances. He had never replied to the messages she
left for him.

"What's she doing here?" Wing was tempted to walk out.

"I think it best that you wait alone with him, Daisy," said McCauley.

"Best for who?" said Wing.

"For her, of course. Look into the sun, Daisy."

"Yes, James."

"Phillip." He bowed and left them together.

"Look into the sun. Look into the sun." He opened the flask. "What the hell does that mean anyway?"

"It's like a koan—a proverb. It takes time to explain." Daisy looked as though she had put herself together in a hurry: wisps of hair fell haphazardly across her forehead and the collar of her mud-colored stretchsuit was turned up. She settled across the table from him and drummed her fingers on a keyboard, straightened her hair, glanced at him and then quickly away. He realized that she did not want to be there either and he took another drink.

"Keep your secrets then. Who cares? I came to see Ndavu."

"He's not here right now."

"All right." Wing pushed the chair back. "Good-bye, then."

"No, please." She seemed alarmed. "He's coming. Soon. He'll want to see you; he's been waiting."

"It's good for him." Wing thought she must have orders to keep him there; that gave him a kind of power over her. If he wanted to he could probably steer this encounter straight into one of the revenge fantasies that had so often been a bitter substitute for sleep. No matter what he said, she would have to listen.

"Are you often like this?" she said.

"What the hell do you care?" He drank and held out the flask. "Thirsty?"

"You haven't returned my calls."

"That's right." He shook the flask at her.

She did not move. "I know what you've been doing."

"What is it you're waiting to hear, Daisy?" Saying her name did it. The anger washed over him like the first wave of an amphetamine storm. "That I've spent the last couple of weeks twisted out of my mind? That I can't stand to live without you? Well, plug yourself. Even if it were true I wouldn't give you the satisfaction."

She sat like a statue, her face as smooth and as invulnerable as stone, her eyes slightly glazed, as if she were meditating at the same time she pretended to listen to him. His anger veered out of control.

"You're not worth it, you know that? It gets me right in the gut sometimes, that I ever felt anything for you. You pissed on everything I thought was important in my life and I was dumb enough to be surprised when you did it. Look at you. I'm suffering and you sit there like you're carved out of bloody ice. And calling it good breeding, no doubt. Fine. Great. But just remember that when you die, you bitch, you'll be nothing but another stinking puddle on the floor."

Then Wing saw the tear. At first he was not even sure that it was hers: her expression had not changed. Maybe a water pipe had leaked through the ceiling and dripped on her. The tear rolled down her cheek and dried near the corner of her mouth. A single tear. She held her head rigidly erect, looking at him. Suddenly he was ashamed.

He leaned forward, put his elbows on the table; his head in his hands. He felt like crying too. "It's been hard," he said. He shuddered, took a deep breath. "I'm sorry." He wanted to reach across the table and wipe away the track of her tear with his finger but she was too far away.

They sat without speaking. He imagined she was thinking serene messenger thoughts; he contemplated the ruins of their marriage. Ever since the party Wing had hoped, secretly, desperately, that Daisy would in time offer some explanation that he could accept—even if it were not true. He had expected to be reconciled. Now for the first time he realized that she might not want a reconciliation. The silence stretched. The telelink beeped; Daisy tapped at the keyboard.

"He'll see you in his office," she said.


Ndavu was actually on a starship in Earth orbit. He explained that what Wing was looking at was a holo-ghost, an image projected through a windowcomm—whatever that was. The messenger's grin reminded Wing of the grin that Leonardo had given his John the Baptist: mysterious, ironic, fey.

"We do not, as you say, keep the message to ourselves." Ndavu's wheelchair appeared to be docked at an enormous desk; in one corner was a model of the Glass Cloud which Wing immediately resented. "On the contrary we have opened missions around the world. We help all who seek enlightenment. Surely you see that it would be irresponsible for us to disseminate such transcendently important information without providing the guidance necessary to its understanding." Ndavu kept nodding as if trying to entice Wing to nod back and accept his evasions.

Wing had the feeling that Ndavu would prefer that he settle back on the couch and think about how lucky he was to have just been invited to visit a starship—the first human ever. But Wing was not having any of it. "Then keep your goddamned secret—why can't you just give us plans to this reincarnation computer and loan us the keys to a starship?"

"Technology is the crux of the message, Phillip."

Daisy sat beside Wing in rigid silence; he wondered if she might not be jealous that he was going to take the tour. "Is she going to be reincarnated?" Wing wanted to pierce her shell; it was beginning to irk him. Or maybe it was just that he was beginning to sober up to a blinding headache. "Is that the reward for joining up?"

"The message is its own reward," she said.

"Don't you want to be reincarnated?"

"The essence does not want. It acknowledges karma."

"The essence?" Wing could feel a vein throbbing just above his right eyebrow.

"That which can be reincarnated," she said.

"There are no easy answers, Phillip," said Ndavu.

"No." He shook his head in disgust. "Does anyone have an aspirin?"

Daisy went to check. "Everything is interconnected," the messenger continued. "For instance I could tell you that it is the duty of intelligence to resist entropy. How could you hope to understand me? You would have to ask: What is intelligence? What is entropy? How may it be resisted? Why is it a duty? These are questions which it took the commonwealth of messengers centuries to answer."

"Just give me the short course."

Daisy returned with McCauley. "What we will ask of you," replied Ndavu, "does not require that you accept our beliefs. Should you wish to seek enlightenment, then I will be pleased to guide you, Phillip. However, you should know that it is not at all clear whether it is possible to grasp the message in the human lifespan. We have only just begun to study your species and have yet to measure its potential."

McCauley stood behind the couch, waiting inconspicuously for Ndavu to finish dodging the question. He rested a hand on Wing's shoulder, as if he were an old pal trying to break into a friendly conversation. "Excuse me, Phillip," said McCauley and Wing remembered something he had forgotten to do. Something that had nagged at him for weeks. He was sober enough now to stay angry and the son of a bitch kept calling him by his first name.

"I'm very sorry, Phillip," said McCauley with a polite grin, "but we don't have much use for drugs here. However, if you're really in need we could send someone out—"

Wing shot off the couch, turned and hit his wife's lover right in the smile. Astonished, McCauley took the punch and Daisy gave a strangled little scream. The sculptor staggered backward, fists clenched. Ndavu looked stunned. Wing turned and whipped the model of the Cloud at the messenger. His ghost rippled and distorted like a reflection in a pond. A window seemed to close on the scrambled image and the messenger was gone.

"That's okay." He sat down, rubbing his knuckles. "I feel much better now."

McCauley touched his bloody lip and then turned and walked quickly from the office. Daisy was staring at the empty space where the ghost had been. Wing settled back on the couch and—for the first time in weeks—started to laugh.

arumen could
tell when Teaqua picked up her shovel; people leaned
toward her like seedlings bending to the sun. Harumen's
view into the garden was blocked as she prowled the far
edge of the crowd. All she saw were backs as people
stood on tiptoes and craned for a glimpse of their goddess. The latecomers jumped up and down in frustration.
They had all watched her ghost before on the link, but
this was different. A chance to see the goddess, in the
flesh, transplanting a tree. She dug a hole and they saw a
spectacle. It depressed Harumen because it reminded her
just how irreplaceable Teaqua was. She was more than
just a symbol; they loved her.

Of course, this lot was pretty raw. Most were either
newly shriven reborns or aged tremblers who had come
to Mateag to yield up their memories and start new lives.

A scattering of farmers had crossed the river to the holy island. The rest were priests or pedants, many more than would have come just a few days before. Word had spread to the temples that Teaqua had made peace with her prophet.

Harumen circled around to where a cordon of blades guarded Teaqua from the crowd. The garden beyond them was small but opulent. It was walled on three sides; the fourth was a marble gallery open to the sun, the air and the devout. The irrigation ditch was lined with azure tile and the well-sweeps were carved ironwood. An agate path wound like a stream of jewels through stands of hybrid messenger wheat, bramble hedges and breadroot mounds. Bright drifts of flowers perfumed the air. There were no weeds, no blotches of mildew, no chewed stems or brown leaves. It was nothing like a real garden and yet it was exactly what these people wanted to see. They did not care if Teaqua herself only visited once or twice a year. It made no difference that there were a dozen unknown gardeners who labored to maintain the plantings. The people wanted a vision of perfection, a dream to sustain them as they weeded their own hardpan fields. It was Teaqua's genius that she had always understood the needs of her people.

Teaqua put her foot on the step of the shovel, drove it into the ground, bent her knees and turned a small clod of soil out of the hole. Step, bend, turn. Step, bend, turn. There was an easy rhythm to her digging; it looked to Harumen like a kind of dance. Ammagon stood uselessly behind the goddess, holding a spading fork and basking in her reflected glory like a snake.

"You watch her now." A farmer in a woven straw hat was talking to a wide-eyed reborn; Harumen eavesdropped. "No wasted effort. And she doesn't try to move too much at once. You can see she's used a shovel before."

The reborn was mesmerized. Teaqua dug methodically. The hole was a meter wide.

"She was born on a farm," said someone behind the reborn. "She knows about work."

"Not like the priest," the farmer said.

"He has soft hands," the other agreed. "They all do."

Teaqua's shovel clicked against a stone. In her first life, before she had risen to greatness, she grown up on a farm in the coastlands. Everyone knew this; it was part of the truths.

"Now here is a surprise." Ndavu came up behind Harumen and caressed her shoulder. "When did you start taking an interest in horticulture?"

She rubbed the side of her face up against his hand. "About the same time he did." She nodded at the prophet. "Actually I've been looking for you. Walk with me for a moment?" She linked her arm through his and steered him from the garden.

They turned onto a cobbled lane. In the blue-green distance to the north were the estates of Temple Kautama; half a kilometer to the south Temple Weekan jutted from the fields like a brick cliff. Harumen waited for Ndavu to speak, offer an explanation, some word of hope. A knot of stragglers trotted past them, hurrying to join the crowd. When Ndavu waved, they waved back. He fooled most people that way; very few noticed he was a messenger unless they were told.

"Were we going somewhere?" Ndavu stopped beside a stone bench in the shade of a mature gold dust tree. "I promised the goddess—"

"I don't understand what you're doing." Harumen could no longer hold her feelings in. She felt betrayed by the two people she loved most. Teaqua and Ndavu.

The messenger brushed the yellow pollen from the bench with his hand. "I should think that it is clear enough." He sat.

"You can't let him win. He's a priest."

"Ammagon is not the problem; you know that. Teaqua has asked us for help. We intend to provide it."

"You've found the world then?"

"There *is* a world about five parsecs away, apparently seeded in the same sweep as Aseneshesh. It is remarkable, actually; the biologies are quite similar. I would like to know how she found out about it."

Harumen goaded him. "Chan came to her in a dream."

"Yes," said Ndavu mildly. "That is one theory."

"But you're encouraging her in it!"

"You want me to lie? There has been trouble enough between us. The commonwealth wants only to maintain good relations with this government—and the next."

"Ammagon hates you, you know."

"We should go back." Ndavu stood. "I promised to tell Teaqua just as soon as I received approval from uptime."

"She's sick, Ndavu," said Harumen. "She hasn't been herself since she stopped sharing pleasure with us. She sleeps alone—all the time now. It isn't normal." Harumen wanted to say what did not need saying: Teaqua was not the only one who slept alone. No one had asked Harumen to the common bed since she had taken Ndavu as a lover. Even scholars had their prejudices. "You've got to help us." Ndavu started walking but Harumen stuck to the middle of the road as if she had taken root there. "She wants to undo everything." She was shouting at his back. "This is madness!"

Ndavu waved without turning. Eventually Harumen chased after him, feeling ridiculous.

"What are you going to tell her?"

"That I will go to this world for her." Ndavu acted as if nothing had happened. "I will try and find someone to build her shrine."

"*You're* going?"

"Who else would you suggest? Besides, I have been downtime here longer than any other messenger—too long."

Just ahead Harumen could hear the peasants hoot in approval and then fall silent. Two more staccato outbursts and then a prolonged screech. Probably Teaqua was saying a few words to the crowd.

"So you're just going to go?" Harumen said bitterly. "It makes no sense. Do you really think Ammagon will lead us into the commonwealth after Teaqua dies? He wants to—"

Ndavu stopped and caught her by the shoulders, spinning her around as if he were fed up with her complaining. He met her gaze boldly, as if to threaten her. As if he were still going to be her lover.

"You should listen if you want to understand," he said. "It is twenty-one years each way, plus however long it takes to convince some poor fool to come here. Those are the facts. Not even a goddess can change relativity. Nothing can happen until I return. Nothing is decided."

"Except that you're leaving me."

"I am going away." Ndavu flagged his impatience. "I am coming back." The ceremony had ended and the crowd spilled out of the gallery onto the road. Ndavu and Harumen were an island in a stream of religious fervor. "If Ammagon does not trust us," Ndavu continued, "hates us, as you say, what is he going to make of the architect I bring back? Even though Teaqua has already convinced herself that this person has been chosen by Chan. Do you understand now? He must be the wedge that drives them apart."

Harumen understood well enough. All her loyalties had been cut from under her; she was falling and there was nothing to catch on to. She could feel people staring as they bumped past.

"Ndavu!" Ammagon called. "Over here." The messenger patted her shoulder and then led her past the cordon of blades to where the prophet stood, beaming at the sapling as if it were a sign from Chan. A few steps away, Teaqua was campaigning for the support of a group of local priests.

"I am sorry to have missed the ceremony," said Ndavu. He bowed and Ammagon bowed; they greeted each other with the polite insincerity of enemies at truce. The prophet ignored Harumen.

"I was just telling Harumen that we will have to sit together under this tree when I come back." Ndavu stooped and brought his hand up under a heavy gold-flecked leaf to admire it. "I will expect her to make a good accounting of the time she has spent."

"I know she'll do her best to please you." The way Ammagon said it made her want to slap him. The prophet was gloating.

Teaqua finally tore herself away from the priests.

"Ah, Teaqua." Ndavu stepped forward to make the sign of supplication. "There is good news!"

**T**he messengers had done a thorough job; Wing's cabin was a copy of the interior of the go-tube he and Daisy had customized on spare weekends just after they were married. They had only used it twice: vacations at the disneydome in New Jersey and the Grand Canyon. Somehow they could never find time to get away. The cabin on the starship had a look-alike oak rolltop desk with a built-in terminal, a queen-sized Murphy bed with a gel mattress and Wing's one extravagance: Chair 31, by Alvar Aalto, one of the Finn's laminated plywood masterpieces. The ceiling was a single sheet of mirror plastic like that Wing had nearly broken his back installing. At the far end was a microwave, sink, toilet and mirror set in a wall surround of Korean tile that Daisy had spent two months picking out. There were differences, however. The gravity was .6 Earth normal; Wing thought he could have lifted the desk over his head had the ceiling been high enough. The floor was not tongue-and-grooved oak but some kind of transparent crystal; beneath him reeled the elephant-skin wrinkles of the Zagros Mountains. And Daisy slept next door.

Wing stared like a blind man at the swirling turquoise shallows that rimmed the Persian Gulf; Ndavu's arduous briefing had turned his sense of wonder to stone. He now knew everything about a planet called Aseneshesh that a human being could absorb in forty-eight hours without going mad. When he closed his eyes he could see the aliens Ndavu called the Chani. Wing had described them to Daisy as twitchy monkeys that had been stretched on a rack, with pink teeth, huge faces and manes that made them look impossibly top-heavy. Not quite escapees from a nightmare but still profoundly disturbing—as much for their similarities to *Homo sapiens* as for their differences.

He knew some of their history. When glaciers threatened to crush their civilization, most Chani had left Aseneshesh. Something had happened to those few who remained behind, something that the messengers still could not account for. Even as they slid into barbarism, these creatures began to evolve at an accelerated rate. Something was pushing them toward a biological immortality totally unlike the hardware-based reincarnations of the messengers. Their cities buried and their machines beyond repair, they had huddled around smoky fires and discovered within themselves the means to intervene in the aging process, by sheer force of mind to tilt the delicate balance between anabolism and catabolism. They called it shriving. With their sins forgotten and their cells renewed, the Chani could live many lives in one body, retaining just a few memories from one cycle to the next. What annoyed the materialist messengers was that shriving was the central rite of a religion based on sun worship. *Look into the sun*, the flourishing remnant had declared to the astonished survey teams, centuries after they had been abandoned. Look into the sun and live again.

The messengers could hardly accept shriving as a divine gift of 82 Eridani, a class G5 main sequence star. Yet since they coveted the biological mechanisms activated by the rite, they embraced some of the trappings of the Chani religion. When delta globulins derived from Chani blood proved beneficial to a number of messenger species, rejuvenation serum became an invaluable commodity. Greed quickly touched off a devastating war for control of the blood supply. The goddess Teaqua's victory made her for a brief time the most powerful being in the commonwealth. However, the messengers soon learned to synthesize the globulins and history once again passed the Chani—and their thearch—by. The goddess continued to rule over her backward, and now profoundly xenophobic, people. Theirs was a proudly static culture, neither in the commonwealth nor out of it. Teaqua had been reborn at least a dozen times; she was the oldest living sentient known to the messengers. But now she had decided to die.

"She wants a tomb, Phillip, and she claims Chan told her a human must build it." Ndavu had given up his wheelchair in the starship's low gravity. As he spoke he had walked gingerly about Wing's cabin, like a barefoot man watching out for broken glass. "You will design it and oversee its construction."

"But if they're immortal . . ."

"No; eventually they all choose death over shriving. We believe there are physical limits related to the storage capacity of their brains. They say that the burden of memories from their past lives becomes too heavy to carry. Think of it, Phillip: a tomb for a goddess. Has any architect had an opportunity to compare? This commission is more important than anything that Seven Wonders—anyone on Earth—could offer you. It has historic implications. You can help lead your world into the commonwealth."

"But why me? There must be thousands who would jump at this."

"Unfortunately, there are but a handful." The messenger frowned, considering. "I will be blunt with you, Phillip; there is no avoiding the relativistic effects of uptime. You will be taking a one-way trip into the future. What you will experience as a voyage of a few weeks' duration on this ship will take decades downtime, on Earth. It could be fifty years or more before you return. There is no way we can predict what changes will occur. You must understand that the world to which you will return may seem as alien as Aseneshesh." He paused just long enough to scare Wing. "You will, however, return a hero. While you are gone your name will be remembered and revered; we will see to it that you become a legend. Your work will influence a generation of artists; schoolchildren will study your life. You could also be rich, if you wanted."

"And you're telling me no one else could do this? No one?"

"There is a certain personality profile. The candidate must be able to survive two stressful cultural transitions with faculties intact. Your personal history indicates that you have the necessary resilience. Talent is yet another qualification."

Wing snickered. "But not as important as being a loner with nothing to lose."

"I do not accept that characterization." Ndavu settled uneasily onto the Aalto chair; he did not quite fit. "The fact is, Phillip, that we have already been refused once. Should you too turn us down we will proceed to the next on the list. You should know, however, that time is running out and that you are the last of our prime candidates. The others have neither your ability nor your courage."

Courage. The word made Wing uncomfortable; he did not think of himself as a brave man. "What I still don't understand," he said, "is why you need a human in the first place. Build it yourself, if it's so damn important."

"We would prefer that. However, Teaqua insists that only a human can do what she says Chan wants."

"That's absurd."

"Of course it is absurd." Ndavu made no effort to conceal his scorn. "We are talking about fifty million intelligent beings who believe that the local star cares for them. We are talking about a creature of flesh and blood who believes she has become a god. You cannot apply the rules of logic to superstition."

"But how did she find out about humans in the first place?"

"We suspect that she got the information from us. At the height of the blood trade, we were forced to grant her unsupervised access to our records. Of course, she claims it was Chan who told her."

"It's crazy." Wing shook his head. "I can't believe I'm listening to this."

"Take time to think." Ndavu stood, shuffled across the cabin and held out his hand. Wing shook it gingerly. "You have qualities, Phillip. You are ambitious and impatient with the waste of your talents. The first time I saw you, I knew you were the one we needed."

Now Wing was alone with an intoxicating view of the Earth, trying to sort fact from feeling, wrestling with his doubts. It was true: he had been increasingly uneasy in his work. Even the Glass Cloud was not all he had hoped it would be. *A tomb for a goddess.* It was too much, too fantastic. Thinking about it made Wing himself feel unreal. Here he sat with the Earth at his feet, gazing down at the wellspring of civilization like some ancient, brooding god. *A legend.* He thought that if he were home he could see his way more clearly. Except that he had no home anymore, or at least he could never go home to Piscataqua House. The thought was depressing; was there really nothing to hold him? He wondered whether Ndavu had brought him to the starship to feed his sense of unreality, to cut him off from the reassurance of the mundane. He would have never been able to take this talk of gods and legends seriously had he been sitting at his desk at the Counting House with the rubber plant gathering dust near the window and his diploma from Yale hanging next to *St. John the Baptist*. Wing could see the Baptist smiling like a messenger as he pointed up at heaven—to the stars? *A one-way trip.* So Ndavu thought he was brave enough to go. But was he brave enough to stay? To turn down such a project and to live with that decision for the rest of his life? Wing was afraid that he was going to accept because there was nothing else for him to do. He would be an exile, he would be the alien. Wing had never even been in space before. Maybe that was why Ndavu had brought him here to make the offer. So that the emptiness of space could speak to the coldness growing within him.

He stood, walked quickly from the cabin. He took a moment to orient himself and then swung across the gravity well to the next landing. There was an elaborate access panel with printreader and voice analyzer and a numeric keypad and scanner; he knocked.

Daisy opened the door. Her room exhaled softly and she brushed the hair from her face. She was wearing the same mud-colored stretchsuit; Wing could not help but think of all the beautiful clothes hanging in her closet at Piscataqua House.

"Come in." She stood aside as he entered. The door

slid shut. He was surprised again at how her cabin duplicated his. She observed him solemnly. He wondered if she ever smiled when she was alone.

"I don't want to talk about it," he said, answering the unspoken question. "I don't even want to think about it. I wish he would just go away." He sat in the chair.

"He won't."

She was about as sympathetic as a concrete wall; he wondered exactly why Ndavu had brought her along. "What I could use is a drink."

"What did you want to talk about?" She leaned against the desk and looked down on him.

"Nothing. I don't know." Wing felt awkward trying to chat with her; it was as if there were a clock ticking somewhere behind her eyes. "I never told you that it was a nice party. The hot dogs were a big hit."

She sniffed. "Snob appeal had something to do with it, don't you think? I'm sure that most of them like vitabulk just fine. But they have to rave about natural or else people will think they have no taste. At the mission we've been eating raw batch and no one complains. After a while natural seems a little bit decadent—or at least a waste of time."

"The essence can't taste mustard, eh?"

Before Ndavu, she might have detected the irony in his voice and bristled at it; now she nodded. "Exactly."

"But what is the essence? How can anything be you that can't taste mustard, that doesn't even have a body?"

"The essence is that part of mind which can be reproduced in artificial media," she said with catechetical swiftness.

"And that's what you want when you die, to have your personality deleted, your memories summarized and edited and reedited until all you are is a collection of headlines about yourself stored in a computer?" He shook his head. "Sounds like a lousy substitute for heaven."

"But heaven is a myth."

"Okay," he said, trying to match her calm but not quite succeeding, "but I can't help but notice that the messengers are in no hurry to have their essences extracted. They use this stuff they got from the Chani to keep themselves alive as long as they can. Why? And since they haven't got an explanation for this shriving trick the Chani do, how do they know heaven is a myth?"

"Nothing is perfect, Phil." He was surprised to hear her admit it. "That's the most difficult part of the message. We can't claim perfection; we can only aspire to it."

"You've been spending a lot of time at the mission?"

"That's a dumb question." Her face hardened. "But I suppose I should expect—" She swallowed the rest of the sentence, although it seemed like she might choke on it.

Wing was confused; he had not been trying to annoy her. It was just something to say. "What?" He came out of the chair and grasped her shoulders. "Go ahead, Daisy. You can tell me."

"I know I can tell you. But you won't understand." She shook herself and Wing let his hands drop away from her. "It's too hard talking to you about this."

"Why?"

"You shouldn't even have to think." She sounded bitter. "Why is he offering *you* this chance? You haven't made any commitment to the message. If he asked me, any of us at the mission . . ." Her mask of detachment slipped, revealing a passion Wing had never seen before. She believed, and nothing else mattered. "I'm sorry." Her voice was very small.

"Right. I'm sorry too."

She went to the sink, splashed water on her face, and let her emotions swirl down the drain. Her skin was pink when she turned again to face him. But the mask was back in place.

"So you'd go," he said.

She sat on the bed and nodded.

"And what about Piscataqua House? Who'd mind the inn?"

She looked blank for a moment, as if trying to remember something that was not very important. "The inn pretty much takes care of itself, I guess. Bechet knows what to do." She frowned. "Business is terrible, you know."

"No, I didn't know."

"We've been in the red for over a year. Nobody goes anyplace these days." She tugged at a wrinkle in the leg of her stretchsuit. "I've been thinking of selling or maybe even just closing the old place up."

Wing was shocked. "You never told me you were having problems."

She stared through the floor for a moment. The starship's rotation had presented them with a view of the hazy blue rim of Earth's atmosphere set against star-flecked blackness. "No," she said finally. "Maybe I didn't. At first I thought the Cloud might turn things around. Bring more tourists to New Hampshire, to Portsmouth—to the inn to see you. Ndavu offered a loan to hold me over. But now it doesn't matter much anymore."

"Ndavu!" Wing stood and began to pace away his anger. "Always Ndavu. He manipulated us to get his way. You must see that."

"Of course I see. You're the one who doesn't see. It's not his way he's trying to get. It's *the* way." She leaned forward as if to stop him and make him listen. He backed away. "He has disrupted dozens of lives just to bring you here. If you had given him any kind of chance, none of it would have happened. But you were prejudiced against him or just stubborn—I don't know what you were." Her eyes gleamed. "Haven't you figured it out yet? He wanted me to fall in love with Jim McCauley."

Wing gazed at her in silent horror.

"And he was right to do it; Jim has been good for me. He isn't obsessed with himself and his projects and his career. He finds the time to listen. To be there when I need him."

"I was there! All you had to do was ask." He felt like hitting someone—but there was only himself. "You let that alien use you to get to me?"

"I didn't know at the time that he was doing it. I didn't know enough about the message to appreciate why he had to do it. But now I'm glad. I would have just been another reason for you to turn him down. It's important that you go to Aseneshesh. It's the most important thing you'll ever do."

"It's so important that his first choice turned him down, right? I should too. Just because I fit some damned personality profile . . ."

"He said it that way only because you haven't yet accepted the message. He's not just some telelink psych, Phil, he understands your essence. He knows what you need to grow and reach fulfillment. He knew when he asked you that you would accept."

Wing was dizzy. "If I leave with him and go uptime or whatever he calls it—zapping off at the speed of light— I'll never see you again. You'll be downtime here. You'll be old, you might even die before I get back. Doesn't that mean anything to you?"

"It means I'll always miss you." Her voice was flat, as if she were talking about a stolen towel.

He dropped to his knees in front of her, took her hands. "You meant so much to me, Daisy. Still do, after everything." He spoke without hope, yet he was compelled to say it. "All I want is to go back to the way it was. Do you remember? I know you remember."

"I remember we were two lonely people, Phil. We couldn't give each other what we needed." She made him let go and then ran her hand through his hair. "I remember I was unhappy." Sometimes when they were alone, reading or watching telelink, she would scratch his head. Now she fell absently into the old habit. Even though he knew he had lost her, he took comfort from it.

"I was always afraid to be happy." Wing rested his head in her lap. "I felt as if I didn't deserve to be happy."

The stars shone up at them with an ancient, pitiless light. Ndavu had done a thorough job, Wing thought. He's given me good reasons to go, reasons enough not to stay. The messengers were nothing if not thorough.

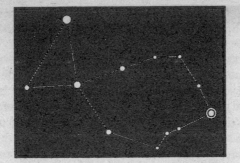

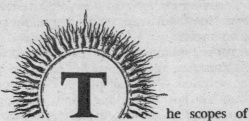

**T**he scopes of Teaqua's windowcomm tracked Ammagon like five unblinking eyes. He fidgeted under their rude stare; he would have preferred to have a priest—or even a scholar—aiming them. But the crew had been replaced by smart machines. Only the messengers would think to give a machine a mind. He wondered what the windowcomm thought of him, if it could know how he hated it.

Onwindow, the chief of the mining town of Netasu was complaining. All the nearby deposits of bog ore were played out. What she wanted was to import partly refined bloom iron from upriver and train local smiths to finish it. An entire village wanted to change over from mining to ironworking! It would wreak economic havoc down the coast.

"And when they hear about this in Kunish and Uncamish?" The prophet wished he could reach through the window and get hold of the stubborn chief. "They'll be all over me." Shake some sense into her.

"My people can't eat slag."

"I'm not asking them to."

"We want to work. That's all."

Chiskat slid into the room, flattening herself against the wall so as not to attract the scopes away from Ammagon. The prophet took a few seconds to get his bearings. Even after all these years, he was not yet used to being in two places at once. Chiskat was here. The chief—Ammagon had already forgotten her name—was actually hundreds of kilometers north. And Ammagon . . . sometimes he was no longer sure exactly where he was. The room was getting warm. He could smell his own sweat.

"Just a minute." Although he signed for the chief to be quiet, she kept arguing her case. Ammagon paid her no attention. Chiskat silently mouthed words; he tried to read her lips. Something about wanting. Or waiting. They were all waiting, thought Ammagon. He signaled to Chiskat that he was almost done.

"You're not listening." The chief loomed upwindow, as if she could get his attention by getting closer.

"No." He pulled back and fixed her with his sternest grimace. "I've listened long enough. I understand the problem. I'm afraid some of you may have to leave and find mining work higher in the mountains. I'll do what I can for the rest. I'll come back to you when I decide." He broke the link. What the chief wanted was a miracle. Ammagon had long since run out of them.

"About time," said Chiskat. "They've been at the table now for nearly an hour."

"Who?"

"You're eating with the scholars."

"Not if I can help it."

"They want to talk about building new galleries at Quaquonikeesak."

"There's nothing to say."

"Teaqua saw them yesterday. She said she'd think about it."

"Then let her eat with them!" Ammagon tugged at his mane. "Is Harumen there?"

Chiskat clenched her fist.

"Probably smirking too. We're going to have to help those miners in Netasu, you know. They can't eat slag. There are just too many people, Chiskat. The world is getting too small for all of us. I'm trying to hold things together but it's changing too fast. And Teaqua is no help—none at all. I never asked to rule. It's not what I do; I'm a priest. If she wants to give orders, fine. Let her come here and tell the miners to pack up and leave their homes. Let her . . ."

Chiskat had a polite but awkward expression on her face, as if the prophet had lapsed into some unintelligible Warm Age tongue. She was loyal to both Teaqua and Ammagon; the prophet's fulminations against the goddess embarrassed her. Sometimes Ammagon was embarrassed himself, but he had reason to be angry. Teaqua was losing her battle with time. She refused to cede power as she doddered toward the end of her life, yet her increasing frailty often left her unable to govern. The thearchy was drifting. That was not Chiskat's fault, however.

"Tell them to eat without me." Ammagon clapped a hand on her shoulder as they walked from the room. "I need to be alone for a while. I'll join them later." He turned down the hall toward to the bedroom. "Tell them I'm praying—that'll give them something to joke about."

The bedroom was empty, although the scents of his lovers lingered pleasantly. Ammagon opened his foot locker and took out a lightweight tunic and slithered into it. He prostrated himself on the prayer rug in front of the window, putting his cheek to the rug, splaying his fingers, turning his feet out. The prayer position was no longer as easy to assume as it once had been. He pressed himself to the floor, flattened his muscles, made himself smaller in the sight of the god. Of course it was evening and Chan had long since turned his face from the world. But then even during the day here in the city of scholars, clouds usually hid the sun. Ammagon was convinced that was why this city was the capital of godlessness.

Ammagon tried to pray, to open himself to the god. He looked for the beautiful blue spot that had once burned within him, but could not find it. He listened for Chan's whisper yet heard only the rasp of his own breathing. For years it had been getting harder to pray. It took a simplicity that Ammagon had lost. His life was too complicated; he knew too much. Despite all his efforts change was everywhere—even in him. When Teaqua had first brought him back to the court and named him her successor, Ammagon had made plans for a return to the old ways. The ways of Chan. He was going to disperse the scholars. Cut back on the use of the links. Enforce the quarantine of the messengers. Nothing had been done. Teaqua had thwarted him at every step—all in the name of maintaining peace and stability. Yet stability was an illusion.

"Chan, hear me!" Ammagon knew that he did not have to see Chan, that Chan was within him. In them all, even scholars. He knew they were probably making fun of him downstairs. It was easier to imagine their voices than to hear Chan's whispers. And it would only get worse, of this Ammagon was certain. Twenty-one years—it had been twenty-one years since the messenger had left. Maybe he had reached his destination and was already about Teaqua's business. Ammagon was not sure. It had something to do with the speed of light. The prophet did not understand the speed of light: a godless idea. Light did not move; it *was*.

Ammagon's leg began to ache. The cold of the stone floor had seeped through the rug and now gripped his knee like a vise. He was tired of waiting for the messenger to come back, waiting for Teaqua to die, waiting for the history of his people to start again. Tired of waiting for his whispers. "Hurry up," he prayed. It was a one-way conversation but it was the best he could do. Ammagon prayed for Teaqua. For Ndavu's success. Let it be soon. "Soon." He prayed despite the terrible silence in his head. Chan was light; Ammagon knew the god could grant his plea.

He tried again to imagine the speed of light. He wondered if it was as fast as the speed of prayer.

**W**ing was dreaming of his father. In the dream his father was asleep on the Murphy bed in his go-tube. Wing had just returned from a parade held to honor him as the first human to go to the stars and he was angry that his father had not been there. Wing shook him, told him to wake up. His father stared up at him with rheumy, hopeless eyes and Wing noticed how frail he was. He reminded Wing of Petropolus. Look at me, Wing said to the old man, I've done something that was much harder than what you did. I didn't just leave my country, I left the planet, my time, everything. And I adjusted. I was strong and I survived. His father smiled like a messenger. You love to dramatize yourself, said the old man. You think you are the hero of your story. His father began to shrink. But surviving takes a long time, he said and then he was nothing but a wet spot on the sheet and Wing was alone.

The telelink rang, jolting Wing awake. He cursed himself for an idiot; he had forgotten to set the screening program. The computer brought up the lights of his gotube as he fumbled the roll-top desk open and hit return. He was home.

"Phillip Wing here. Hello?"

"Mr. Wing? Phillip Wing? This is Hubert Field; I'm with the Boston desk of Infoline. Can you tell me what's going on there?"

"Yes." Wing tapped a key and opened a window on his monitor. He could see the skyline of Portsmouth against a horizon the color of blue cat's-eye; the status line said 5:24 A.M. "I'm sitting here stark naked, having just been rudely awakened by your call, and I'm wondering why I'm talking to you." The pull of Earth's gravity had left him stiff and irritable.

Field sounded unperturbed; Wing could not remember if he had ever been interviewed by this one before. "We've had confirmation from two sources that the messenger Ndavu has offered you a commission which would require that you travel to another planet. Do you have any comment?"

"All I can say is that we have discussed a project."

"On another planet?"

Wing yawned.

"We've also had reports that you recently toured the messenger starship, which would make you the first human to do so. Can you describe the ship for us?"

Silence.

"Mr. Wing? Can you at least tell me when you'll be leaving Earth?"

"No."

"You can't tell us?"

"I haven't decided what I'm doing yet. I'm hanging up now. Make sure there're two *l*'s in Phillip."

"Will we see you at the ceremonies today?"

Wing broke the connection. Before he could roll back into bed the computer began playing his Thursday morning wakeup: the Minuet from Suite No. 1 of Handel's *Water Music*. It was 5:30; today was the dedication of the Glass Cloud.

He folded the gel mat with its nest of blankets and sheets back into the wall of the go-tube. Most of his clothes were scattered in piles on the oak floor but Daisy had bought him a gray silk Mazzini suit for the occasion which was still hanging in its garment bag on the towel rack. Twice he had returned it; she had sent it back to him three times. He tried it on: a little loose in the waist. Daisy had not realized that he had lost weight since he had moved out.

Wing walked briskly across the strip to the USTS terminal where he was just in time to catch the northbound red-white-and-blue. It seemed as though everybody in the world had offered to give Wing a ride to North Conway that day, which was why he had perversely chosen to take a bus. He boarded the 6:04 carryvan which was making its everyday run up Route 16 with stops in Dover, Rochester, Milton, Wakefield, Ossipee and North Conway. The spectators who would flock to the dedication were no doubt still in bed. They would arrive after lunch in hovers from New York or in specially chartered 328 double-deckers driving nonstop from Boston and Portland and Manchester. Some would come in private cars; the vice-president and the secretary of the interior were flying in from Washington on Air Force One. New Hampshire state police estimated a crowd upward of half a million, scattered along the ninety-seven kilometers of the Glass Cloud's circuit.

A crowd of angry locals had gathered at the bus stop

in Ossipee. They hustled a clown on board and then banged the side of the carryvan with open hands to make the driver pull out. The clown was wearing a polka-dotted bag that came down to her ankles and left her arms bare; the dots cycled slowly through the spectrum. She had a paper-white skin tint and her hair was dyed to match the orange circles around her eyes. A chain of tiny phosphorescent bananas joined both ears and dangled beneath her chin. A woman up front tittered nervously; the man across the aisle from Wing looked disgusted. Even New Hampshire Yankees could not politely ignore such an apparition. But of course she wanted to be noticed; like all clowns she lived to provoke the double take and the disapproving stare.

"Seat taken?" she said. The carryvan accelerated abruptly, as if the driver had deliberately tried to make her fall. The clown staggered and sprawled next to Wing. "Is now." She laughed, and shoved her camouflage-colored duffel bag under the seat in front of her. "Where ya goin'?"

Wing leaned his head against the window. "North Conway."

"Yeah? Me too. Name's Judy Thursday." She held out her hand to Wing.

"Phillip." He shook it weakly and the man across the aisle snorted. The clown's skin felt hot to the touch, as if she had the metabolism of a bird.

They rode in silence for a while; the clown squirmed in her seat and hummed to herself and clapped her hands and giggled. Eventually she opened the duffel bag and pulled out a small grease-stained cardboard box. "Popcorn? All natural."

Wing gazed at her doubtfully. The white skin tint made her eyes look pink. He had been on the road for two hours and had skipped breakfast.

"Very nutritious." She stuffed a handful into her mouth. "Popped it myself."

She was the kind of stranger mothers warned little children about. But Wing was hungry and the smell was irresistible. "They seemed awfully glad to see you go back there," he said, hesitating.

"No sense of humor, Phil." She put a kernel on the tip of her tongue and curled it into her mouth. "Going to the big party? Dedications are my favorite; always some great goofs. Bunch of us crashed the dedication of this insurance company tower—forget which—down in Hartford, Connecticut. Smack downtown, tallest building, the old edifice complex, you know? You shoulda seen, the suits went crazy. They had this buffet like—real cheese and raw veggies and some kinda meat. We spray-painted the entire spread with blue food coloring. And then I got into the HVAC system and planted a perfume bomb. Joint must still smell like lilacs." She leaned her head back against the seat and laughed. "Yeah, architecture is my life." She shook the popcorn box at Wing and he succumbed to temptation. The stuff was delicious.

"Hey, nice suit." The clown caught Wing's sleeve as he reached for another handful and rubbed it between thumb and forefinger. "Real silk, wow. How come you're riding the bus, Phil?"

Wing pulled free, gently. "Looking for something." He found himself slipping into her clipped dialect. "Not sure exactly what. Maybe a place to live."

"Yeah." She nodded vigorously. "Yeah. Beautiful country for goofs. The whole show is gonna be a goof, I figure. What do you think?"

Wing shrugged.

"I mean like what is this Glass Cloud anyway? A goof. No different from wrapping the White House in toilet paper, if you ask me. Except these guys got permits. Mies van der Rohe, Phil, you know Mies van der Rohe?"

"He's dead."

"I know that. But old Mies made all those glass boxes. The ones that got abandoned, they use 'em for target practice."

"Not all of them."

"I think Mies musta known what would happen. After all, he had four names. Musta been a goof in there somewhere." She offered him another handful and then closed the box and stuck it back in her bag. The carryvan rumbled across the bridge over the Saco River and headed up the strip that choked the main approach to North Conway.

"These guys on the link keep saying what a breakthrough this gizmo is and I keep laughing," she continued. "They don't understand the historical *context*, Phil, so why the hell don't they just shut up? Nothing new under the sun, twist and shout. The biggest goof of all." Wing noticed for the first time that her pupils were so dilated that her eyes looked like two bottomless wells. The van slowed, caught in strip traffic; even in daylight the flash bars seemed to pulse with garish intensity.

"Me, I thought it was kinda unique." Wing could not imagine why he was talking like this.

"Oh, no, Phil. No, no. It's the international style in the sky, is what it is. Study some architecture, you'll see what I mean." The carryvan crawled into a snarl of USTS vehicles near the old North Conway railroad station which had been moved to the airport and converted to a tourist information center. An electroluminescent banner hung from its Victorian gingerbread cornice. Green words flickered across it: *"Welcome to North Conway in the Heart of the Mount Washington Valley Home of the Glass Cloud Welcome to . . ."* Hovers were scattered across the landing field like seeds; tourists swarmed toward the center of town on foot. The line of busses waiting to unload at the terminal stopped moving. After ten minutes at a standstill the carryvan driver opened the doors and the passengers began to file out. When Wing rose he felt dizzy. The clown steadied him.

"Good-bye, Judy," he said as they stood blinking in the bright May sunshine. "Thanks for the snack." He shielded his eyes with his hand; her skin tint seemed to be glowing. "Try not to get into too much trouble."

"Gonna be a real colorful day, Phil." She leaned up and kissed him on the lips. Her breath smelled like popcorn. "It's a goof, understand? Stay with it. Have fun."

He fell back against the bus as she pushed into the crush of people, her polka dots saturated with shades of blue and violet, her orange hair like a spark. As she disappeared the crowd itself began to change colors. Cerulean moms waited in bathroom lines with whining sulphur kids in shorts. Plum grandpas took vids while their wrinkled apricot wives shyly adjusted straw hats. Wing glanced up and the sky went green. He closed his eyes and laughed silently. She had laced the popcorn with some kind of hallucinogen. Exactly the kind of prank he should have expected. Maybe he had suspected. Was not that why he had taken the bus, to give something, anything, one last chance to happen? To make the final decision while immersed in the randomness of the world he would have to give up? Maybe he *ought* to spend this day-of-all-days twisted. He kept his eyes closed; the sun felt warm on his face. Stay with it, she had said. "Have fun," he said aloud to no one in particular. He laughed and opened his eyes. An ocher policeman was staring at him. Wing gave him an jaunty salute and went off to find the other VIPs.

"It's a tribute to the American genius." The vice-president of the United States shook Wing's hand. "We're all very proud of you."

Wing said, "Get out of Mexico."

Daisy tugged at his arm. "Come on, Phillip." Her voice sounded like brakes screeching.

The vice-president, who was trying to pretend—in public at least—that he was not going deaf, tilted his head toward an incandescent aide in a three-piece suit. "Mexico," the aide repeated, scowling at Wing. The vice-president at ninety-six was the oldest person ever to hold the office. He nodded sadly. "The tragic conflict in Mexico troubles us all, Mr. Wing. Unfortunately there are no easy answers."

Wing shook Daisy off. "We should get out and leave the MBF to sink or swim on its own." The vice-president's expression was benignly quizzical; he cupped a hand to his ear. The green room was packed with dignitaries waiting for the dedication to begin and it sounded as if every one of them was practicing a speech. "I said . . ." Wing started to repeat.

The vice-president had leaned so close that Wing could see tiny broken veins writhing like worms under his skin. "Mr. Wing," he interrupted, "have you stopped to consider how difficult we could make it for you to leave this planet?" He kept his voice low, as if they were making a deal.

"And what if I don't want to leave?"

The vice-president laughed good-naturedly. "We could make that difficult too. It's a beautiful spring day, son. Could be your day . . . if you don't go screwing yourself into the wrong socket. Ah, Senator!" Abruptly Wing was staring at the great man's back.

"What is the matter with you?" Laporte appeared beside Daisy and he was hot, a shimmering blotch of rage and four-alarm ambition. "You think you can just stagger in, twisted out of your mind, insult the vice-president—no, don't say anything. Once more, once more, Wing, and you'll be watching the Cloud from the ground, understand? This is my project now; I've worked too hard to let you screw it up again."

Wing thought it unfair of Laporte to criticize, since only a few months ago he himself had come twisted to Wing's party. Unfair but irrelevant. Wing was too busy being pleased with himself for mustering the courage to confront the vice-president. He had been certain that the Secret Service would whisk him away the moment he had opened his mouth. Maybe it had not done any immediate good but if people kept pestering it might have a cumulative effect. Besides, it had been *fun*. The crowd swirled; like a scene change in a dream Laporte was gone and Daisy was steering him across the room. He knew any moment someone would step aside and he would be looking down at Ndavu in his wheelchair. He glanced at Daisy; her mouth was set in a grim line, like a fresh knife wound across her face. He wondered if she were having fun, if she would ever have fun again. What was the philosophical status of fun vis-à-vis the message? A local condition of increased entropy . . .

"I must have your consent today, Phillip," said Ndavu, "or I will have to assume that your answer is no." The messenger's face looked as if it had just been waxed.

Wing picked a glass of champagne off a tray carried by a passing waiter, pulled up a folding chair and sat. "You leaked my name to telelink. Told them about the project."

"There is no more time."

Wing nodded absently as he looked around the room. "I'll have to get back to you." The governor's husband was wearing a kilt with a pattern that seemed to tumble into itself kaleidoscopically.

Ndavu touched his arm to get his attention. "It must be now, Phillip."

Wing knocked back the champagne: ersatz. "Today,

Ndavu." The glass seemed to melt through his fingers; it hit the floor and bounced. More plastic. "I promise."

"Ladies and gentlemen," said a little green man wearing a bow tie, gray morning coat, roll-collar waistcoat and striped trousers. "If I may have your attention please."

A woman from the mission whispered to Ndavu, "The vice-president's chief of protocol."

"We are opening the doors now and I want to take this opportunity to remind you once again: red invitations sit in the north stands, blue invitations to the south and gold invitations on the platform. We are scheduled to start at two-fifteen so if you would please begin to find your seats. Thank you."

Daisy and Wing were sitting in the back row on the platform. On one side was Luis Benalcazar, whose company had designed both the Cloud's ferroplastic structure and the software that ran it; on the other was Fred Alz. Laporte, as official representative of the Foundation and Solon Petropolus, sat up front with the vice-president, the secretary of the interior, the governor, the junior senator and both of New Hampshire's congresspeople, the chief selectman of North Conway, a Hampton fourth-grader who had won an essay contest, the Bishop of Manchester and a famous poet whom Wing had never heard of. Ndavu's wheelchair was off to one side.

The introductions, benedictions, acknowledgments and appreciations took the better part of an hour. . . . *A technological marvel which is at one with the natural environment* . . . The afternoon seemed to get hotter with every word, a nightmare of rhetoric as hell. . . . *the world will come to appreciate what we have known all along, that the Granite State is the greatest* . . . On a whim he tried to look into the dazzling sun but the colors nearly blinded him. . . . *their rugged grandeur cloaked in coniferous cloaks* . . . When Wing closed his eyes he could see a bright web of pulsing arteries and veins. . . . *this magnificent work of art balanced on a knife edge of electromagnetic energy* . . . Daisy kept squeezing his hand as if she were trying to pump appropriate reactions out of him. Meanwhile Benalcazar, whose English was not very good, fell asleep and started to snore. . . . *Reminds me of a story that the speaker of the house used to tell* . . . When they mentioned Wing's name he stood up and bowed.

He could hear the applause for the Cloud several moments before it drifted over the hangar and settled toward the landing platform. It cast a cool shadow over the proceedings. Wing had imagined that he would feel something profound at this dramatic moment in his career but his first reaction was relief that the speeches were over and he was getting out of the sun.

The Cloud was designed to look like a cumulus puff but the illusion was only sustained for the distant viewer. Close up, anyone could see that it was an artifact. It moved with the ponderous grace of an enormous hover, to which it was a technological cousin. But while a hover was a rigid aerobody designed for powered flight, the Cloud was amorphous and a creature of the wind. Wing liked to call it a building that sailed. Its opaline outer envelope was ultrathin Stresslar, laminated to a ferroplastic grid based on an octagonal module. When Benalcazar's computer program directed current through the grid, some ferroplastic fibers went slack while others stiffened to form the Cloud's undulating structure. The size of the envelope could be increased or decreased depending on load factors and wind velocity; in effect it could be reefed like a sail. It used the magnetic track as a combination of rudder and keel or, when landing, as an anchor. Like a hover its envelope enclosed a volume of pressurized helium for lift: 20,000 cubic meters.

The Cloud slowly settled to within two meters of the

ground, bottom flattening, the upper envelope billowing into the blue sky. Wing realized that people had stopped applauding and they were looking up with an awed hush. The Hampton schoolgirl climbed onto a folding chair and stood twisting her prize-winning essay into an irretrievable tatter. Wing himself could feel the goose-flesh stippling his arms now; the chill of the Cloud's shadow was strangely sobering. The secretary of the interior sank slowly onto his chair, shielded his eyes with the flat of his hand and stared up like a lumberjack in Manhattan. Pictures would never do the Cloud justice. The governor whispered something to the bishop, who did not seem to be paying attention. Wing shivered. Like some miracle out of the Old Testament, the Cloud had swollen into a pillar that was at least twenty stories tall. It had accomplished this transformation without making a sound.

Fred Alz nudged Wing in the ribs. "Guess we got their attention, eh Phil?" The slouch-backed old man stood straight. Wing supposed it was pride puffing Alz up; he could not quite bring himself to share it.

Daisy squeezed his hand. "It's so quiet."

"Sssh!" The governor's husband turned and glared.

The silence was the one element of the design that Wing had never fully imagined. In fact, he had been willing to compromise on a noisier reefing mechanism to hold down costs but Laporte, of all people, had talked him out of it. Not until he had seen the first tests of the completed Cloud did Wing realize the enormous psychological impact of silence when applied to large bodies in motion. It gave the Cloud a surreal, slightly ominous power, as if it were the ghost of a great building. It certainly helped to compensate for the distressing way the Stresslar envelope changed from pearl to cheapjack plastic iridescence in certain angles of light. The engineers, technicians, and fabricators had worked technological wonders to create a quiet Cloud; although Wing approved, it had not been part of his original vision. The reaction of the crowd was another bittersweet reminder that this was not his Cloud, that he had lost his Cloud the day he had begun to draw it.

The octagonal geometry of the structural grid came clear as the pilot hardened the Cloud in preparation for boarding. Ndavu wheeled up and offered his hand in congratulations. They shook but Wing avoided eye contact for fear that the messenger might detect Wing's estrangement from his masterpiece. A hole opened in the envelope and a tube shivered out; the ground crew coupled it to the landing platform. Ndavu shook hands with Alz and spoke to Luis Benalcazar in Spanish. Smiling and nodding, Benalcazar stooped toward Ndavu to reply. "He says," Ndavu translated, "that this is the culmination of his career. For him, there will never be another project like it."

"For all of us," said Alz.

"Thank you." Benalcazar hugged Wing. "Phillip. So much." A woman with a microcam came to the edge of the platform to record the embrace. Wing pulled away from Benalcazar. "You, Luis"—he tapped the engineer on the chest and then pointed at the Cloud—"it's your baby. Without you, it's a flying tent." "Big goddamn tent, yes," said Benalcazar, laughing uncertainly. Laporte was shaking hands with the congressman from the First District. The chief of protocol stood near the entrance of the tube and began motioning for people to climb through to the passenger car suspended within the envelope. Before anyone could board, however, Ndavu backed away from Wing, Benalcazar and Alz and began to clap. Daisy stepped to the messenger's side and joined in, raising hands over her head like a cheerleader. People turned to see what was going on and then everyone was applauding.

It felt wrong to Wing—like an attack, as if each clap were a blow he had to withstand. He thought it was too late to clap now. Perhaps if the applause could echo backward through the years, so that a nervous young man on a stony path might hear it and take sustenance from it, things might have been different. But that man's ears were stopped by time and he was forever alienated from these people. These people who did not realize how they were being manipulated by Ndavu. These people who were clapping for the wrong cloud. Wing's cloud was not this glorified special effect. His cloud was forever lonely, lost as it wandered, windborne, past sheer walls of granite. A daydream. You can't build a dream out of Stresslar and ferroplastic, he told himself. You can't share your dreams. He thought that Daisy looked very pretty, clapping for him. She was wearing the blue dress that he had bought for her in Boston. She had been mad at him for spending so much money; they had fought over it. The glowing clearwater blue of the material picked up the blue in her eyes; it had always been his favorite. Daisy had taken five years of his life away and he was back now to where he had been before he met her. She was not his wife. This was not his cloud. These were not his people. For some reason he found himself thinking about the Chani goddess Teaqua, a creature of such transcendent luminosity that she could send messengers to run her errands. He wondered if she could look into the sun.

"Tell him to stop it," Wing said to Daisy. "Tell him I'll go."

The applause ended eventually. Several hours later Wing happened to watch Infoline's evening report. Hubert Field noted in passing that the architect was not among those who boarded the Glass Cloud for its maiden voyage.

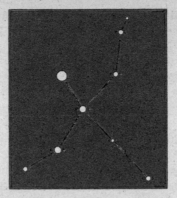

**T**hree days out,
Wing began to itch. When it was bad, it was as if his skin
had desiccated and was flaking away, cell by cell. He
thought he had caught a rash, prickly heat from outer
space, but the messengers' tests said there was no need
to worry. Ndavu said it might be a physiological manifes-
tation of his anxiety. At first Wing accepted this; he was
anxious, all right. The starship had already come .67AU
and was almost a quarter of the way to Ceres, the base
from which the messengers would create the discontinuity they called the mass exchanger. According to
Ndavu, once through the aperture there would be no
way to rebundle the strings of space-time into a configuration where Phillip Wing, the year 2054 and Earth
were contiguous. Or something like that.

Then Wing began to smell things. One morning his

urine smelled like boiled carrots even though he was on a diet of vitabulk and flavored waters. The air in the gravity wells had the faint scent of wet lumber. Ndavu reeked of dog. When Wing spilled coffee on Chair 31, the smell that lingered on the foam upholstery gave him hallucinatory flashes of breakfast in bed with Daisy. He wondered if they were spiking his bulk with something. Ndavu had warned that there could be no consciousness-altering behavior on the starship, that the journey itself would alter his consciousness. More anxiety. At least it helped pass the time as he lay in bed scratching himself, awash in his own odd cinnamon stink, alert and exhausted at the same time.

Wing never managed to get to a first-name basis with the starship's crew. There were three: the Pilot sisters and the Biologist. They floated through the ship's gravity wells in mobile life-support systems. When they spoke, which was rarely, their English was barely comprehensible. The Pilot sisters' identical red capsules had four specialized limbs and an array of sensory protuberances that suggested a kind of whimsical femininity. All he ever saw of the Biologist was a box that might have been an oversized telelink monitor, except that the screen was an unvarying blue. The Pilots usually carried the Biologist to where it was needed. Ndavu had warned Wing not to waste any curiosity on the crew, who were ill-equipped and too busy to interact with him. Still, Wing persisted in drifting through the gravity wells watching them do things he did not understand. He found these inarticulate gadget-creatures less threatening than studying vids of the Chani. Besides, looking at the starship's monitors gave him a headache.

By the fifth day he had headaches whether he looked at a screen or not. He knew the pain was coming when he saw sparks swirl at the periphery of his vision. Even when his head did not hurt, he felt a little feverish. And he needed a shave. When he had been at Yale he had tried raising a moustache, but the woman he had been trying to coax into bed had told him that it looked like spiders' legs. His beard had always been sparse at best; he was accustomed to going several days without a razor. Now he had a stubble every five or six hours. And black hair sprouted on his arms, his neck, his legs. There were even wisps on his chest!

On the seventh day Wing rested—never did manage to get out of bed. He tried to cheer himself up with some Laurel and Hardy two-reelers that had been unsilenced and 3Ded but it was too much effort to laugh. So he settled for a walkthru vid of the Louvre. That had just enough action for him. It was the first time he had delved into the library he had brought from Earth; before he had been afraid it would depress him. It did not matter now; he was already depressed. When the documentary ended, he was content to watch static. Ndavu watched him. After dinner, which he skipped, the Pilots toted the Biologist into Wing's cabin and set it at the foot of the bed. Ndavu assured him that there was nothing to worry about. The Biologist stared bluely at Wing for about ten minutes, said "Normal is," and then its bearers took it away. Ndavu stayed behind.

"We will turn the gravity down in here," said the messenger. "It should help."

Gravity had nothing to do with it, thought Wing. If gravity was the problem he could go out into the wells or up to the control room, where there was no gravity. He knew that they had done something to him. Poisoned him, or maybe it was some kind of vaccine. Wing said nothing; it did not matter. Part of him wanted to scream but the fear seemed to come from very far away, its urgency lost in transmission.

"We are approaching significantly relativistic speeds, Phillip." Even Nvadu seemed to be receding. "You are the first human to go uptime. It is the beginning of a great adventure."

"Dying." Wing wanted it on the record.

Ndavu pulled up the desk chair and straddled it. "Listen to me, Phillip. You are not a tourist. You are going to another planet to live and work. The atmosphere on Aseneshesh is different, the biosphere is different. Solar radiation is more intense, gravity less. You would hardly be able to wander around in your shirt-sleeves. As you are now, you would be a biological catastrophe waiting to happen." Ndavu's face was very big; it seemed to fill Wing's cabin. "We have given you a genetically sculptured cancer, Phillip. It is metastasizing rapidly through your body, reshaping you into an organism which is adapted to life on Aseneshesh. You won't have to be tied to life support or experience the world through a ghost. You are going to be something very like a Chani."

Wing said, "Human."

"You will not lose that, I promise you. We are not tampering with your essence, only your externals. You can be changed back; that was why a human was chosen. You are cousins, you and the Chani. The reshaping is not all that radical."

There is a war going on inside of me, thought Wing. I can feel things dying.

"Soon we will put you on life support. Your internal systems will fail temporarily until they have been fully reshaped. We have taken steps to see that you are not in pain. By the time we pass through the aperture, the worst will be over."

He touched Wing's hand. There was a prickling of fine hair. They were turning him into an animal.

"I will not lie to you," said Ndavu, "and tell you this will be easy. It will probably be one of the most difficult times of your life. However, you are not dying. You will survive and you will prosper. I expect great things of you, Phillip Wing."

Wing began to pant.

His mouth was dry and the hot wind was in his face. He stood on the east girdle wall and looked across the festival court toward the step pyramid at Saqqara and Wing knew he was standing in the place of the great Imhotep himself. The first architect known to history, the pyramid builder. The sun burned like the eye of god; dust devils stirred the sands. Two thousand brown men swarmed like bees across the construction site. He could smell the rock dust and sweat a hundred meters away. A long sloping causeway, roofed over to protect the workers against the fierce sun, climbed the four stacked mastabas. The fifth was nearly completed and on it would be constructed a sixth. Many of the master stonemasons had returned to the base of the first mastaba and were casing the rough-dressed core of the pyramid with a chiseled limestone facade. In his mind, Wing could see it finished: sixty meters tall, bone white against the red, pebble-strewn sands. The tallest, the grandest structure on Earth.

He realized that none of it was real when the stone wall beneath his feet began humming. A metallic note disturbed the silent dream of stone. The whole burial complex began to throb, as if the vision itself was oscillating. The laborers set their blocks down, the masons dropped their chisels and looked up. The sky was shrieking at them.

The god's eye blinked.

It lasted only a millisecond and yet Wing screamed in horror. For in that brief time he understood chaos. He knew that the god did not care for man or stonework;

the god had no feelings at all. The god was a discontinuity; to worship it was to honor randomness.

Then the eye of the god opened again, but with a cold and indifferent light, and it started to snow from an ice blue sky. The brown workers spilled down off the pyramid and milled about the courtyards in confusion. They sprouted fur and capered like chimpanzees. Their arms swung wildly and knuckles almost grazed the ground. They threw the snow up in the air as if to make the god take it back.

"It is all right, Phillip." Ndavu's voice seemed to come from everywhere. "We are decelerating, coming back to downtime. The aperture is behind us."

Wing wanted out. He wanted to see his cabin and argue with Ndavu. He wanted Daisy back; he wanted to wake up in his bed in Piscataqua House beside her. Instead, the Glass Cloud scudded across the Nile basin until it hovered directly overhead. Swollen as the pyramid, it eclipsed the sun. As it re-formed above him a hole opened in the bottom and the boarding tube snaked out. He climbed through the tube into the passenger car suspended within and swayed down the empty center aisle, catching at the empty seats to steady himself. He flung open the door of the control room and the smiling pilot turned to greet him. John the Baptist.

Wing was in bed, cheek pressed against the gel mat. He was facing the wall on which hung his print of Leonardo's Baptist, the only personal possession he had brought from his office. It was an excellent reproduction; even the cracks in the master's brush strokes were there. He realized he had been staring at it for some time. He worked to sort its reality from the vision of the pyramid builders.

His mouth was wrong. His tongue felt oily and too thin. He ran it across the inside of his teeth; several came to a point. Slowly he brought his hand up to touch his face. It was covered with short bristly fur. His nose had melted away and in its place was a pad of nose leather pierced by two slits the size of old-fashioned warded keyholes. He probed gingerly with a fingertip; damp inside. Then he sneezed. This is what you get, he told himself, for not reading the contract.

"Phillip," said a voice, "it is time to acquire new data." Someone rolled him away from the wall and he flopped onto his back like a dead man. Now he could see the center drawer of his desk; someone's thighs moved through his field of vision. He wanted to look up but his muscles did not respond. He felt as if he had been stretched on a rack; all the strength had been wrung from him.

Wing heard the Biologist's hum and felt a puzzling resonance in his own mind. Its screen was only about thirty centimeters from his face; he could see nothing but blue. There was a familiar scent in the room.

He tried to ask what was happening but could not manage his strange tongue and stiff lips.

"Do not try to talk yet." He felt pinpricks as someone pressed things into his skull; blue lightning struck his optic nerves. Wing could feel a huge nest of hair on his head, a mane. And now he recognized Ndavu's doggy scent in the room. Wing drooled on his bed, remembering.

"You are recovering," said Ndavu. "Life support is no longer necessary, although you are still very weak. Now we are providing you with information to speed your adjustment."

On the Biologist's screen, or perhaps in Wing's mind—he was not really sure—a vast glacier calved into a gray ocean. Wing did not want to adjust. What he wanted to do was cry. But he could not.

John the Baptist helped Wing realize that the reason

he could not cry was because he no longer had tear ducts. Now Wing understood that if he needed to manifest sadness, he would experience a mild rhinitis, an inflammation of the nasal mucous membrane. Instead of crying, he would sniffle and perhaps sneeze. Wing was offended.

The Glass Cloud flew impossibly high; it was practically in low orbit. Below Wing spun a world in shades of two colors: rumpled white land and dark ocean the color of twilight. He saw ice deserts, snow-swept mountain ranges with turquoise shadows, vast reaches of gunmetal tundra. Then more ice: islands of dark ice streaked with light ice rivers, floating sheets of ice, cracked blue here, frozen over there. Wing was numbed by ice. Yet still he watched, searching the ice in vain for signs of a civilization: a city's grid, the patchwork of farms. But there was no sign of people from this altitude.

The Baptist nodded and the Glass Cloud dived so steeply that Wing cried out in alarm. For a second the cockpit seemed to flicker and Wing could see reflections on the surface of the Biologist's screen. Then he resonated back to the world in his mind. They were flying over a chain of islands that led like stepping stones to a brown coastline. The Baptist's names for them were nonsense words: Ataki, Wunshesh, Emat, Nish. There was a Sea of Nish too, and a port of Nur. Wing spotted boats like seeds floating in a puddle. Closer. Nur had more buildings than he could count. Its streets were paved and its waterfront bustled. Still he could not imagine it housing a population of more than fifty thousand. He wondered if this was the Chani's largest city.

Abruptly the Cloud shot spaceward; the continent fell away until Wing could see it whole. It was called Aseneshesh and was all of the world that the Chani knew. It was roughly triangular, widest to the west, tapering to an eastern point. Ranged along the western coast was the continent's mountainous backbone. To the east the rain shadow of these mountains had created a desert. Wing caught a glimpse of a great river, the Chowhesu, that spoiled the desert's arid perfection like a carelessly dropped blue rope. Then the Cloud roller-coasted back down to the western shore of Aseneshesh. On the narrow coastal plain, at the head of a long bay, was Kikineas. It sprawled across the bay; the Baptist estimated that as many as half a million Chani called it home. Wing realized this was the City of Scholars, seat of the Coastal Protectorate and home of—

"Stop!" was what Wing tried to say. What came out was a chirping sound that sounded like Gilbert and Sullivan on fast forward. "Stop!" The Baptist seemed to understand. He froze at the controls of the Glass Cloud and the city of Kikineas ceased to unreel beneath them.

Who are you and how are you doing this? Wing did not try to speak the words. He realized that he did not have to. There was an odd quality to this realization, an *otherness*. He was about to realize that John the Baptist and the Glass Cloud in his mind were aspects of the interface for the memory implants that the messengers had made in his brain for the purpose of—

But he fought against this flood of information like a drowning man. He focused on the Biologist, desperately afraid that he had cracked wide open. He was looking at the blank blue screen. No, not quite blank; he could see his own reflection in it. A face stared back out at him, unguessable emotions playing across its alien features.

Wing had become Chani. He touched his black cheek, feeling the nap of the short lustrous fur. His mane stuck out in every direction. There were flaps of skin—the color of well-done steak—around his nostrils; they fluttered when he exhaled so that each breath sounded like a low snore. The contours of his face had changed: it was as if he were pressed up against a pane of glass. He shut his eyes.

John the Baptist was waiting in the darkness. It was impossible to give Wing direct access to all the data he would need without major psychological reconstruction. Wing was made to visualize the two implant nodes at the base of his skull: primary and backup, marvels of miniaturization. The interface was designed to reflect Wing's personal symbolism. All necessary information about the Chani would be channeled from memory implant through John the Baptist, a tutelary icon, into Wing's own memory. Both the implant and interface were purely for his own convenience; the alternative was decades of intensive study. Then Wing realized that the interface would also reflect an important aspect of the *Chani* psyche. Most Chani hallucinated an inner voice in times of high cognitive dissonance. They believed they were being directed to right action either by the voice of Chan or Teaqua. The Chani heard the whispers of their god; so too Wing would hear whispers of data. This was an important congruity which would enable Wing to—

He sat up in bed. "T-turn it off!" His tongue contorted as if it had a will of its own. *"Off!"* There was no one, not even the Biologist, to hear his strangled cry. It was certainly not English; he had never made sounds like that before. He could feel his heart—he hoped it was his heart—pounding. He swung his legs off the bed, pushed himself forward, tottered across the deck and collapsed onto his desk chair. He heard an odd clicking as he tapped at the keyboard to summon help. He stopped typing to stare at the six stubby digits on his right hand. Wing found that by concentrating on his anger at the messenger he could trigger thick centimeter-long claws from fleshy sheaths in his fingertips. He did not have to concentrate very hard.

Wing was angry. He was sick of listening to Ndavu's all too reasonable arguments, enraged by his new body, indignant over the invasion of his mind and, above all, furious at how he had been tricked. He wanted nothing more than to pound the messenger's face to jelly and then turn the starship around and go home. Except that he knew it was impossible. There was no home and he just barely had the strength to stand on his own. Even the muscles in his face ached when he tried to talk. Angry as he was, however, he found it easier to listen to Ndavu than to be lectured by a creature of his own imagination. Whenever he closed his eyes, John the Baptist was there waiting.

"Digestively, you are very nearly unchanged," said Ndavu. "You can continue to eat vitabulk; you probably will not find much of the Chani diet to your taste at first. However, should you decide to sample it, try to start with small portions."

Ndavu had a new head. A velvet fluff of thick, straw-colored underfur covered his face; his mane was red. He was wearing a long-sleeved gray tunic, baggy gray pants and no shoes. He was well over two meters tall; the two of them seemed to fill Wing's cabin to overflowing. And yet for all that, he was certainly Ndavu. Wing recognized something in the voice, or perhaps it was the officious attitude.

"I regret that I cannot do very much to help you gain control of your interface, although I assure you that you can. You might reconsider the icon; we chose John the Baptist in the Glass Cloud because we believed you would find familiar images comforting. Change them if you like."

Wing found himself wondering about Ndavu's genitals, since there had been some disconcerting changes in his own. His testes had ascended into his body cavity and his penis . . . His penis had shrunk: it was about the size of a nipple. It seemed unlikely that he could perform. Not that he had any erotic inclinations; the very idea of sex made him queasy. Wing decided it was probably best not to think about it. Still, he could not help comparing himself to Ndavu. As best he could tell, both of them had been completely transformed into Chani. He was amazed how the messenger could stay so calm when he himself was falling apart. Wing felt overwhelmed by what had happened to him. He was very much afraid that he had lost himself.

"Our passage through the aperture was without incident. A pity you had to miss the mass exchange, but it was unavoidable." Ndavu paused, noticed that Wing had stopped paying attention. "I really do not know what else to tell you, Phillip."

"S-say it's g-going to be all right." His new voice was a continuing surprise; he sounded like he was practicing bird calls underwater.

"The worst is over." Ndavu smiled, showing sharp pink teeth set in gray gums. "I know, I have been re-shaped many times."

Wing nodded and then dismissed him with a wave of the hand. After Ndavu had gone, Wing stripped off his wet diaper and clumsily bundled himself into a fresh one from the pile the messenger had left. The worst would not be over, he thought, until he regained control of his body. And his mind.

Wing concentrated fiercely as he turned his attention inward. He was determined this time to confront and control the interface. He grabbed John's shoulder and spun him around. The Cloud's control yoke pitched forward as the Baptist released it and the horizon indicator began to tilt. Wing hauled him out of the pilot's seat. Fifty gigabytes on a device the size of an acorn: everything the Chani had ever thought about abstract relations, space, physics, matter, sensation, intellect, volition, affections . . .

This can't go on, Wing thought.

The Baptist shrugged. It was his sly smile that most enraged Wing; it put an ironic twist to everything that he brought to Wing's attention.

Wing pushed him out of the way and slid into the pilot's seat. Through the main viewscreen he could see a glistening snow field rushing at him. He eased back on the yoke and the altimeters stabilized. Red lights turned green; slowly the horizon leveled. In the co-pilot's seat next to him, John the Baptist circled thumb and forefinger and flashed him the okay sign. Wing was not exactly sure how he had done it or what he would do next, but he was flying the Cloud.

Ndavu was speaking over the intercom. Wing was not sure whether it was the intercom in his head or in the cabin. "We have achieved orbit, Phillip."

They were downtime. Wing set the autopilot and at last slumped back against the headrest. He was exhausted.

John the Baptist waited patiently while he slept.

**T**he sun was an ember in an ice blue sky; its pale light provided only a feeble blessing of warmth. Harumen rammed her shovel deep into the drift and scooped up a nearly weightless cake of powdery snow. It was like lifting smoke. She slung it over her shoulder and the load scattered in the wind. A few stray flakes blew back at her and caught in her mane.

"If you don't try so hard, you'll get more done." Wekiti was leaning on her shovel a few paces ahead.

Harumen grunted as she attacked the drift again.

"Keep your blade low. That's it." Wekiti flagged approval. "Now let the snow slide off."

They did not understand at the scholars' palace why Harumen volunteered for these kinds of jobs. She told them she needed the exercise and it was true. But that was the least of her reasons. She enjoyed working with strangers like Wekiti: people who treated her as nothing more, or less, than an able body. People who did not need to assume things about who she was and how she must feel about it. She also liked getting things done. If she turned around now, she could see that she and Wekiti had cleared a path that stretched back some thirty meters to the side entrance of the library. An accomplishment. But what she liked best about snow clearing was that she did not have to think much while she was doing it. Old Ipposkenick would have been horrified— she could hear him now. *A scholar's work is to think. You can't understand life unless you think. People who don't think are slaves to their whispers.*

"Lift with your knees." Wekiti bent to demonstrate. "Not your back."

The blade of Harumen's shovel grated over the buried cobblestones. The snow hissed softly when the wind moved it. Clouds of her breath curled into the chill air. She advanced another five meters. They were almost to the Northway. The street smelled of dung and was streaked black where they had spread wood ash over the ice. Her hands were cold. She wondered if Wekiti liked her.

Harumen tried to picture the body beneath Wekiti's oilskin. Solid but lithe, she decided. Although the hair on her arms was coarse, the fur on her belly would be fine as new grass. Harumen admired Wekiti's ropy arms for a while and wondered how she would feel if they were wrapped around her. Wekiti's lips would be tender, her tongue firm. Harumen went on like that as she worked, playing a game of hard and soft with an imaginary Wekiti. Taking her as a lover, sharing pleasure and clearing away the snow at the same time.

Sometimes Harumen worried that she had begun to live too much in her own imagination. It was because

**110**

she carried another world around in her head. Earth, that strange and terrible place, was as real to her as the mud in the Northway. The messengers had given her an alien planet to understand and now, after all these years, they were finally giving her the alien. But that was exactly what Harumen did not want to think about. She tried instead to concentrate on Wekiti's hands. Soft and hard.

She knew that was yet another reason why the other scholars did not often ask her to share pleasure: because of two hard implant nodes at the base of her skull. Her colleagues treated her with an uneasy mixture of awe and pity; a combination that did not make for satisfactory lovemaking. She could not blame them; there were times when she was so totally involved with her interface that everything else was mumbles and mist. Who wanted to take a haunted lover to the common bed?

The dirty wall of snow along the edge of the Northway was not quite as tall as Harumen. It had frozen to the consistency of brick. Wekiti kicked at the base with her boot and a chunk of ice skittered toward Harumen. "We'll need the pick to break this up."

"Back at the library." Harumen leaned her shovel against the bank. "I'll go get it."

"Take your time." Wekiti yawned. "It's almost lunch."

As she hurried back down the path, Harumen could see the scholars' palace at the far end of the plaza. She picked out her room—and his right beside it. She had spoken to Ndavu yesterday. The starship had already made planetfall; they were bringing him down tomorrow. The messenger had said that Phillip Wing was nervous.

*He* was nervous. Harumen chittered as she slung the pick over her shoulder. She had been waiting forty years for him. She had undergone an operation that had set her apart from her people and, in a way, from herself.

She had spent years in a mental wrestling match with the messenger interface, pushing it through half a dozen personas in a desperate attempt to keep it from controlling her. In the process she had learned everything about Phillip Wing and his world that the messengers could tell her. She could name the colleges of Yale and recite the history of Piscataqua House. She knew about the war in Mexico and Wing's favorite telelink channels and the rules of basketball. She could explain who Bramante, Inigo Jones, Alvar Aalto and Takekazu Tobata were and why they were important to Wing. She knew about Daisy Goodwin—but she did not understand her. Or Phillip Wing, for that matter. *He* was nervous?

Harumen set the pick down beside the shovel. Wekiti had propped herself against the snowbank. Her eyes were half-lidded, her face to the sun. She was moving her lips the way some people did when they were talking back to their whispers.

"Wekiti?"

She blinked. "What? Did you run all the way?" She waggled a finger at Harumen. "You're in too much of a hurry. Take it easy, would you?"

It was an odd coincidence. Wekiti was not the only one telling her to slow down. The interface counseled patience too. But Harumen could not help herself; she had waited forty years! She had a right to be impatient.

Wekiti put her arm around Harumen and steered her away from the snowbank. "It's not going anywhere," she said. "It'll keep until after we eat."

She did not understand; Harumen wanted the work. But there was no escaping lunch, or her preoccupations. As they trudged back across the plaza, Harumen could feel the comforting weight of Wekiti's arm. It sent an inexplicable shudder of desire through her. What was she thinking of? She did not understand herself today, but then ever since Wing's arrival she had been surprising herself. Her life—this world!—was finally going to change.

Harumen wondered how long she would have to wait before Phillip Wing would be interested in sharing pleasure with her.

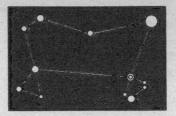

et snow spun out of the sky. The wooden cart rattled down an icy track, breaking the crust beneath its wheels. It was loaded with crates filled with Wing's personal belongings. Wing rode between his Chani liaison and Ndavu in the driver's box.

"Reminds me of . . ."—what Wing wanted to say was Christmas, but there was no word for it in Chani—"Kautama's day." A snowflake caught on the fur on the back of his hand; he licked it off. "Just like the ones I used to know."

The liaison, Harumen, wore a tunic and trousers made of a coarse red fabric. She could be Santa's helper, except that as the snow melted on her, she smelled like a wet rug. At two meters plus, she was too tall for an elf but there was definitely something fairylike about her. In the eyes, maybe: all yellow iris with only a rim of white.

They seemed fixed in their round sockets. Her eyes spooked Wing because they were his eyes too.

"Dashing through the snow," he sang, "in a something open sleigh."

Actually there were four surunashes pulling the cart, beaked creatures the size of wolves. A second cart, driven by a pair of silent Chani, followed with the components of Wing's CAD workstation and a load of vitabulk. Behind them were the transport pod and the snow-covered domes of the messengers' base.

"Is something the matter, Phillip?" said Ndavu.

"Chittering all the way," Wing chanted, "Chi-chi-*chit*."

"Chi-chi-*chit*," said Harumen. She gazed past him owlishly.

Wing chittered again and had difficulty stopping. He knew he was making an awful impression. He blew into his cupped hands to warm them and then rubbed his forearms. Although his new fur had thickened up nicely and he was wearing isothermals, he felt cold. Maybe it was the wind or perhaps it was because Harumen looked under, over and around him but never met his gaze. He wondered what she thought of him. Was he handsome? Ugly? Harumen kept bobbing her head in a way that suggested that she was sympathetic. At first he had attributed them to the roughness of the road but now the Baptist reminded him that her quirky head movements were called flagging. Since the Chani only made eye contact as a sign of intimacy or rage, they communicated on a nonverbal level with a repertoire of twitches, a kind of emotional sign language using patterned head movement. For some reason that struck him as funny, and he continued to chitter.

The entire messenger base was surrounded by a log stockade. Harumen stopped at the gate and Chani guards came down from their towers to inspect the carts. Wing had expected Ndavu to do the talking but it was Harumen who explained who they were and where they were bound. One of the guards circled around the front wagon and lifted the tarp that covered the Aalto chair. He noticed her left arm ended in a stump; stiff hairless nubs were growing into new fingers.

"Leave it!" called the driver of the second cart.

The guard pulled her good hand back abruptly and went to help her comrade crank open the gate.

Once outside they turned onto a road that paralleled the base until it entered a village. Ascowen butted right up against the stockade. Most of it was constructed of rough-sawn lumber but there were two brick buildings which carried the weight of public architecture. It seemed a new and prosperous place; the main street and many of the alleys were paved with split logs. Even the greenest shacks had at least one glass window. Yet while the village thrived, the stockade behind it was falling into ruin. The wall was made of six-meter lengths of tree sunk into the ground and cabled together; the trunks were warped and rotting. Wing could see slivers of the messenger domes through the gaps.

All around him was evidence of commerce between the base and Ascowen. While most people wore tunics, trousers or both, several sported transparent sheaths that could only have come from offworld. They did not shy away, as Wing had expected, but rather trotted alongside the carts, grabbing at the tarps and shouting offers of trade. They held up baskets of orange berries for inspection, strips of leather or dried meat that smelled like mushrooms; they tore the clothing off their backs to exchange for the contents of his crates, whatever they might be. They waved carved statues of wood and stone, and brazenly enough, considering the messenger quarantine, prisms that played airy music, necklaces made of flashing pinlights, ghostly images of the goddess.

"I thought they didn't like outsiders." Wing chittered nervously.

"They don't." Harumen spoke directly to Wing for the first time. "But they'd be happy to take your goods."

Ndavu said nothing, although he seemed pleased by what he saw. Wing was not pleased. He quashed an inexplicable urge to punch someone, anyone, flail at the hairy hands which clutched at his belongings, curse the would-be traders. Voices swirled around him. When he clapped hands to ears his new mane felt like a basket perched upside down on his head. He thought he could feel the planet itself spinning. He had seen too much; he felt battered by the relentless onslaught of surprises. Trembling, he focussed on a knot in the floorboard of the driver's box. He shut out the swarming strangeness of the world until there was nothing but wood grain and the sound of his own breathing and stayed that way until the cart passed out of Ascowen.

"She knows," Harumen was saying. "Ammagon gripes about it all the time. To hear him tell it, Ascowen has been thoroughly corrupted; he'd like to see it burnt and the ashes scattered."

"He will not stop change that way," said Ndavu. "Technology is part of the message. Your people are hungry for it. They will have their way eventually."

"Their way may not be what you think. All they want are your machines—not your message. They're proud of who they are."

Wing could follow what they were saying, but understanding was elusive. He was still thinking in English, so he had to take an extra mental step in each direction of a conversation. It reminded him of a game he used to play as a child: *The goddess knows; pass it on.* He grunted and sat up.

"Are you all right?" Ndavu patted him on the back. "I am worried about you, Phillip."

"I just felt a little dizzy." He brushed the snow from his fur. "I guess . . . Maybe that village was too much, too soon. But I'm better now."

"You haven't seen Kikineas yet," said Harumen.


The skyline of the city was wrong. At first Wing thought it had to be a trick of perspective. The towering spine of Kikineas seemed out of proportion to the low-rise sprawl around it, like a shack with a steeple. Then, as the carts trundled down the ridge road, Wing began to worry about his new eyes. Ndavu had claimed that they had not meddled with his essence; all the changes had been external. Yet the way he *saw* the world was at the heart of his talent. If he could not trust his eyes, how could he work?

The central grid of the city was surrounded by slums of mud and scrap wood; someone's careful master plan had come undone. Split-log streets on the outskirts were jammed with ragged people and their animals. The air was thick with smells: smoke and fresh bread and rot and frying fish and urine. Dirty ice clogged open sewers; the carts jolted through potholes. Many Kikineans seemed to have nothing to do but tag after them. Unlike the people of Ascowen, however, they had very little to trade. They seemed more interested in mobbing Wing, screeching and tugging at his isothermals and pinching his fur as if to make sure he was real. Eventually Harumen had to stop at a squat brick keep to request escort from the local police. The keepers carried cudgels and used them to punch through the crowds. Their callousness shocked Wing despite John the Baptist's assurances that the Chani's ability to regenerate body parts was linked to a high threshold of pain.

He shut his eyes then and fixed on the Baptist's face, not for information but rather as an anchor against the madness surging around him. There was a palpable humanity in the features of that smiling, womanish man that steadied him. The face helped Wing remember what it had been like before he had been reshaped. He was already having difficulty imagining himself as a human being.

The mob would not follow the caravan into the center city. Within the span of a few blocks Wing passed from near riot to a surreal, muffled stillness. Here he was in a neighborhood of stone; its snowy bulk seemed to swallow noise. The loudest sound was the clatter of wheels on cobbles and the creaking of the cart's bolsters. The few Kikineans about kept their distance from the little caravan. The keepers marched them to a colonnade and then turned back without a word. Beyond the tapered columns was a square lined with fantastic buildings.

"The courts of Tetupshem," said Ndavu, "are the oldest part of the city."

To Wing, this place was far more upsetting than the crush of street people. While the Chani seemed all too real, none of their wooden huts or squat brick lodges had prepared him for the dizzying impossibility of the courts. Stone could not take that kind of shear. *These buildings could not stand!* It was as if the pyramids had been made of papyrus or skyscrapers molded of sand. His sense of the potentialities of architecture tilted; most of what he knew was now proved wrong in Aseneshesh's lower gravity. He could not imagine drawing moment diagrams that could explain these loads; the momentum of a falling snowflake ought to be enough to bring the arena crashing down. And the gilt dome over there was an eggshell. . . . It was a nightmare and worse: it was a nightmare from his past.

When Wing was five, he would often wake up at night screaming. It was just after they had arrived in the States. His father came sometimes but more than once he was left to cry himself to sleep. Later Wing called them his geometries but when they began they were too terrible for words. In the earliest nightmares he was flying—sometimes in a plane or a hover, sometimes naked—and he would look down and see a runway below him like a line drawn with a ruler and he would swoop down toward it because he had to land. As he descended the landing strip would rise up to meet him until he could see that it was not tarmac runway but a geometric line, a collection of points with length but no breadth, impossible to balance on. But in his dream he would try, waving his arms in a desperate attempt to tightrope on less than a thread until at last he fell and fell and finally woke up. The child psychiatrist on the telelink said it had something to do with grieving for his mother. As he grew older the dream changed and he would be sneaking through a city; all around him office towers stretched to the clouds. They rested on vanishingly small foundations, like great pencils of glass and steel balanced on their points. Then someone, his father or a teacher or a character from a favorite vid, would wander too close to one of the towers and Wing would scream a warning not to touch it. The impact of his voice made the skyscrapers teeter and domino into one another until huge black chunks of steel and stone were falling toward him and falling, falling and . . . *"No!"* he screamed as strong hands held him down so that he would be crushed by the falling debris. *"It's balance."* He writhed in the grasp of those hands and he opened his eyes and there were monsters holding him down, hairy creatures with no noses and sharp pink teeth. They were the ones who had brought back the scary geometries and now they had him and they had made him into a monster and he would never get away.

"It is all right, Phillip," said one of the monsters as it

pressed something into Wing's arm. Who would trust a monster? "We will take care of you."

Wing lay in a darkened room for two days and worried about what he had seen. He unpacked the things he had brought from Earth and studied them obsessively until he was no longer sure whether they had changed or not. Sometimes, at his worst, he imagined that his eyes were actually parasites that had slithered into his head and settled there. John the Baptist haunted him; he had visits from Harumen and Ndavu. The messenger assured him that his breakdown was a temporary and understandable setback and that he would soon adjust to his new world. Wing wanted to believe it.

They had moved him into the messengers' dormitory at the scholars' palace, the only place in the city where offworlders were allowed to live. In time his curiosity overcame his fear and he began to explore his new place on this world: cautiously, a handsbreadth at a time.

The room was a three-by-seven-meter rectangle with a door at one end and shutters at the other. Harumen reported that the shutters opened onto a balcony; Wing was still too demoralized to see for himself. The room smelled as if the wooden floor had recently been sealed and the plaster walls whitewashed. Alternating strips in the high ceiling radiated light and heat; the messengers had fixed it so that he could control the ceiling from his workslate or the CAD workstation which they had built into his rolltop. They had left the desk near the door, next to Chair 31. The door had a mortise lock; nobody offered Wing the key. Stacks of plastic crates from the starship lined the walls. Wing's gel mat was spread on a carved wooden bedframe.

Harumen prowled around his room when she visited.

She liked to touch things. "It was like what where you came from?" She picked up his workslate and played with the keyboard.

"There were flowers." Wing threaded fingers through his mane as he gazed up at the strip lights. "We kept a greenhouse; even in winter we had"—he wanted to say impatiens and begonias and orchids but could not—"many kinds. Do you have flowers?" He felt silly because the Baptist compressed images of the hundred most common species into a data squirt. Harumen seemed to sense what he was really asking.

"After thaw," she said, "baby's mane blooms along the shore. Yellow petals. We pick the flowers to share with friends." She fitted the slate back into its slot on the workstation. "They are sweet to the taste, delicious with breadroot." Sometimes when she grinned her pointed canines glinted in the light. "So some things *are* the same, yes?"

Wing felt distanced from himself. He observed his own behavior closely now that he knew how brittle he could be. As long as he did not have to deal with anything new he would be all right. He was getting used to his room; at least it had his things in it. But by the end of the second day, Wing had yet to work up the courage to open the shutters.

He spent a lot of time in front of his reproduction of *St. John the Baptist*. He was intrigued that Leonardo's saint did not look much like his Baptist. The Baptist seemed more feminine somehow; the features were perhaps softer, although Wing realized that it had not been true until he thought it. The Baptist's imagery was in flux; now he looked a little bit like Shane Darcy, the transsexual vidstar. The differences were not in themselves surprising; Ndavu had told Wing he could customize the interface. What was surprising was that the Baptist had changed without Wing's knowledge. His unconscious at work—doing what? Wing stepped back from the reproduction, considering it as a clue. He remembered seeing the original at the Louvre; he could even picture the museum shop near the Winged Victory of Samothrace where he had bought the print. He could not remember much about the painting's history, however, even though he knew he had once read a biography of Leonardo and had seen several documentary vids. A late work, he thought. He queried the Baptist, who could not help. There was nothing about Leonardo in the implant. Wing wondered if the Baptist might be able to pry the forgotten information out of his own memory. The Baptist led Wing to realize that a data interface could not cross personality boundaries without an invitation, a safeguard which protected the integrity of the host essence. Wing could not help but wonder what integrity he had left to protect. At least the Baptist was someone he trusted, a creature of his own imagination. His only friend? The idea left him feeling as light as air. Leonardo's fey saint seemed to taunt him to it. Wing chittered and asked the Baptist to access his memory.

When Leonardo died in exile, he had three paintings with him: the *Mona Lisa*, *St. Anne with the Virgin and Child* and *St. John the Baptist*. *St. John the Baptist* is generally considered to be Leonardo's last painting. It caused a minor scandal and was for a time suppressed because of its unserious treatment of Christ's stern precursor. To many it was a clear admission of Leonardo's homosexuality.

(And that's all you remember.)

Wing shuddered, at once terrified and fascinated. He had not expected a voice. It had certainly come from inside his head. Human but androgynous. Now he was sure that he had gone crazy.

(If you keep it a secret, no one will know but you.) and then the voice went silent.

"Hey," said Wing. *"Wait."* Immediately he felt foolish for speaking aloud. He was determined, but he could not get the Baptist to speak again. He could visualize the face and access information in the implant but there was no personality, no voice behind the data. Finally he had to consider the possibility that he had merely hallucinated it. After all, the Chani claimed to hear the whispers of their god. Now he was one of them—sort of. But calling it an hallucination resolved nothing. Even if the voice had not been real in the strictest sense, he had perceived it. At some point he would have to trust his perceptions, bizarre as they might seem, or else he *would* go mad.

It was the first pleasant surprise he had had in a long time. Wing's lack of appetite had distressed Harumen; she had decided to sit with him at dinner to make sure that he ate. In her view, vitabulk was the problem. She did not like anything about the stuff: the doughy color, its bitter scent of yeast, the squeeze tubes in his flavor palette. As he took a steaming bowlful out of the microwave, she produced a small cloth bag, like a sachet.

"Here," she said, unwrapping it, "we have flowers."

Inside was a wad of dried yellow petals and brown seeds with puffy tails. He brought the bag to his nostrils and sniffed; there was a sharp fragrance. He was touched by her gesture. He knew she was trying to be friendly—despite her unnerving eyes, for all her twitching.

"Eat," she said.

He brought a pinch of baby's mane to his mouth. Harumen cocked her head to one side. At first there was nothing but a dry, papery taste—then his tongue caught fire. It was as if he had gotten a mouthful of chili powder. When he coughed it out, Harumen launched herself backward off her stool and dropped into a fighting crouch. "'S hot!" Wing sucked air. *"Water."* He rubbed his tongue on the roof of his mouth while she ran to fetch him a cup. Afterward he sniffled and twittered at the same time. "That was fierce. My tongue is numb; even Dad's curry wasn't that hot."

The baby's mane had touched off an unexpected burst of feelings. For the first time since he had left Earth, Wing stopped watching himself. He took both of Harumen's hands and did an impromptu dance. "Get your hot stuff. Hot, hot—double hot!" She eyed him as if wondering whether she would have to sit on him to calm him down.

"Here, watch." He took a careful pinch of the baby's mane and sprinkled it over his vitabulk. "I *like* hot. We just have to work out the dosage." He ate with something approaching gusto. "Great." He savored the familiar burning at the back of his throat. "Best I've had since I left home."

She flagged her confusion.

"I appreciate it, Harumen." He smiled. "I really do." She was smiling now too.

After Wing finished eating, they chatted for almost an hour. They did not discuss his mission or the messengers or other matters of galactic import. Rather they talked about the weather and growing baby's mane and what Harumen liked to eat. Wing made her promise to dine with him sometime and she said she would bring him another surprise if he wanted. For her part Harumen was very much interested in his things and so Wing tried to explain Leonardo's chiaroscuro and why Alvar Aalto had used laminated birch to make his chairs. She seemed to understand most of what he said. He was at ease with her; certainly it was different—better—than being with Ndavu. When it was time for her to go, he actually felt disappointed.

"I want to help you." Slowly, she reached out and ruffled the fur on the back of his hand. He fought the impulse to shy away; it was the first time he had been touched by a Chani. "Is that all right?"

"Yes." He was having such a strong physical reaction to her that he had to squeeze her hand to keep from shivering. "Oh, yes." He had no idea what had possessed him.

She clenched her fist, the Chani sign of assent. He chittered as she closed the door behind her. It was a breakthrough! He had not felt quite like this since he was in the seventh grade. He was so giddy that he strode up to the shutters, flung them open and stepped onto the balcony.

It was late and the city was dark. While the messenger dormitory was electrified, the Chani depended on oil lamps and candles for illumination, even here, in the City of Scholars. Kikineas did not seem so intimidating now; darkness helped tame the shadowy monuments. Familiar white heaps were scattered throughout the courts of Tetupshem; Kikineas had the same problems with snow removal that Portsmouth and Boston had. In the distance Wing could hear a priestess chanting like a loon on amphetamines. But it was the moonless sky which commanded his attention, a vast canvas of stars and the night, untouched by human imagination. He looked for but could not find any trace of the familiar constellations; no boastful Cassiopeia or bold Orion, no bears or dogs or swans.

He gazed at the stars, trying to figure out who he was and why he had come to this strange place. Back on Earth he had been the Brave Young Architect, the Hero of the New Millennium, Humanity's First Representative to the Stars. Or at least, that was what his clips said. The Greeks would probably have named a star for him, or maybe even a whole constellation. He liked it: Orion the Hunter, Aquarius the Water Carrier, Wing the Architect. He twittered. Since there were no Greeks at hand, he would do the job himself. He decided that his attributes ought to be a workslate and a hard hat. Then he searched the sky for a suitable pattern of stars. Just as he had planted his imaginary feet on the horizon, he heard the door bang open behind him.

"Phillip, what are you doing?" Ndavu raced across the room toward him, as if he were afraid that Wing was about to jump.

Wing stepped down. "Making myself at home."

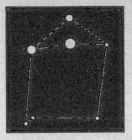

**T**he next morning Wing felt strong enough to wrestle the entire city. All at once or one at a time; it made no difference. Instead he was persuaded to settle for a tour of the scholars' palace.

Ndavu and Harumen slept across the hall from Wing. Ndavu's room was sparsely furnished: cot, plastic chest and a windowcomm. The window that overlaid the far wall opened onto the teeming floor of a pink ocean. It was covered with what looked like upside-down plants, anchored to the carnelian mud by leafy straps, topped by nests of white roots waving languidly in the current. Confetti creatures spun by in gaily colored schools and there was something wriggling through the stalks. Wing was fascinated; they had to drag him away.

Harumen's room looked and smelled as if it had been

lived in for some time. Wing was getting used to her scent; he tried to think of it as meadowy. She had a beautiful wooden locker with panels carved in flower motifs, a rack stuffed with egg-colored scrolls and some flimsy books. A faded red oilskin hung from a hook on the back of the door. She had sketched charcoal landscapes on walls which had gone gray from previous drawings and erasures. Her bedframe was identical to Wing's; her mattress was filled with feathers.

Most messengers preferred to stay at one of the bases, so the only other resident of their dormitory was Menzere, who lived above them on the floor reserved for special environments. She met them at the landing at the top of the stairs, hands clasped together in the sign of supplication and greeting.

"I am glad to meet you, Phillip Wing." Her fur was dark brown and she wore a gray tunic with a blue waist-sash. "I have been looking forward to your coming. Perhaps we can be strangers together in this place?"

"Yes," said Wing. He was not sure exactly what she meant. "And what do you do here?"

"I have been correlating data for the planetary climatologists."

Harumen nudged past him.

"We are developing a model of the glaciation cycle."

Harumen seemed intent on walking head-on into Menzere. Wing was about to reach out and yank her back—

"We hope to advise the Chani on reclaiming lost land."

—when Harumen penetrated Menzere's body. The messenger smeared and rippled and then reorganized as Harumen passed through her.

"Of course this is a ghost," said Ndavu, a beat after the Baptist supplied the same information, "Menzere must remain in her room; the environment here is too stressful for her."

Harumen turned to watch his reaction.

"You must visit me later," said Menzere. "I have an observatory."

"I'd like that," said Wing.

It took most of the morning to go through the palace. At the center of the complex was a domed assembly hall. The dome rested on a forest of stone columns and was fenestrated by an asymmetrical pattern of stained-glass peepholes, giving the ceiling the effect of stars at twilight. Beneath the great hall were four levels of underground lecture rooms, workshops and storage space. All empty.

"Where is everybody?" said Wing.

"Waiting in the commons," Harumen said. "We'd like you to share a meal with us. But I wanted to be sure you were all right."

"I promise not to bite." He clicked his teeth with mock ferocity. "So let's get on with it."

On their way to the commons, they had to pass the main entrance to the palace. Wing insisted that they step outside for a moment so that he could see how the exterior of the palace worked. He was testing himself and they all knew it. The surface of the dome was gilt; a reflecting pool circled it. From the edge of the pool amber brick dormitories radiated like the rays of a stylized sun. Each was connected to the main structure by a second-story arcade bridge over the pool. There was irony here: the architecture of the scholars' palace referred directly to the god they did not believe in. Thinking about that prompted Wing to move out of the shadow of the palace into the light.

Chan was as swollen as the sun at the end of a sultry August day, yet it had a dreamy, jewel-like quality. It was the color of topaz. Wing worried that his new eyes did not burn when he looked into this sun; in fact Chan had a compelling quality for which the messenger implant had not prepared him. Wing was unexpectedly elated to see Chan for the first time; he was reminded of the way he had felt at the dedication of the Glass Cloud. At the edge of his consciousness he was aware of the Baptist explaining things he did not want to know: that Chan was .719 times as bright as the sun with an average surface temperature of 5805 degrees; the orbit of Aseneshesh was .881 AU at its closest approach to the primary and .899 AU at its farthest. Wing thought about turning away from Chan but did not; he had the sense that if only he kept staring long enough, important things would come clear. He understood for the first time how these people could make a god of their star.

"It is cold." Ndavu tugged at his arm. "We should go in."

Most of the other dormitories, it turned out, were empty too. There were not so many scholars as Wing had expected: forty-three, according to Harumen, and eighteen apprentices. At first Wing found them slightly pathetic. They seemed lost in the vastness of their own dining hall; rows of empty tables behind them stood as telling reminders of a long decline. The stillness of the grand room seemed to swallow their learned debate.

The prophet Ammagon had not dared strike at them directly; Teaqua would not have permitted it. Over the years, however, he had conspired with his fellow priests to cut back the number of reborns sent from temple to the palace. Elderly scholars were shriven and given new lives; there were few replacements. As the community of scholars had dwindled, Ammagon announced an ambitious plan to reform education. He founded new schools, organized on a religious model and dedicated to defending the purity of Chani culture against the pollution of new ideas. His pedant-priests taught practical skills and obedience to the whispers. Those who might once have become scholars now learned to regard the palace of free inquiry as a dangerous anachronism.

The scholars who had survived Ammagon's reform were a suspicious and dispirited lot. Wing was introduced to them one by one; he tried to be polite to each. They had nothing to ask of him and replied to his questions with a terseness that bordered on hostility. They were not sure what to make of him.

Most were historians and archaeologists engaged in cataloging Warm Age artifacts from a nearby trove, yet they refused to speculate on possible applications of their studies. "We seek to know only for the sake of knowing," said Ipposkenick, an architectural historian who was the most forthright of the lot. "Our job now is to learn, not teach." One of his colleagues flagged a warning; Ipposkenick shrugged it off. "What goes on in the world today or tomorrow means nothing to us. All we ask is to study yesterday's things in peace. What has been forgotten. Let the pedants show people how to grow barley and build dams. We serve the goddess by damming the past. We stop up the truth."

"What Teaqua says is the truth." His colleague squirmed.

"The truth." Slowly Ipposkenick clenched his fist in agreement. "The truth is that the Warm Ages have passed. Teaqua also will pass."

Harumen asked if Wing still wanted to stay for the midday meal and he told her to stop fussing over him. She was a scholar and these were her people; he needed to earn their trust. He chose a place at table opposite Ipposkenick, while Ndavu and Harumen slid into places on either side of him. The others, including Menzere's ghost, found places at the long table at the front of the commons; Wing had a view of empty chairs marching into the gloom. They were served by their apprentices, who spooned glutinous cold porridge into bowls. They sprinkled it with green berries and quequa, which looked like pickled slugs. Ndavu and Harumen received this fare as well; an empty bowl was set before Menzere. Someone had heated Wing some vitabulk. As he squeezed parti-colored lasagna paste from a flavor tube, the scholars' reserve finally slipped: they looked disgusted.

Nobody ate, nobody spoke, not even after the food had been doled out and the servers had taken their places at table. Taking his cue from Harumen, Wing waited. A stringed instrument twanged. As the entire front wall of the commons shimmered and opened into a window, the Baptist informed him that he was about to witness thanksgiving, one of the goddess's two daily windowcomm audiences. Thanksgiving was primarily religious; the emphasis of the evening gathering was entertainment.

The worshipers onwindow prostrated themselves on a stone floor. Horns sounded, drums crashed, scratchy chords were plucked. As a procession shuffled through a temple, the window made a slow and reverent pan. Using the congregation for scale, Wing estimated that the walls soared at least thirty meters from the floor. Gray light filtering through clerestory windows hinted at a barrel vault high overhead. Wing wanted more time to study the architecture but the window followed a litter carried by twelve blue-jacketed blades. They set it beside a stone altar and dropped to their knees, being careful not to impale themselves on their scabbards. After a moment, a form uncoiled from the nest of pillows on the litter, ducked under the canopy and stood. Arms outstretched, revealed in all her glory, Teaqua accepted the thanks of her people.

The goddess was dressed in a golden robe which trailed along the floor. Her fur was the color of new brass. Her crown was a cut-glass helmet with a fist jutting from the forehead; a torque of prisms hung around her neck. As she came to the edge of the altar, the window shifted perspective. Now Wing could see the worshipers over her shoulder. They were surging, prancing, waving, flagging and calling to her in a frenzy.

"Praise her! The star of Chan!"

"Help us . . ."

"Chan is great."

"Bless you, Teaqua, bless us."

"We hear, we hear you always and everywhere."

"Teaqua, oh Teaqua!"

The scholars were unmoved by the fervor of the people onwindow; they fidgeted and whispered to one another. Ipposkenick waved his spoon. "Send us better food, oh Teaqua." There was a ripple of embarrassed chitters.

When at last the faithful subsided, the window returned to Teaqua. She raised her hands in supplication. "They thank you, Chan. Hear their prayers!" Her voice rang across the commons; she did not plead, but rather commanded her god. Even Wing felt a thrill at her voice. Then she turned her head with a ponderous grace, no doubt to keep the crown from slipping, yet at same time creating the illusion that she was making eye contact with her far-flung audience—a familiarity only the goddess would dare assume. Wing noticed a scholar down the table surreptitiously dip a finger into his porridge and lick it clean. Meanwhile a priest in a blue jacket came onwindow, bearing a wooden platter heaped with food. He offered it to her but Teaqua opened her hand in refusal, saying, "Eat now, all of you, while I speak to Chan on your behalf." With that she retreated carefully to her litter, balancing the glass helmet on her head. The window stayed with the priest, who set the tray on the stage and sat cross-legged beside it. At this, Ndavu picked up a spoon that looked like bamboo split lengthwise. The commons filled with the mutter of conversation as the scholars began to eat.

"The prophet Ammagon," muttered Harumen, flagging her disapproval at the window. "The goddess's flea."

Ammagon popped a berry into his mouth. "Tomorrow," he said, swallowing, "we'll be leaving this fine town to go on with Teaqua's tour. I, for one, will be sorry to go. I must say I've enjoyed my stay here. Kunish is a wonderful place and its people have much to be proud of." He paused while the local audience cheered.

"Kunish is a mudhole and its people stink of fish," said Ipposkenick. There were several grunts of agreement. Wing tasted his vitabulk: lukewarm.

"I've been impressed by the fishers here," Ammagon continued. He selected a choice fillet from the platter and ate it in a gulp. "Yes, very tasty." He quickly took a drink of water. "The whole fleet has been working very hard in honor of Teaqua's visit. I'm pleased to tell you that they've gone over the plan for this year by a thousand tons." More cheers in Kunish, groans in Kikineas. "As a result we'll make up any grain shortfalls in the Coastal Protectorate with half weight in fish."

"Make the pedants teach 'em how to preserve it!" said a voice from the far end of the table.

"But first teach the pedants," someone else called. All the scholars twittered.

"And now," said Ammagon, "let's listen to the music of Owena while you and I enjoy this fine meal. She'll be singing 'The Lamp Toad' and 'Wicked, Wicked We-quassin.'"

The window shifted to a stiff group of musicians pluck-ing stringed instruments. The singer had a voice like a squirrel. Wing scooped up a glob of vitabulk. He was surprised to see Menzere eating too; he wondered how a ghost could manipulate real objects. She smiled at him as she picked up her cup. Closer observation revealed the trick. The cup rippled slightly as the messenger's hand closed around it. What she sipped from was a ghost cup; the real one was masked by her window. He smiled back at her, puzzling again over the messengers' thor-oughness. There was something obsessive about the care with which they created their illusions.

Ammagon returned. "Thanks once again to Owena and her fine musicians. I can't say enough about the way the hard-working people of Kunish have treated us dur-ing our stay here. Now before we end today's visit, Tea-qua has asked me to tell you that she's changing her plans. The next stop on our tour was to have been Netasu, known to all for its wonderful mines. But we've just learned that the human, Phillip Wing, has finally landed at Kikineas. Since he has come to us at Teaqua's request, it seems only right that she go to welcome him at the end of his long journey. I know you're all as eager to meet him as I am. I don't need to tell you how impor-tant his work is to us. With Chan's help and Teaqua's blessing, he'll bring us a new age of peace and holiness. So we'll see you all in Kikineas and until then, look into the sun."

"And hear the whispers," replied the congregation and the window closed. The audience was over.

"Congratulations, Phillip," said Ndavu, "this is indeed an honor for you."

Wing could not help but overhear Ipposkenick say to

Harumen, "I don't know why she has to come here. She has never loved this city."

When Wing had boarded the messenger starship, he had carried on with him intellectual baggage which, he *knew*, he could not afford to lose. For instance, he believed that the principles of project management were as immutable and universal as the laws of physics. Any complex design problem, no matter whether it involved building robot welders or a maglev system or a tomb for a goddess, was subject to the logic of the flow chart. So Wing had imagined that, when he arrived, he would immediately launch into the fact-finding and analysis phase of the project. He would work with Teaqua to establish her needs and goals. He would refine this information into a program of spatial requirements for the proposed building. In consultation with his client he would then proceed to site selection and preliminary sketches and when they were approved he would produce a final plan. Probably the messengers would have to translate his ideas into working drawings that the Chani building trades could use. While he did not want to supervise construction on a day-to-day basis, he was sure he would find some master builder who could do it. Process was all, he had thought. Follow the steps in the right order and success, or at least completion, was assured.

But he could not bring himself to start. Wing had expected all along that the initial study phase of this project would be the hardest: quantitatively different from any he had ever tried. He knew he would have to climb the steepest learning curve of his life. Now he realized just how difficult the study was going to be—qualitatively different from anything he had ever done. He felt overwhelmed; he did not believe he had the capacity to master all the facts in their labyrinthine interconnections. The messenger implant and the Baptist were actually part of his problem: he *knew* far more than he *understood*. Psychological defenses, over which he had little control, sprang up. He was nothing like a sponge which, when immersed in a new culture, effortlessly and inevitably soaked up information. He was a stone—impermeable—dropped into a murky sea. He had lost control of his ability to learn.

His trouble was not immediately apparent to those around him. While he waited for Teaqua to arrive, Wing seemed to adjust to his life at the scholars' palace. He took both his daily meals in the commons. He interviewed scholars about their specialties. He toured Kikineas. He worked to make a friend of Harumen and he was polite to Ndavu.

However, it was not unusual for Wing to forget the way from his room to the commons. When someone would find him wandering the halls, completely lost and fighting panic, he would claim that he was exploring. He was constantly embarrassed because he could not remember people's names, no matter how often he was reminded. Sometimes he would wake up in the middle of the night and stare into the darkness and not know where he was. He had dreams about motionless eyes that turned him to stone. By day he was shown the city: the fortresslike library which had been converted from barracks, an arena where twenty thousand could watch a mamaskish or share a worship feast, the sprawling public courts, the municipal granary, Temple Nurusquan. He toured the waterfront and was escorted through the seething, shabby new town along the Northway. He traveled Chan's Path, passed through the Fishgate, crossed over the Sweetwine River on the Wensbridge, and climbed Chemish Hill, where he visited the ruins of

Wequassin's villa. He remembered hardly any of it. He knew he had seen stonework but could not recall the rustication. Somewhere there was a whole neighborhood of identical timber-framed houses with burnt brick walls. Had the arches of the Wensbridge been elliptical or circular? The city's architecture was a snow-covered blur in his memory. Eventually he stopped paying attention altogether. He drifted along with whomever he was with, making appropriate noises, impersonating an architect at work. His plan was simple: he had decided to wait for Teaqua. She would know what she wanted.

It was easy to fool the scholars; they never noticed that he was daydreaming. Like unappreciated experts everywhere, once they got used to him they would loose torrents of explanation, their conversational restraint swept away by enthusiasm for their own work. Ndavu did not seem to notice either. The messenger had receded since their arrival. At times he seemed to be busy wrestling with his own problems. Harumen, however, noticed everything.

"What're you thinking, Phillip?"

He had been at the window, dreamily searching for the stars of his constellation. He turned away, blinking. "I'm sorry, what?"

Her expression darkened. "How come when I talk, you don't hear?"

He did not want her to be angry with him. "I was thinking of a plant, actually. I left it in my office, back on Earth; Daisy gave it to me. It had big leaves." He twisted his hands to show her what a rubber tree looked like. "I used to have to dust it all the time. I was . . . I was just wondering if anyone was taking care of it. Probably not; probably it's long gone."

"Are you happy, Phillip?"

He tried to smile for her. He was still not quite used to

the way a smile worked; he had to curl his lips away from his teeth. "I'm not sure happy enters into it, really."

"Maybe you're ill." Harumen went to the window and closed the shutters. "What's 'homesick'?" She nibbled at the word as if it were a fruit she was tasting for the first time.

"Something like loneliness. When you miss home." He balked at explaining nuances: too much work. "Look, it's late. Let's call it a day. Sorry I wasn't listening to you before but I'm tired."

She flagged a pattern he did not recognize. "He says you've had a shock."

"Who? Ndavu?" Wing stared at his hands for a moment. "Maybe he's right. But I'm getting better. A little rest and I'll be"—he flicked the claw of his index finger—"good as I ever was."

Wing heard a swish behind him. Something touched the side of his head and lingered there. He turned and found himself in Harumen's arms. She had slipped off her tunic. She looked him right in the eye and cooed.

"Harumen!" He fought the impulse to break away. "What're you doing?"

"You want rest." She brought a knee up against the lower part of his thigh. "We'll rest together." Her breath smelled of fish.

"I meant by myself."

"Alone? But you'll be cold alone." She pushed back from him. "Alone isn't lonely?"

"*No.*" He was very near to hysteria. "Get away from me." He was responding to her despite himself; his fur seemed to tingle as each hair rose up in its follicle. "You have to leave." He felt strange flesh unfolding between his legs. He could not think diplomatically, he could not think at all. "Now, Harumen. Just *go!*"

"You want someone else?"

He put up his hands to fend her off. The farther away she was the better he felt. "Harumen." He drew a deep breath. "I just have to be alone for a while." She cocked her head to one side. "Alone is all I want. I'm sorry."

She considered. "You're not ready." She tousled the fur on his shoulder as if he were a sick dog. "I can wait." She left him.

Wing could not stop shaking. He was not sure exactly what had just happened. Did she really want to sleep with him? It was unthinkable. Yet her intentions were not so disturbing as his own response. He had been aroused—against his will. The memory of her touch left him seething with desire and revulsion. He could still see her pink teeth, feel the smolder in her owlish eyes. He had panicked precisely because some part of him desperately wanted her. Who was he? Was he the mind that had reeled at Harumen's advance? Or the body that still tingled? He wondered if Phillip Wing might not be dead, his place in the universe taken by a biological and psychological corruption. A monster.

The Baptist did not offer an opinion.

Wing fell on his back into bed, gazing numbly at the water stains on the wall. He grieved for his lost self. It would have been more satisfying had he been able to cry, but all he could do was sniff. When he wiped his nostrils with the back of his wrist his fur matted down. Not for the first time, he felt ridiculous. He wanted to sleep but could not.

Instead he drifted into a daydream, a comforting no-place, neither of Earth nor Aseneshesh. At first it was a field: tall grass and wild flowers whispering in a summer breeze. Then he was in a room with his workstation and his rubber plant and he was thinking of Daisy. He missed her so much. He fantasized that she was next door, waiting at the door for him to call her.

(Phil.)

It was the first time he had heard the voice since the day he had made his peace with the Baptist. He had taken it then as a sign that he was going crazy; now he took solace from it. Company for his misery.

Where are you? he thought.

(Let me in.) Definitely a woman's voice.

Wing clenched a fist. That was all he had to do. A door that did not exist opened.

John the Baptist was no longer male. She had been transfigured by his imagination and was now a creature of light. The rough brown robe had slipped off one shoulder and had caught on the curve of her breast. Her skin was luminescent. Wing was mesmerized by her hands: the long, slender fingers, the subtle play of muscles beneath the skin. His face burned. He could not see hers.

"Who are you?"

She knelt beside the bed and touched his cheek. He realized that she could be anyone. He tugged at the robe and it slid down and gathered at her waist. She kissed him; her lips brushing the thin slit of his mouth, her tongue flicking against his pointed teeth. When he pulled her onto the bed she seemed as real as anything in his room: the rolltop workstation or Chair 31 or the stink of Aseneshesh. He did not question how it was that her beautiful fingers could comb through the fur on his belly until his misshapen body throbbed with sensations that were at once utterly alien and deliciously familiar. He embraced her whether she was a miracle or madness. At the moment of climax she bit his shoulder and he cried out her name in ecstasy.

Afterward she groomed him, untangling the snarls

their lovemaking had left in his coat. He could not stop looking at her; he kissed a red spot on her hip where his fur had chafed her skin. She laughed and he thought he could forgive her anything, even the fact that she was not real. It was enough that she was human and had not been repulsed by him.

Although he could not see her the next morning, he knew that she was still with him.

*Daisy.*

She was his secret. Wing thought that if he told Ndavu about her, he would try to take her away. Again.

**T**here were too many boats in his life, Ammagon thought queasily. Crowded barges and ferries in Riverside, flimsy luggers whipping along mountain lakes—he hated crossing water. It was almost enough to make him leave the traveling court, retire to some village temple. Worst of all were the ships that sailed the ports of the Coastal Protectorate. At least ferry passengers went ashore at night and slept in beds that stayed in one place. On a ship, you were trapped for days, bouncing around like the stone in a rattle. And the air was always so foul below decks: the stink of the sea mingled with the old scents of all the nauseated wretches who had wanted only to be somewhere else. He would take fifty kilometers of bad road any day.

When he was feeling old, Ammagon sometimes joked about using messenger pods to move his court, once he became thearch. He had made many secret flights for Teaqua and had been impressed despite himself. Qutta was thirteen hundred kilometers up the Chowhesu from Mateag. Only two hours by pod but he would have to spend at least three soggy weeks on the river in packets—and who knew how long it would take afterward to recover from the journey? It bothered Chiskat that Ammagon would dare speak of such an accommodation with the aliens, even in jest, but then Chiskat was a zealot with no sense of humor. Ammagon, however, could see good reasons for using messenger transport, even if he did not really intend to. The thearchy could not exist without messenger wheat and windowcomms had become as much a part of the people's lives as whispers. Meanwhile the traveling seemed to get worse every year. There were too many unruly people; even the most remote lands were filling up. The court had to keep scurrying from emergency to emergency and pods would actually make their lives so much easier . . . but of course, Chiskat was right. It was a question of principle. Ammagon knew he was probably doomed to spending the rest of his days cursing boats.

He stretched wearily; his feet grazed a stanchion and his mane was matting against the bulkhead. He was constantly tired these days but sleep rarely came. His mind spun with the troubles ahead. Not only did he have to run the thearchy and the temple and protect Teaqua from herself but soon he would have to deal with the new alien. No doubt the obscenely mutilated Harumen had already turned Phillip Wing against him. There was no help for that now. Anyway, Phillip Wing was nothing but a tool the scholars would try to use to pry the goddess away from him. Ammagon knew that the scholars were the true enemies of the thearchy—his enemies. They did not accept the whispers. Not only did they not resist change, they wanted it. The messengers, on the other hand, were a necessary evil; as long they did not interfere they certainly had their uses. When Teaqua died, the struggle for power between the scholars' palace and the temple would begin in earnest. And then . . .

The ship heeled over and Ammagon had to cock his hip to keep from sliding off the bunk. Something rattled across the deck beneath him. It was a bad time to be feeling old. Sometimes he was not sure whether the creaking he heard came from his bones or the ship's timbers. If only he had been shriven ten years ago; it could have been arranged. He would have had plenty of time to grow back into power, relearn the skills of governance. But there had been the barley blight and pedants to train and Teaqua to watch over and he knew the scholars would take advantage. And who could he have trusted as a caretaker? Chiskat, who had started as his dresser?

The real reason, however, that Ammagon had not been shriven was because he had no whispers to call him. His secret fear was that Chan no longer whispered to him because he had strayed into error. But how could he know when there were no whispers to guide him? It was maddening. What he needed most was to look into the sun again and yet he was left groping in the darkness.

Someone knocked on his door. Ammagon grunted in acknowledgment.

Chiskat stuck her head into the cabin. "She wants you."

"Again?" Ammagon heaved himself up. "What?"

"I don't know. I was grooming her and she started talking very fast. Something about Wequassin and the war. Couldn't understand most of it. All of a sudden she says 'Get Ammagon.'"

"I'll come."

He wondered which Teaqua would be waiting for him.

She might be her old cunning self and minutes later she would not know where she was. Sometimes she raved but then she could spend days without speaking at all. "How is she?" he asked Chiskat as he followed her down the companionway.

"Muddy." Chiskat shook her hand as she walked, overplaying the palsy. "Not sure she'll even know you."

Ammagon was not sure he knew her. He did not understand Teaqua; he could not imagine himself doing what she was doing. To give up shriving and never to be reborn, to let herself drown in her memories.

Teaqua was sitting in a chair, propped upright with pillows and tucked in place with blankets. Her head listed with the cant of the deck. "You left me alone," she said. "They came while you were gone."

Ammagon made the sign of supplication and said nothing; no one on board would have dared disturb the goddess. Chiskat seemed relieved as she bowed and retired from the cabin.

"I've been with Chan tonight. I've seen the past changing." Teaqua's voice was small and indistinct, like the squeak of old floorboards. "Only the future is fixed. Why is that?"

"I can't say, Teaqua." Ammagon worried when she skirted the edges of meaning like this. "It's different for me."

She clenched a fist in acknowledgment. "I'm one with the god. You're not."

Ammagon shrugged.

"You're like everyone else."

He sat on the bunk. "I try to be."

"But you would take my place?"

"Someone must," he said carefully, "if that's Chan's wish. But it's your—"

"You want what I have. Say it!"

"I hope to serve Chan."

She sniffed. "I'm tired of your lies. You want me to hate Wequassin so you can raze his palace." She seemed pleased with herself, as if she had discovered a hidden truth. Ammagon knew it was pointless to contradict her, especially when she was wrong.

"Yes, he had failings," she continued, "but you forget that he helped me make this world. We grew up together, do you understand? No one can say what he was thinking at the end. I'm telling you that he took the grain reserves from his own city and sailed to feed the starving in Riverside. You see, unlike some, he couldn't eat while others went hungry. He fasted until he went mad, the whispers howling in his head—*I've heard them!* And then things were done. You can't imagine the horror of it, the horror."

Ammagon kept his head so still that his neck ached; he could not afford inadvertent flagging now. He thought he knew what she wanted. She needed to be shriven of her memories of the Hunger War. Of her guilt. It was not something Ammagon could do.

"He thought it was all his fault. The deaths. He was vain that way; sometimes he acted as if he were the only adult on Aseneshesh and everyone was a cub. Even me."

Her head jerked abruptly toward the door to her cabin. At first Ammagon thought that Chiskat had returned. He twisted around to see: the door was still shut.

"Ah, Wequassin, come in," she said. "We were just talking about you." She followed her hallucination with her eyes across the cabin to the bunk. "You know, I had you killed." She was staring right at Ammagon.

The prophet could not help himself; he flagged his disbelief. "Why would you do that?"

"Because you wanted to take my place," said the goddess. "No one is going to take my place."

Ammagon was stunned. This was what he had always feared most: that Teaqua would crumble and undermine the thearchy before the transfer of power. He wanted to say something, argue with her but he knew it was futile when she was in her mood. All he could do was pray that the madness would pass. And if it did not? For a horrifying moment he considered her pillows. She was so weak; if he were to pick one up, press it to her face . . . The ship shivered through a wave and Ammagon lost his balance. He staggered backward and bumped the cabin door. The blasphemous temptation passed but left him feeling as if nothing he knew were true. It was at that moment of utter emptiness that his prayers were finally answered. A wordless voice filled the void within him. *The messengers.* It might have been the wind sighing or the timbers complaining or the squeak of Teaqua's breath. It was at once sound and blessed silence; Ammagon knew immediately what it was. *The messengers will help you.*

For the first time in years, the prophet heard his whispers.

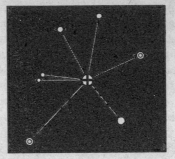

ing was dreaming of Daisy. In the dream he was human again. He and his wife were lying together, naked, next to the garden at Piscataqua House. The flowers nodded and he could smell the honeyed scent of nicotiana and the spice of carnations. A warm breeze whispered down Wing's belly; he brushed his fingertips slowly across the silky underside of Daisy's breasts. I'd like to make love to you, he said and when she smiled in reply he could see all of her teeth. She leaned over him and they kissed. He wanted to hold her but his arms were too heavy. Finally she pulled back from the kiss. The sun hung over her shoulder, firing her hair. It hurt Wing's eyes to look at her and he sat up. It was then that he noticed that in every window of Piscataqua House was a Chani face, twitching with astonishment at the sight of humans making love. Their heads were as big as barrels. Harumen came out the back door, looking like a botched special effect. She stood over them, flagging a pattern he thought he ought to recognize. Her shadow chilled him.

"Get up, you."

He started. A strange Chani was standing beside his bed. She wore a blue jacket and gray diapers from which hung a knife in leather sheath. When Daisy informed him that this was a priestess, Wing was totally disoriented. He would have had trouble enough distinguishing the Daisy of his dream from the Daisy of the interface. Now he had to deal with an uninvited guest. She did not seem particularly friendly.

He blinked and sat up. "Didn't I lock the door?" he said. He was getting used to surprises but this was the first time the craziness had started so early.

"You're a sly one, aren't you?" She stared directly at him, a clear breach of courtesy.

Priestesses rarely ventured into the scholars' palace. Wing realized on his own who she must be. "Teaqua sent you." He reached for his tunic. "She's here."

She gave him a hard stare. "How much do you know?"

"I just woke up."

"Come along then." She stood. "My name is Chiskat."


Teaqua had not actually honored the city of scholars with a visit. Instead she had taken up residence across the river at Temple Quaquonikeesak. Wequassin had built Quaquonikeesak near the farm where he and Teaqua had lived as cubs. From its perch on the summit of Chemish Hill, the temple commanded the entire city. It was enclosed by a triangular wall, a massive puzzle of stone with mortarless joints tight enough to pass an Inca's inspection. At each corner of the triangle was a tower fenestrated with archers' loopholes. To Wing, Quaquonikeesak looked more like a fortress than a place of worship.

At the end of the Warm Ages, those who remained on Aseneshesh had tried to preserve what they could of their world. Chemish Hill was not the result of geological processes; it was a vast underground museum. Its true nature had long been forgotten—until a farmer's cub named Wequassin had uncovered the entrance while digging post holes for a new fence. He and his sister, Teaqua, were the first in centuries to enter the vault. Sixteen years later they ruled Aseneshesh. They had kept the vault a secret during their rise to power; only after their rift was it revealed. The scholars claimed it had been looted Warm Age technology that had created the miracles upon which Teaqua had built the thearchy.

While the vault itself remained forbidden, Teaqua had brought some of the preservers' treasures up to the temple which guarded its entrance. There the blasphemous collection was displayed, so that the people could see for themselves the wickedness of the Warm Ages. No one but the goddess knew the full extent of what lay buried beneath Chemish Hill.

Chiskat left Wing, Harumen and Ndavu at the gatehouse, while she went to report their arrival. She returned with the news that Teaqua had gone into the vault and could not be disturbed. The prophet had ordered her to make Wing and his party comfortable.

She showed them to a shabby cloister hiding behind a colonnade. It normally served as housing for resident priests, reborns, penitent tremblers, visiting scholars and the great flocks of pilgrims who came to be piously horrified by the excesses of the Warm Ages. Almost everyone had been moved down to Kikineas, however, to make room for Teaqua and her retinue. The rooms were closet-sized and simply furnished with feather mattresses, chamber pots, an occasional mirror.

"You sleep here." Chiskat pulled aside the curtain that served as a door, revealing a closet with a glass window that overlooked the stables. Three crates of vitabulk took up most of the floor space. "She's here, the messenger there. I'm across the hall." Wing realized then that his chances of seeing Teaqua anytime soon were not good. Hurry up and wait: it was the classic power snub.

Harumen asked Wing if he would be interested in seeing the Warm Age collection. He said he was, hoping he might thus escape the dour Chiskat. However, she attached herself to the tour without waiting for an invitation.

While the cloister was boxy and uninspired, the temple beyond celebrated the curve in teardrop windows and sinuous buttress walls. Six arched doors opened into a large and murky hall, jammed with the faithful from Kikineas who had come up to participate in the first thanksgiving of Teaqua's visit. For every person there seemed to be a wall lamp flickering in its niche. Although he was glad for the extra light, the smoky, twice-breathed air made Wing's eyes sting. As he adjusted to the gloom he saw that three tapestries, about five meters by nine, hung from the ceiling vault above the entrance to the exhibits at the far end of the hall. Chiskat bumped against him, trying to steer him away from Harumen and Ndavu as they threaded through the crowd toward the tapestries.

In the background of the first was the absurdly top-heavy skyline of a city, a structural engineer's nightmare. Part of the city was ablaze. Several fat Chani squatted on a foreground beach and watched as two of their number fought with knives. The beach was strewn with wreckage. Chiskat explained that it depicted the wickedness of the Warm Ages.

The second showed a vast and desolate winter landscape. A sliver of Chan glimmered behind a dark cloud. A pack of fearsome creatures that looked like pocket dinosaurs had backed a lone Chani into a corner of the tapestry. The survivor's coat was frosted; his only weapon was a staff. "The reckoning," said Chiskat.

In the last, two figures crouched on an icy precipice and gazed down at an Edenic valley. One was a skeletal Chani, the other a surreal creature of light. Her mane and fur were woven from the same gold thread used to portray Chan, now fully visible. According to Chiskat, Kautama the Upright was rescued from death by Hanu, Chan's daughter. They became the parents of a new race.

Wing had a crick in his neck; he stared at the tapestries as if they were a message from home. Ndavu had spoken of similarities between humans and Chani but Wing had not expected to hear variations on a theme of Adam and Eve. For the first time, he felt that he understood something important about these people. He tried to tell Chiskat.

"Then Chan has turned his face from the humans?" She interrupted him.

"No, Chan doesn't . . . We don't know Chan."

"But you have a sun," she said. "All suns are forms of Chan." Wing had never heard this doctrine before; neither had Daisy. "Then your kind has never sinned?" Chiskat sounded skeptical.

"Many believe there has been sin. Some also believe that there was a punishment." Wing could not resist turning the logic of this new doctrine back on his inquisitor. "But Chiskat, if all suns are Chan, then doesn't that mean that all things that live under the suns must be his creatures? Even the messengers?"

"Once you look away from Chan, Chan also looks away from you." Chiskat's lips curled in contempt. "What is a messenger? One who goes to the uptime. One who forsakes her sun."

"Phillip," Ndavu called, "come this way."

Wing waved back. "And so just being here makes me a messenger?" He rested a hand on Chiskat's shoulder: a friendly gesture. "But you're wrong, you know. I never joined."

Chiskat pinched the fur on Wing's forearm, not quite hard enough to hurt. "This is how you have always looked?"

"No."

Tugging at the fur, Chiskat removed Wing's hand from her shoulder. Silently, she nudged him on, as if nothing more needed to be said.

The Warm Age collection was displayed in a series of interconnecting galleries around the periphery of the great hall. The rooms were deserted now, since all the pilgrims were busy jostling for choice spots at the thanksgiving. This part of the temple was unheated; the insides of many windows were laced with frost. Wing recognized the cold as a none-too-subtle reminder of the wages of sinful pride.

He could understand immediately how some of the collection offended against current belief. The space probe, for example, pitted and charred from its mission; the ancients had used it to study their sun. With other artifacts, the sacrilege was more subtle. There were glass cases filled with golden flatware, spun-gold cups and tureens ornamented with repoussé reptiles, enamel perfume boxes with gold filigree flowers, golden jewelry and gilt candlesticks. Wing realized that modern goldsmiths were not allowed to debase Chan's metal by using it for the profane arts.

"Why do you keep asking, when you have already made up your mind?" said Ndavu, his voice calm. He and Chiskat had been skirmishing ever since they had entered the galleries. She muttered something which Wing could not hear. "You do not know enough to have an opinion." They passed out of earshot into the next room.

Some of the Warm Age collection was alarming. Across one room shimmered a wall of globular color. Tiny polychrome planets and their spinning moons were suspended in white light. It reminded Wing of Jim Mc-Cauley's work, except that this light sculpture was made to be disturbed. Harumen pushed through the wall, setting off a chain reaction of collisions which produced a cacophony of sudden and violent discord: explosions, rock crack and thunderclap, the shriek of rending metal, and something very much like screams. As if that were not distressing enough, the next room was filled with pictures of dying Chani. Each had been swaddled with some lightweight gauzy material: an after-the-fact censorship demanded by the death taboo. However, by squinting through the modern wrapping, Wing could see through to the ancient pictures, uneasy crosses between portraiture and vid. In each, the most telling—often the most grotesque—detail moved; everything else was stopped in time. A mortally wounded Chani slumped against a wall; blood dripped from the end of her finger and pooled on a stone floor. Another plunged like a statue in horrified freefall against a roiling sky. Yet another's chest had been crushed by a boulder; her foreshortened leg twitched against a clump of blue flowers. Sickened, Wing turned away from the pictures.

"You can't look? You're upset?" Chiskat came up behind him; she seemed pleased by his reaction. "It is said that these are the very pictures which drove Wequassin mad."

"Nonsense," said Ndavu. "Hunger drove Wequassin mad."

"Yes," said Chiskat. "You were here, weren't you? You knew Wicked Wequassin."

"I would not call him wicked."

"Of course not. He did exactly what you wanted."

Harumen intervened. "Now you're boring us," she said, linking arms with Wing. "Phillip does not care about Wequassin and neither do I. I believe you were charged to watch us, not rehash history." She marched Wing away from the argument.

Harumen had been acting strangely that day. She seemed subdued; he had the sense that she was being careful around the priestess. It irked him that he knew so little about her: why should she have to be careful? What did she have to be careful about? What exactly was her place in the thearchy? He concentrated on these questions intensely but no realization was forthcoming from Daisy. Not for the first time, he felt frustrated with his command of the implant. Thanks to the messengers, Wing probably knew more than any human who had ever lived. Yet he understood but an infinitesimal fraction of this information. What good was expanded memory when he had no idea of the dimensions of his knowledge, when something he "knew" could take him by surprise?

The temple rang with the sound of bells. It was time to give thanks.

Wing, Ndavu and Harumen waited as Chiskat unlocked the gate. It was not so long ago, Wing thought ruefully, that a day like this would have left him cata-tonic. He had an image of the inside of his head as a switchboard on which all the lines were beeping. Not so long ago the only way he could have coped would have been to disconnect everything, sit alone with his eyes shut and listen to himself breathe. But he was making progress of a sort: he was learning to live with the din. The gate swung away and Chiskat ushered them through.

In the middle of the paved courtyard a stairwell de-scended into the pavement. It would have been hard to notice had not two blades been standing guard over it. One of the blades gave Wing a threatening yawn that showed pink teeth. They did not politely glance off to one side; there was nothing polite about them. Chiskat stopped at the top step; she appeared to be waiting for someone. The blades said nothing. Then the prophet himself burst from the building opposite them.

"Phillip Wing! Finally! Glad to meet you!" Ammagon could scarcely speak. "Such a big place, easy to get lost." He rested a hand on his breast as he caught his breath. "Fine thanksgiving, wasn't it? Yes, very nice. I know what they say about Kikineans but . . ." He waved a hand to dismiss such slander. "Couldn't you just *feel* their love for Teaqua? Washing over us like waves?"

Wing gave him a polite but noncommittal grunt.

Then Ammagon pushed the nearer blade toward the stairwell. "Well, go on, let them in. Don't blame me: *she* sent for them."

At the bottom of the flight was a heavy wooden door clad in iron. The blade put his shoulder to it. Warm air from the vault billowed up the stairs.

"Go ahead now." Ammagon ushered Harumen down. "But try to remember that she tires easily." He waved Wing on. "Good to see you, Phillip Wing." He said

Wing's name like it was one word. "We'll have to get to know each other later." When the messenger tried to follow, he caught at his tunic. "No, I'm afraid not, Ndavu. She doesn't want to see you."

"What do you mean?" said Ndavu as Chiskat and the other blade closed around him. Wing hesitated momentarily on the stairs but Harumen tugged him into the vault.

"Besides," said Ammagon, putting his arm around the messenger's shoulder, "you and I have things to talk about." The door shut, cutting the prophet off.

The vestibule smelled of damp concrete. The only light came from behind the two huge red doors which stood open before them. They passed through onto a glowing ramp which corkscrewed down a shaft. Wing knelt and scratched at the ramp. It felt like a textured plastic: rockhard but warm to the touch—not a very good heat conductor. He peeked over the edge: about thirty meters to the bottom of the shaft.

As they descended, Daisy oriented Wing. The preservers always built their vaults on five levels; counting from the top down would be living quarters, an information access/utility/storage level and three floors housing the collection. Daisy expected that Teaqua would receive them on the topmost floor; the goddess was very secretive about this vault's treasures.

Solon Petropolus had once warned Wing never to believe in anything he had not seen for himself. Now the wisdom of that advice was proved. The goddess was nothing like the luminous ghost her people saw. Wing and Harumen found her sprawled in a nest of pillows on a low couch, a cape of blue feathers gathered around her like a quilt. Her fur was so thin that Wing could see the loose skin beneath it. An invisible weight seemed to pin her to the cushions and there clung to her the papery odor of slow corruption, the smell of an attic where something had long ago died. She watched with a burning, rheumy stare as he and Harumen knelt and extended their arms in supplication. Wing could not help but think that he had arrived too late, that he had little chance of finishing a tomb before this shriveled creature would have need of it. As he sat back on his heels, Wing kept his eyes down lest she read his dismay.

"Wait outside, Harumen." Teaqua's voice was small and indistinct. Harumen withdrew without saying a word.

The goddess lapsed into a long and unnerving silence. It was as if she had forgotten Wing was still with her. He had no idea what to expect; all he knew was that he was not going to make the first move. As he waited, he glanced around the room in which she had chosen to receive him.

The ceiling glowed, filling the space with a hard, white light. He was kneeling in the middle of an enormous dollhouse, ten by seven meters. Teaqua's couch was in its courtyard. The little rooms surrounding him were filled with hundreds of stone figurines, all prostrated to the goddess. There was an array of tiny worshipers on the floor around her, dusty rows in each compartment. The statues were squirrel-sized and exquisitely detailed. Although all wore Chani clothing, many were clearly alien. Some had reptilian heads; others appeared to be flagelliform flowers. There were lumps with no arms and multilimbed creatures whose robes had been cut to their bristling anatomy.

"Chan and Teaqua, one and the same one," murmured the goddess.

Wing blinked and leaned toward her. She was hard to hear.

"We're speaking only to you." Teaqua's head lifted off the pillows. "Secrets, do you understand?"

The fur along his spine prickled. "I'll keep them."

She pressed a hand to her throat. "This body is ending."

"I'm sorry." He hesitated, wondering if it were even appropriate to offer condolences. But he was too flustered to steer a diplomatic course. The best he could do was to blurt out whatever came to mind. "How long will I have? To do the work?"

"Time enough; it's Chan's will." Her hand flopped to her side. "But you must hurry. It's only because people love and fear Teaqua that our peace holds. Some think that the end of this body means the end of Teaqua. The messengers believe this. Those who've turned to the messengers believe it too. They deny that Chan and Teaqua have become one and the same one. They want to end our peace so they can change the world."

"Who?"

"They say Teaqua is this body and that Chan is a sun. That's a lie."

"Can't you stop them?"

Teaqua's voice rose. "A lie. Say it."

"A lie," said Wing. "Of course."

"Once—long ago—Teaqua *was* like other Chani; that's why the lie spreads." Her eyes were bright, almost feverish. "She hungered. She had feelings anyone could have. But no longer, no . . . she gave up everything for her people."

Teaqua subsided again. For a time there was no sound at all except for her breathing. The silence stretched. Wing wondered just how long this interview was going to take. Maybe he should have packed a lunch.

"The past," said Teaqua finally. "Cold, so deep. Sometimes . . . it feels like we're drowning." She shifted uncomfortably in her nest of pillows and appeared to notice Wing again. He sensed that she did not know who he was.

"Are you all right?" he asked. "Ammagon said we shouldn't tire you."

"Ammagon?" She started as if he had slapped her. "Come here." Wing rose with difficulty: his knees were stiff from kneeling on the stone floor. She reached out, took his arm and smelled him. "The stink of true flesh. You're real. That's good." Teaqua's grip tightened. "Ammagon has nothing to do with this." She twisted Wing hard enough to hurt him. "Let him look out for himself." Then she let him go. He stood in front of her, rubbing the spot where she had grabbed him, mystified.

"Does this room please you?" Teaqua chittered, a small wet sound like water boiling. "But you don't know what you're seeing. A whim, years old. We wanted to leave something behind in this place. Add Teaqua's story to all the stories buried here. Look at them." She cocked her head, waiting. Wing realized that it was not an invitation but an order. To humor her he turned completely around once and revised his estimate upward. There were at least a thousand statues, maybe fifty rooms.

"You see shaped stone. We see the lives we've shaped. We can change our thoughts into stone, we can change people's lives. These stones are speaking to you, Phillip Wing. Listen to them. They're saying, 'We're the ones who Teaqua held in her hand.'"

The more she talked about herself, the stronger she seemed to become.

"When the messengers first came to this world," she continued, "they treated us like animals. They mocked our ways. Now they're on their knees to Teaqua. Here and everywhere. How can that be? Because Chan is great. They fear Teaqua because Chan is great."

She paused and Wing could no longer contain his impatience. "What do you want me to do?" he said.

"Someday Chan may find a new voice. Another body,

a fresh mind." She flagged annoyance and he realized that she had not finished boasting. "Then the end of this body won't matter. But Chan doesn't often choose to become one and the same one with flesh. A made thing. It's an honor to live in such an age, to serve a goddess. The age of the god will end with us. The one who rules after will be Chani, but not Chan."

This was news not only to Wing but to Daisy as well. The messengers had always assumed that Teaqua's successor would be allowed to claim godhood. Now the goddess wanted to take her divinity with her to the grave. Wing could feel Daisy weighing the possibilities.

"It can't be the same, change will come. But still our peace must hold. Change *and* peace, do you understand? So Teaqua must go on. Not for our sake but for the sake of those who might believe the lie. They need a sign— you make it. Like a body, something that's of the world. A house of stone as hard as a mountain. To last forever. A sign that Teaqua goes on."

"But you—the body—won't really be alive in it? I just want to understand."

Teaqua growled. "Sit down, Phillip Wing."

He sat.

"The body ends," she said, "only the body. Chan and Teaqua, one and the same one, go on forever. The god does not die. This is what Teaqua's shrine must tell the people. If Teaqua goes on, the laws go on. Let the law of Chan steer change and our peace will hold. What you believe does not matter, but when the others say Teaqua is dead, what you build must answer."

"Where do you want it built?"

"Where all Chani can see it."

"What do you want it to look like?"

"You make it."

Wing could not help but chitter. So here it was: the

163

proverbial blank check. Every architect's dream. Yet he found himself wishing for some direction—a hint, at least, of the vision that lit those fierce eyes. Teaqua did not want a building, she wanted architectural propaganda. Like Solon Petropolus. Suddenly he was struck by the similarities between them. This was, after all, what Seven Wonders had been all about. Was that the real reason that Ndavu had asked him? Because he had already proved that he could design a building that a megalomaniac could love? Except that he had designed the Glass Cloud for himself; Petropolus had only come into the project afterward. And Teaqua's conceit was even more grandiose than Petropolus's. She expected him to build a structure that could prop up not only her ego but the entire culture. He was not sure that mere upright stones could carry such a weight. Nor was he sure he understood these people anywhere near well enough to do the job. "I'll need to get out of Kikineas," he said, flicking off points on his claws. "See other cities, visit your quarries, look for a site, talk to the crafts—"

"Ask and Harumen will take you wherever you want."

She made a motion with her hand and the door to the gallery slid open.

"No, wait!" Wing held up his hands to stop her. "I'm not done yet." He had so many questions he did not know which to ask first. "I want to know . . . Ndavu said you had a vision. He said that Chan told you that a human must do this. Why a human? Why couldn't one of your own builders do this for you?"

"Ndavu, yes." Teaqua paused, as if considering his question. "A terrible thing to be messenger. To live with the message, to do the things they must do. You didn't want this work, did you, Phillip Wing? You didn't want to come here?"

"Not at first, no. He persuaded me."

"The messengers tried to overthrow us, you know. By starving our people. Instead we brought them to their knees"—Teaqua tilted her head toward the statues—"but at a cost. A high cost."

Again the silence; Teaqua was sliding back into her memory.

Daisy prompted Wing. "Cost?" he said. "You mean the Hunger War?"

"Someone had to learn from them," said Teaqua. "Find all the secrets. Hear the message. But there was no one to trust. Only we could take this up burden." She glared at the statues, as if accusing them. "Now we would forget but such is not Chan's will. Instead he took Teaqua into himself and we became one and the same one. The god can't be shriven; we can never forget."

Wing had no idea what to make of Teaqua's rambling discourse until he noticed that she was sniveling in grief. Then he was afraid. She was not a messenger but she knew the message, or at least part of it. Wing realized then that *he wanted to know too*. Of course he wanted to know.

"We asked if the Chani were alone," she said. "It was then that the messengers told us of the seeding. We had a vision of flowers. Chani and humans are flowers in the same garden. Perennials and annuals. To live but a single season makes you unhappy. Angry. Because your lives are short, you make many bright and beautiful flowers, an angry flowering of art. The Chani live many times; their flowers are rare. They don't make things to quarrel with death. They've no need. Their lives are long and full; the people welcome an end when it comes. They climb Hanu's mountain and build a nest on the ice of Firstlight and call to Chan to take them. But not Teaqua.

We're no longer of the people, the message changed us. We're like you. Come here."

Once again Wing approached the couch on which Teaqua lay and once again she grasped his arm. This time she tugged him close to her and spat on the back of his wrist. He resisted the urge to pull away. She rubbed the spittle into his fur with her thumb and let him go.

"Ammagon will know my scent," she said, "you'll have what you need." Harumen came up behind him. "Find us when you have something to show."

"Let's go." Harumen touched his arm. "She's tired."

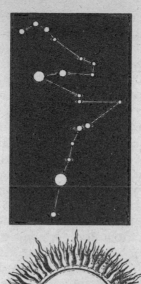

"**B**etter," said Wing, changing his mind. "Not bad at all." He held the last sip of the hot wine in his mouth. It was syrupy, yes, but the stuff volatilized like brandy and had a woody finish that reminded him of walnuts. Ipposkenick refilled his mug, although Wing was in no hurry to have another. This was the first alcohol he had drunk since . . . since . . . it was hard to remember. *Earth*. He had not felt the need. Maybe because this world was itself like a drug. And he had certainly taken a massive dose, he thought. He closed his eyes and Daisy loomed out of the darkness, laughing at his joke. Had he made a joke? Very strange indeed; they were both drunk. When Wing shook his head to clear it, Daisy's hair danced.

Ipposkenick told him again to visit Temple Weekan when he was in Mateag. "You have to see the masonry."

167

It had been Ndavu's idea to throw the going-away party. These people did not give parties. They came together at inns and taverns, attended festivals to dance and chant and tell stories, assembled in public places to give thanks to Chan and govern themselves and complain about their governance. These were all social occasions, but with a purpose. These people expected there would be some event at the center of any gathering: an entertainment, news telling, the sharing of pleasure or—at the very least—a hot meal. The notion of whiling away a few hours in pursuit of some tenuous experience of good fellowship was alien to them. They were, in fact, only doing it to humor the alien.

The wine had been Harumen's idea. She understood quite a bit more about Earth customs than Wing had at first suspected, or perhaps she had realized that wine would lubricate a sticky situation. At the start Wing's guests had seemed ill at ease; it was clear that some did not know exactly what they were doing and did not much care to be doing it with one another. Most had come only because Teaqua had anointed Wing. Yet as the evening passed and the wine flowed, the awkwardness faded. Ndavu had been right. Wing was enjoying himself. He derived a curious satisfaction from the fact that all of these creatures—people—who disliked each other had crowded into *his* room for *his* sake. Wing settled back on the gel mat, rested his head against the wall and let the babble of voices wash over him. Menzere was chatting with Chiskat. Ndavu and Ammagon were sitting on the floor; their heads were very close together. They made an unlikely pair. Ndavu was still trying to get the prophet to arrange an audience with Teaqua and did not seem to be above using flattery to get his way. And the messenger was drinking wine! Wing noticed Harumen trying to eavesdrop on their conversation at the same time she was showing Osh, Uttaro and

Arinash Wing's workstation. She kept calling up scenes of Earth but her audience seemed more interested in playing with the slatted rolltop. Wing was impressed at how quickly Harumen had mastered the workstation; she had gone through the tutorial in an hour.

"Wish I was going with you," said Ipposkenick. "Haven't been to Mateag in . . . let's see . . ." The architectural historian's voice trailed off.

Ammagon began grooming the fur on Ndavu's shoulder. The messenger cooed as if he enjoyed the prophet's caresses. Surprised and slightly embarrassed, Wing inspected the dark wine in his mug.

"Wish I was going . . ."

Wing knew this but Ipposkenick had a scholar's tendency to lecture. It was enough that Wing had allowed his friend to prepare the itinerary for the trip. Wing wanted to see the local architecture for himself, find inspiration on his own. He was about to explain this when Ipposkenick started to snore. He had passed out on the bed beside Wing.

Chiskat got up to watch Harumen's demonstration and Menzere's ghost glided over. Wing felt vaguely guilty that he had never taken the messenger up on her invitation to visit her quarters but he *had* been busy.

"Sure you want to talk to me?" said Wing, tipping a shoulder toward the sleeping Ipposkenick. "I do this to people."

Menzere chittered politely. "I will take my chances, Phillip."

"I'd offer you a drink—if you were really here."

"Ethanol does not agree with me." The messenger shrugged. "However, I should warn you that I am stunning myself in an analogous way, to get into the spirit of your party."

"Very good." Wing saluted her with the mug and then

took a drink. "Very good. Except how is it that Ndavu can drink wine and you can't?"

"Ndavu is capable of many things which I would not care to attempt," said Menzere.

Wing glanced across the room in time to see Ammagon licking the bristles on Ndavu's cheek. "Not all messengers are created equal, then?" he said.

"All essences are equal."

"Yours and mine?"

Menzere made a fist.

"Chani and messenger?"

"This we believe. Of course it has never been fully tested."

"But it has been tested on humans?"

Menzere cocked her head to one side and made a gesture which invited Wing to consider his own case.

That was what he was afraid of. "Chiskat keeps claiming I'm a messenger," he said with boozy impatience. "You telling me she's right?"

"As they define the word, you are. As we define it, you are not yet a messenger. There are potentials which are as yet unrealized."

"And who decides if they get realized?"

"You do. It could hardly be otherwise."

"Thank you," Ammagon interrupted, "for asking me to your party." He had Ndavu in tow. At this point it would have taken a laser torch to separate them.

"Glad you came," said Wing brusquely, still provoked at the thought that he might become a messenger. It was bad enough that he had become . . . whatever he had become.

Ammagon twitched Ndavu's arm.

"We are going now." The messenger looked slightly lopsided; Ammagon nudged him upright. "It is late. We are going." Ndavu sniffed the air as if he had just caught an interesting scent; whatever he smelled seemed to please him. "To another place, he knows someplace. To . . ."

The messenger swayed and Wing had an unexpected glimpse of Harumen behind them. She was scowling at Ndavu and Ammagon; their sudden closeness seemed to have stirred strong emotions within her. Then she saw him watching her and she looked away. Wing felt the briefest twinge of . . . something. He did not know what. He was glad he was drunk; at least now he had an excuse for being confused. A bellyful of wine made it easier being an alien.

"Very nice, very nice." Ammagon kept saying the words like an incantation as he steered his prize toward the door. "Very, very nice."

Without thinking Wing tried to give the ghost a worldly dig in the ribs. "Oops, 'scuse me." Menzere's abdomen shimmered as Wing's elbow passed through.

The ghost shrugged good-naturedly. "It happens all the time."

Wing decided he liked Menzere. "On Earth, we have a saying. 'Politics makes strange bedfellows.'"

"It is a truth," said the messenger solemnly. Like a heat mirage, Menzere's image continued to waver. "You will excuse my appearance," she said, "but I'm afraid I may have overstimulated myself."

Wing wanted to clap her on the back but thought better of it. "'S okay. I feel a little out of focus myself."

The guests from the temple gave Ammagon a five-minute head start before getting up. Wing was glad to see Chiskat go; she looked as if she wanted to break something. The scholars followed soon after. Harumen shook Ipposkenick awake; grumbling, the historian staggered off. Finally Menzere's shimmering hologhost stood, grimaced as if she were about to be sick and then her window closed abruptly with an audible crackle of static. After everyone had left, Harumen helped Wing clean up. "I thought it went well. Were you happy with it? Was it what you wanted?" That peculiar intensity came over her again; Wing read it now as a kind of desperation. He assured her that the party had been a great success. "I'm glad," she said. "I want you to be happy here." She lingered at the door as if waiting for him to say something. He was too tired to think of what it might be.

"Good night, Harumen," he said. "And thanks." She reached out then and, without looking directly at him, shyly tried to touch the side of his face. He realized that she wanted to stay the night with him, had been hoping all evening for an invitation. Wing could not help himself: he flinched. Instantly her expression hardened. She turned, walked and then ran down the hall.

He closed the door, flopped onto his bed. He felt angry, not necessarily at her. He did not want to hurt her; he liked Harumen very much. But just because Ndavu was headed for the common bed with Ammagon did not mean that he . . . it was nothing personal . . . he couldn't possibly . . . Wing closed his eyes. Laughing drunkenly, Daisy wrapped her legs around him.

Wing peered through the transparent fuselage of the transport pod at the valley of the Chowhesu River, which the Chani called Riverside. When he closed his eyes he could still see the land, or at least the version of it stored in the implant. He was intrigued by the differences. The images that Daisy produced were as idealized as an architectural rendering and just as static. Here was a lonely boat with a shining white sail, there a laden cart stopped among verdant fields. But today the valley was overcast by a smear of high thin clouds; its colors were duller. The Chowhesu was dirt brown with black mud banks; from above it looked like a great unpaved highway. All kinds of traffic plied the river: canoes, crude rafts, ferries barging from shore to shore and narrow open-decked lateeners with sails faded by Chan's merciless glare. The Chowhesu was at a seasonal low and the reed swamps along its banks had died back. Most of the fields of Riverside were fallow but a few farmers were trying to squeeze a late crop out of the rich bottom land. Wing could just make out jade rows sprouting from the dark earth.

From the air Wing could see that Riverside's crooked grid was defined not by its roads—little more than dusty tracks—but rather by irrigation canals cut between the fields. At the farthest reach of the last ditch the desert waited: straw-colored dunes corrugated by the wind, weathered cliffs which stuck out like bones. There was little rain here in the lee of Aseneshesh's mountains and the desert squeezed Riverside constantly. Even at its widest the valley was scarcely more than twenty kilometers across. Yet the majority of the people lived on this long ribbon of muddy water and fertile land. If the Chowhesu were ever to fail, Riverside would dry up and blow away. However, as long as snow fell in the mountains, the melt would have to find a way to the sea.

"We just passed over Hush's Ferry," said Ndavu, pointing. "On the other side is Keekaysak."

The messenger was studying Riverside as intently as Wing. Harumen, on the other hand, had a blanket over her head and had lowered her seat back. She had not made a sound since they had flown over the highlands; sporadic changes in the contours of the blanket were the only hints that there was yet life beneath it. Harumen did not much care for flying in a fishbowl piloted by a computer.

Ndavu pointed. "There is Mateag."

Some called it the island city, others the city of temples. According to the truths, it was on the fertile island of Mateag that Chan's daughter, Hanu, had taken Kautama, the last Chani, as her mate. On Mateag she had taught him the secrets of shriving. They had shared pleasure and prospered there, sired a new race. Now most of the people of this most historic of cities busied themselves with the ecstasy and terror of shriving. Mateag imported the old, the weary, the sinful and it exported reborn innocence. Although people could be shriven anywhere in the thearchy, most thought of Mateag when the trembling began. It was said that Chan bestowed special favors to those who chose to forget and start over in the city of temples.

Mateag had burned during the Hunger War. Afterward it became the centerpiece of Teaqua's reconstruction program. Old temples were restored, new and more ostentatious ones begun. The island itself was now dedicated entirely to the spiritual; secular functions had moved across the river branches to the north and south shores. The old city had been ruthlessly stripped of ordinary architecture until only the monuments remained, paeans in brick and stone to Teaqua's greatness.

The island reminded Wing of the campus of some extravagantly endowed agricultural college. Temples, cloisters and outbuildings were sited in precise clusters, surrounded by gardens and orchards and trellised arbor ways. Every centimeter of land was in production. A breadroot crop was wintering over for harvest after thaw, sweetening in the cool soil. There were muddy fields of dormant messenger wheat; a variety of hardy greens thrived in tidy raised beds. The bare hedgerows would yield clawfruit in season; among other things, Mateag was known for its preserves and jellies. Wing had never been to a place that was so relentlessly ordered. What he saw looked more like Versailles—or the disneys—than working farms. Certainly no farm had ever had such buildings; even the barns were palaces! Yet strangely enough, no one seemed to be working. Wing's party had the paths to themselves. The fields were empty.

Despite the visionary scope of the planning and the beauty of the landscaping, it was the architecture that most tantalized Wing. From what Daisy had shown him, from what Ipposkenick had told him and from what he himself had read at the scholars' palace, he had come to the city of temples with the idea that he might build the tomb here. Now that he could actually see Mateag for himself, he had doubts. He could not help but remember the way he had felt the first time he visited Rome. He had taken the maglev to Montuori's sleekly modernist Termini station, itself a landmark, and had immediately started to walk, making an architectural pilgrimage through the narrow streets. To San Carlo alle Quattro Fontane, Borromini's little jewel of the Baroque. He had gazed with disdain at the bloated and kitschy neoclassic monument to Vittorio Emanuele and passed quickly on to Marcus Agrippa's serene Pantheon. And then to the strange and yet beautifully mutated Castel Sant'Angelo—which made the Church of the Holy Spirit in Portsmouth look like a model of good planning and orderly design. Finally he had come to St. Peter's, where Bramante, Michelangelo, and Bernini had created the grandest masterpiece of the High Renaissance. His tour had left him at once awestruck and downcast. He had measured himself against Rome's masterpieces and found that he was an unpromising graduate student, barely fit to contemplate genius. Now he was back again, on a different world but in the same state of mind. How could he possibly build on Mateag? It would take him a lifetime just to master a single idiom, much less grasp the entire history of Chani architecture on display here. He knew exactly what would happen if he tried. He thought again of the embarrassing Vittoriano, the monument which proclaimed the mediocrity of its builder to the ages. At least poor Sacconi had been Italian—and human. Wing did not even have the advantage of belonging to the same *species*. The idea of trying to compete here struck him as hopelessly arrogant.

A priestess met them in the courtyard of Temple Weekan. Open windows breathed the warm and yeasty aroma of bread into the yard. Wing was instantly hungry.

"I'm Timmin." The priestess made supplication to Harumen.

"Harumen." She returned the sign. "This is Wing; you've heard of him. He's Ndavu—the messenger."

Timmin did not repeat the sign but rather gave Wing a disapproving stare. Her only acknowledgment of Ndavu's presence was a snort, as if she were trying to clear a stink from her nasal slits. "Come in then." Timmin addressed the space between Harumen and Wing.

Wing understood immediately why Ipposkenick had wanted him to see Temple Weekan. It had been built to honor Kautama's daughter Weekan, known as the Baker. The complex was situated on a canal near the river and reminded Wing of a New England mill—except that no mill had ever looked quite like this. The brick makers had added pigments to the clay, producing half a dozen muted colors: brown, dark red, plum, gray green, straw and terra-cotta. The mason had used this limited palette to make every wall into a mosaic. The designs were at once abstract and representational, a kind of bricklayer's pointillism. There were stylized images of scythes and wains, the spikes of various grains, mill gears and grinding stones. Timmin led them quickly through the main hall of the temple, a damp, gloomy space filled with the sound of running water. An interior canal passed through one end and the altar could only be reached by a bridge. The commons were brighter and the cloisters were airy and brighter still. All were deserted.

"Where is everybody?" It had finally begun to bother Wing.

Timmin blinked at Wing as if she had not understood. Harumen repeated the question sharply.

"We'll show you our temples for Teaqua's sake." The ferocity of Timmin's dislike surprised Wing. "But you're not going to corrupt the shriving, do you understand? We've gathered all the reborns together in small groups to pray and tell the truths. If you must force yourselves on them . . . just one group. Only a few will suffer. And no tremblers."

"Never mind." Now Wing was sure he had made a mistake coming to Mateag. "Let's go," he said to Harumen.

"You never learn, do you?" Harumen ignored him; she struck out angrily and grabbed Timmin's mane. "It's not for priests to say whether Wing is corrupt. He serves the goddess; she has blessed him. Or maybe you have a problem with that?"

Timmin gave her a conspiratorial grin, as if inviting her to consider Teaqua's condition. Immediately Harumen yanked Timmin's mane harder, twisting her head around until the grin turned into a grimace. "Speak!"

"H-he may see whatever he wishes."

"And if he wants to call an assembly? See everyone on the island?"

"If he . . . wishes."

"You serve here at Teaqua's pleasure." Harumen let her go. "Make sure your friends understand that."

*　　*　　*

The tremblers lived in a ward that Piranesi might have recognized. The dark room smelled of smoke and dirty clothes. Wing counted about twenty cots; seven were occupied. An incessant drone of voices filled the room but there was no conversation. Many of the tremblers buzzed or hummed to a sprung rhythm. One rocked back and forth on her cot, knees grasped to chest. Another just sat at the edge of the bed, stared at the floor and shook. She had lost much of her fur; Wing was surprised at how grotesque bare skin looked to him.

"But-but-but . . ." she said to no one.

"You're *wrong*." The trembler in the cot next to her had a tic. His head kept jerking toward his left shoulder as he tried to focus on Wing. "Your body doesn't fit." He gave an alarmed hoot; others picked up the call.

Wing did not know what to do and neither did Daisy; the messengers had yet to understand trembling. They suspected it began as control mechanisms in the motor cortex shut down. Some argued that shriving progressively disrupted the integrative functioning of the Chani brain until the tremblers became as helpless as newborns, their behavior reduced to reflex and instinct. But there was no theory to explain why or how this could happen.

Ndavu reached out and brushed the side of the trembler's head. He stopped hooting and his twitch abated. Wing thought Timmin was going to slap Ndavu's hand away but she held back, no doubt in fear of Harumen.

"You are right," Ndavu said. "He does not belong here. We are just visiting for a little while and then we will go away."

"I have nightmares," said the trembler. "They're wrong too."

"They will pass. Ask Chan to burn them away."

178

"Chan is great," the trembler said fervently. "Praise him!"

"Look to Chan," said Ndavu. "Look into the sun."

The priest on duty hurried across the ward, carrying a small golden cup. "It's a bad time," he said. Ndavu withdrew his hand and the priest held the cup to the trembler's lips. "Sip it, only a sip."

"We should go now." Timmin sounded outraged. "Now."

"Now-now-now . . ." The balding trembler in the next cot echoed.

The trembler whom Ndavu had comforted hugged the messenger. "Soon, lord?"

"It will not be long," Ndavu said.

"Timmin's right," said Wing. This place was giving him a headache. "Let's go."

The tremblers' priest bowed to Ndavu in gratitude for his help. Timmin, meanwhile, looked as if she were about to explode. As they left the dark room, Wing realized that the priest had mistaken the messenger for a Chani.

Timmin stalked through an open-air arcade to a shadowy vestibule. She explained that it led to the retreat where tremblers were taken for the final acts of shriving. Wing could hear what sounded like barking within; a low calm voice was repeating the words, "The smell of light, the touch of Chan." Timmin said Wing could peek in if he wanted but warned him not to speak. Wing hesitated. He did not really want to enter but for some reason he felt obligated.

(Go, go in! No offworlder has ever seen it!)

Wing yelped in alarm; it was as if something had sprung at him from the shadows. He had often tried to coax Daisy into direct conversation, yet now that he heard her unbidden whispering, he was scared. He turned away from the vestibule and staggered blindly away, stunned by the knowledge that it had been Daisy who had held him, however briefly, at the entrance to the retreat. She . . . it . . . something alien was influencing his behavior. Maybe he should have expected it; after all, he had allowed himself to create sexual fantasies in which she acted independently, as a real person. But he had always thought he was in control, had believed that when he was not paying attention to her that Daisy shut herself down. He realized—on his own!—that he had never really thought enough about her, any more than he would have bothered to analyze his intuitions or consciousness. He had just experienced her without contemplating what she was doing in him. To him. For if Daisy was curious then she was more than just a fancy interface to a data bank; she was an intelligence. Not a construct of his own imagination but a cybernetic parasite. He had been *violated*; the very thought made him dizzy and sick. Even now he imagined he could feel her trying to batter through the wall of fear in which he had sealed her. Or perhaps it was just the blood pounding in his head.

"Phillip, slow down!"

"What's wrong?"

Hands grabbed him and pulled him down onto a bench. The stone shot its coldness up his spine. He thrashed blindly against whoever it was trying to restrain him. He knew they only wanted to make him their puppet, to strip away his freedom.

"What's the matter with him?"

Wing felt something prick his forearm and he tried to throw himself to the floor to escape.

"Turn it off," a voice yowled. Wing thought it might have been his. "She's *wrong*." Or was he hallucinating? And how could he ever hope to tell?

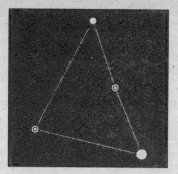

**H**arumen perched on the edge of the couch and watched Wing sleep. Ndavu claimed that Wing would be himself again when the sedative wore off. She was not so sure; the messenger was not very imaginative about pain. Wing had curled into an odd shape: knees drawn to chest, arms closed in, chin lowered. His nasal slits shivered as he breathed; from time to time he moaned as if his dreams troubled him. Even asleep he looked so unhappy that she wanted to take him in her arms and carry him to bliss. But he needed rest.

She loved him. She did not know how it had happened but there was no denying it now. Still, she wondered how much *he* really understood about love. Human notions of it made no sense to her. They were so possessive of one another; it was unnatural. In her opin-

181

ion the entire species needed to spend a few steamy weeks in common beds until they had discovered the joy and necessity of pleasing many partners. While there was no doubt that Wing's people were more technologically advanced than hers, when it came to pleasure the humans were backward.

Wing's arm twitched and he muttered in an unintelligible singsong. She reached out and rubbed his shoulders lightly. That seemed to settle him. She liked touching him—very much. She would have liked it better if he were awake and was touching her too. She let her hand slide up his neck to the side of his face. The messengers had given him such a beautiful body. She thought he was crazy not to share it.

But he was crazy. To be human meant to be crazy. They were so obsessed with death that it was a wonder they knew anything about sex. Even though Wing was Chani now and his mortality was no longer an immediate problem, he still thought like a human. She was not sure whether he would ever change.

He rolled over and mumbled again. This time she was able to make out one of the words. "Daisy."

"S-s-sh." She breathed into his mane. "You'll wake yourself up." It was hard to keep from nuzzling him.

The information about Wing in her implant was maddeningly incomplete. He loved this Daisy so much that he had to run away from her? Harumen could hardly accept that. He was supposed to be ambitious yet he had freely chosen an irrevocable exile. Harumen wanted to understand exactly why he had come to Aseneshesh. Ndavu said that it was because he was a creature who had learned how to fit in anywhere but not how to belong. It was his fate to be an alien no matter where he was, even on his own world.

Maybe that was why she loved him, because he was just like her. And she was so lonely.

"No, *don't*." Wing's arm shot out wildly as if to ward off a blow and he struck Harumen's leg. His eyes shot open and for a moment she thought he might attack her. Then he moaned and clamped a hand over his face. "It's you." He sounded disappointed. "I was dreaming."

"Sounded like a nightmare." She resisted the urge to give him a comforting hug. "You were afraid?"

"She had a knife. Daisy. The blade was smeared with messenger blood. Yellow and like honey. Thick. She was going to cut me with it, infect me with the message. We were in the Counting House. She said if I were a messenger I'd never have to feel anything again. I didn't want that. Didn't want to be like her." There was a silence; Wing let his hand fall back to the mattress. "Where are we?"

"The cloister at Temple Weekan." Finally she could no longer resist. "I'm worried about you." She took his hand in both of hers. "Ndavu gave you something. He said it would calm you down." Wing did not pull away.

"He was right about that."

"How do you feel?"

"Me?" He stretched and then sat up. "I don't." Harumen squeezed his hand and let it slip out of her grip. She was not sure whether he had even noticed the contact.

"What happened to you?" she said.

He scratched his shoulder, considering. "I guess Daisy was curious."

"Your wife?"

"No," he said. "I don't know how to explain. It's something the messengers did to me—not really sure you'd understand."

"You have Daisy in your head." She knew exactly what he was talking about. "And she whispers to you."

Wing seemed taken aback that she had guessed so easily. She wanted to tell him then that she had a memory implant too, how she also had struggled with it—was still struggling. But she was fearful of what he would think; she had seen all too often how people's attitudes changed when they knew her secret. Besides, Ndavu had specifically warned her not to burden Wing with new information until he recovered. In a moment of hesitation, she lost her chance.

The messenger entered the room. "Up already, are you?" He seemed very pleased with himself. "I told Harumen there was no need to worry."

It was all so neat, she thought. Maybe Ndavu had always meant for her to love Wing, had sowed the seeds of desire deep within her implant. The messenger had meant so much to her once, but over the years he had receded and Wing had loomed larger and larger in her imagination. However, she did not really care anymore how it had happened. She was in love. It was enough.

**W**ing felt as light
as a handful of air as he gazed up at the two of them.
Ndavu seemed very pleased with himself; Harumen
looked edgy. There was something different about her,
but Wing could not decide what it was. He glanced
down to see if his feet were actually touching the floor.
Whatever the messenger had given him had drained the
terror and pain and most of the life from him; Wing was
not himself. He wished he could reestablish contact with
his feelings, awful as they had been. However, this was
an abstract sort of desire; nothing he cared to do anything about.

"I want her turned off." He had not known he was
going to say it. "Cut out of me, you understand?"

"What are you talking about?" said Ndavu.

Wing felt the rough contours of the stone floor with his toes.

"His interface," Harumen explained. "Daisy whispers to him."

Wing had never intended to tell Ndavu that John the Baptist had become Daisy. Now all his hidden fears and pleasures spilled out. It was easier than he had imagined because he spoke as if about someone else. A stranger. Still, he resented Ndavu for interrogating him while he was defenseless. Just the sort of thing a messenger would do: take advantage of a crazy person. It was not until Wing heard himself talking about the stranger's sexuality that he experienced even a flicker of embarrassment. The intensity with which Harumen was listening made him shy and he changed the subject. "So how do I get rid of it?"

"You need the interface, Phillip. You could not possibly do your work here without it. Believe me, whatever personality it has is the one you have given it. The sole purpose of its existence is to serve you, not us."

Wing was surprised that the stranger—he—was sniffling. "I'm not sure I believe you anymore." He brushed the back of his hand against his snout and tried to clear his double vision. Being two people was confusing him.

"The interface is built into the implant."

"Then I'm crazy. Can't do the work. Stuff me in a box and ship me home."

"If you want to, you can suppress her." Ndavu was pleading; part of Wing was pleased. It was true that Daisy usually emerged only when Wing was curious. All he had to do was not care. Maybe the solution was to have Ndavu keep shooting him up with depressants so he could spend the rest of his stay scuffling around like some schizophrenic zombie.

"I am sure the worst is over," said Ndavu.

"That's right," Wing said. "We realize now that poor

Wing is three sizes too small for this job so we're sending him home."

"You can't go home," said Harumen.

"He is not going home," said Ndavu wearily. "You are not going home."

"You said you were helping him," Harumen said. "You've made him worse."

"You will remember that I warned you he was not ready for this trip. He needs more time to adjust. You were the one who could not wait."

"It's what Teaqua wanted."

"Teaqua wants to leave this world to the pedants, Harumen."

"That's a lie!"

"Now, now, you two." Their arguing pricked through Wing's detachment. "You'll upset the patient. Maybe we should all calm down." He saw no reason why he should have to be the peacemaker. They were supposed to be taking care of *him*.

"Someday, Harumen," the messenger said coolly, "you are going to have to decide whose side you are on."

"There's nothing to decide. I know."

"Do you know what kind of world Teaqua is going to leave behind? Will there be a place in it for you?"

"This is my world." She stiffened. "I'm Chani."

"Yes"—Ndavu shrugged and gestured at Wing—"and Phillip here is human."

"What are you two talking about?" Wing realized that there were secrets between them that he wanted to know.

Harumen's expression was hard as ice. "I'm not stupid, Ndavu. I know you'd say anything, do anything. You shut your eyes and wormed into Ammagon's bed and what did it get you? Next you'll start begging to share pleasure with me so I'll do what you want."

"Maybe I would not have to beg."

She shrank back, fumbled at the door. "Call if you need me, Phillip." Wing could see that Ndavu's words had wounded her.

It was only after she had gone that he felt his heart—something inside him—fluttering. "What are you doing to us?" His voice caught.

"I am only doing what must be done," said Ndavu.

"That's not an answer!"

"Phillip, what you are asking is very complex; any response would only raise more questions and more, until we might well end up discussing the message itself."

"So?" Anger rumbled like distant thunder in Wing's voice. "Tell me what's really going on here. Or are you just going to keep evading questions until I crack?"

"You know everything you need to know to do your job." Ndavu looked distracted, as though his attention were elsewhere. Wing wondered then what kind of interface a messenger might have. "As for the rest, it is not yet the right time. This is serious, Phillip. The message could change your life in ways you might later regret."

"The forbidden fruit, is it?"

"You ought not taste unless you are willing to accept the consequences."

Wing struck his chest, ruffling the nap of the guard hair. "I've suffered consequences already."

"The message is not only information. To hear it is to make an irrevocable commitment. Once you pick the forbidden fruit, you cannot put it back on the tree."

"I want an answer, Ndavu."

Ndavu retreated toward the door. "The answer is no." He turned and was gone before Wing had a chance to protest.

Wing was not sure whether he had won or lost the skirmish. All he knew was that he did not have the energy to chase after Ndavu. The stranger inside of him chittered and Wing decided maybe they—he—ought to lie back down.

Later that evening, Harumen brought him dinner and stayed to eat with him, at first in silence. His fare was a bowl of raw hot vitabulk and a flavor palette of ham, corn, asparagus, cheese. Harumen ate what looked like cockroach soup. They shared a loaf of fresh bread from the temple bakery and a small bowl of clawberry preserves.

"You're well?"

"Well enough to get out of here."

"Good, good."

The bread was delicious; Wing was losing his appetite for bulk. He jammed the scoop into the stiff cooling bulk and left it standing there. "What is it between you and Ndavu?"

"I—we had great hopes for Ndavu." Wing had the sense that she was choosing words very carefully, using precision to mask her pain. "He seemed to understand what the scholars were trying to do. He—we shared pleasure many times; once I thought I loved him." She stirred her soup unhappily. "When Teaqua decided that she was going to—that she wanted not to be shriven, everything changed. He asked me to . . . prepare myself to help you. He said you'd need someone to understand. Teaqua gave her permission. But then *he* left to get you. That was a surprise. I wasn't expecting it."

Wing waved for her to stop. She had already said too much. She was telling him the kinds of secrets that only people with commitments share with one another. He was not ready for that kind of responsibility. "So what are we going to do?"

"Do?" She slumped back into her chair. "What must be done. Tomorrow we fly to Uritammous."

It was actually two days before Wing was ready to travel. He dressed himself and walked out of Temple Weekan on his own. When he was hungry, he knew enough to eat. He could carry on intelligent conversation and was only rarely confused by jokes. He smiled and sighed and even flagged some of his feelings. On the surface he gave what he thought was a convincing performance of normality. Inside he waged an oddly mundane and yet furious war for self-control; his mood swung wildly with each little victory and defeat.

Doing without Daisy was like trying to ignore an itch. At the first prickle of curiosity, there she was—inescapable, exasperating. Nevertheless, Wing had resolved not to consult her in any way. It was not that he doubted her information; he worried she was eroding his viewpoint. He had not realized how thoroughly she had penetrated his thoughts. If he let his concentration slip even for a moment, she would wrap him in cobwebs of explication that clung despite all his efforts to break loose and experience the world for himself. He did not want the official version, the messenger slant.

He decided to ask more questions, although he knew that even this strategy was suspect. After all, Daisy supplied his vocabulary. Ndavu and Harumen accepted his new inquisitiveness good-naturedly. As they had disembarked from the transport pod, he overheard the messenger reassuring her that it was a phase he was going through. Although his companions had clearly come to some private accommodation, there was still a noticeable strain to their relations.

The messengers' base in the highlands reminded Wing of all the warehouses he had ever seen. Its domes were cold, dim and artless as two-by-fours. The first was abandoned; much of it was taken up by dusty processing and storage mechanisms, the purpose of which was not immediately clear. The storage racks had been cleared, the machines stood idle. A stale vinyl smell hung in the still air.

"At one time this was our central blood-processing and shipping facility," replied Ndavu. "It was closed down after we began to synthesize the rejuvenation serum." He brought the lights up. "When I first came here we were processing about two million liters of blood a year. We collected the blood in sterile thermoplastic pouches, centrifuged it over there." He pointed to an enormous blue drum. "While in the centrifuge the pouches were subjected to an electrical charge which caused them to compartmentalize. The plasma was discarded; the cells were frozen and stored until they could be boosted to orbit for zero-G processing. Now, of course, the Chani have nothing to export and so we use the spaceport exclusively as a transfer station for the wheat."

The airlock to the next dome was protected by a soap bubble. Wing popped through its shivering wall, leaving a rainbow eddy in his wake as he entered the grain elevator. They climbed to what appeared to be an empty control center. On the bank of monitors above them were six views of a pneumatic robot vacuuming wheat out of a transport pod through a conveyor tube that shuddered like a dying snake.

"We store most of our reserves in orbit," said Ndavu. "They keep for years in space. As the growing season approaches, we begin to ship seed. From time to time we also provide wheat for consumption; the level of imports depends on the yearly crop. Everything comes to this facility first. The mountain climate helps keep down pests and prevents storage blight. From here we distribute to other bases and then to the Chani."

"It must cost to ship grain through the mass exchanger." Wing could feel Daisy twitching with explanations. "Can't you raise it here?"

"Tetraploid triticale does not breed true and the Chani refuse to learn the techniques of hybridization. Teaqua has denied our request for land so that we can grow the necessary grain ourselves. We have even offered to reclaim the glaciated continents for this purpose. We can grow most of the seed grain in orbit but yes, it is very expensive to bring wheat in bulk through the mass exchanger. Some say that Teaqua enjoys putting this strain on the resources of the commonwealth."

Harumen was studying the robots. She seemed not be listening although Ndavu clearly wanted to draw her into the conversation.

"Then why do you do it?"

"They would starve otherwise." He shrugged. "You see, we are not quite the monsters they make us out to be. Besides, it is a situation we hope to change."

At the loading dock outside of the elevator, grain squirted from the conveyor tube into a wagon that looked like a log cabin on wheels. Two others were parked behind it. They were drawn by a team of a dozen surunashes, wolf-sized reptiles with ugly beaks and gray feathered flanks. Wing, Harumen and Ndavu were to hitch a ride down to Uritammous, some thirty kilometers away.

As they jolted down the cobbled road, Wing saw that a fourth wagon had joined the end of their train. He craned for a better look; its flatbed was covered with a tarpaulin beneath which he detected boxy contours. Not grain, certainly. He asked his Chani driver about it. "Parts," she said. Hostility shimmered off her like heat from a tar roof. Wing had seen her kind before; some of these people simply could not abide aliens, even if they did serve the goddess. He faced forward and shut up. He could not help but notice Ndavu chatting amiably in the wagon ahead.

The city of Uritammous was a port on the Skywater, a huge, shallow lake near the center of the plateau where most highlanders lived. The mountain winters were not quite so harsh here and the lake provided both food and easy transport. Wing had not been impressed with Uritammous during flyover. Wooden, weather-beaten, badly laid out, it was the most primitive of the cities he had seen. Uritammous had been heavily scarred by fire and no wonder; with all that wood and those narrow streets and squeezed development, what chance would bucket brigades have? Yet it had become Wing's first choice for a tomb site, now that he had decided against Mateag. Uritammous was big enough to accept a horde of pilgrims and it lay astride the major trade route between the Coastal Protectorates to the west and great Riverside to the east.

The grain wagons slowed as they negotiated the streets of the city. Pedestrians and handcarts and carriages and several species of pack animals squeezed past them. Nobody seemed interested in him; that was a blessing. Wing's appearance with Teaqua at the thanksgiving had made him a minor celebrity. Better the rude silence of the xenophobic wagoneer than the attention of the crowd. The solitude helped Wing relax. Chan's strong light warmed him like a pat on the back and he believed that he might have left his troubles behind in Riverside. Maybe it was only the thin mountain air making him giddy, but so what? The more of Uritammous he saw, the more convinced he was that he was in the right place. Anything he put up here would be an advance over the local state of the building arts. No competition. Maybe he would build just out of the city, look for higher ground. It made sense: the metaphor of ascent and all that, the god on the mountaintop. He could see the possibilities. Let it be a hard climb to some astonishing view, something even the slowest pilgrim would understand. From such a vantage, Teaqua would look down on her people. Wing took a deep breath as the idea swelled within him; he had to try it out on someone.

He swung from his perch in the driver's box and landed on knees and palms in the street. His hands stung but he picked himself up and waited for Harumen.

"This is it!"

"Get back on the wagon."

"Right here, Harumen, this is the place." He gestured up at the shining blue sky.

She spoke to the wagoneer beside her. "He says just a little further."

"No. Yes, all right." People were stopping to watch. Wing twittered and danced away. He did not mind making a fool of himself. "Doesn't matter," he called.

The last wagon had pulled up and on an impulse Wing jumped up beside the wagoneer. "What're we carrying here, friend?"

"Spare parts." The wagoneer flagged his amusement. "For the fixers."

Ndavu had twisted around to see what was happening.

"And just what do fixers fix?"

"Ghosts."

Wing's mood had swung again. He decided it was time to indulge himself—show these people just who was in charge. "I'd like to see that." After all, the goddess had spat on him.


Kitawog, the chief of the repair shop, had a thin face and small dull eyes. She sniffed the air regularly, as if trying to smell out an ambush. The fixers lugged five crates of windowcomm components into the shop. "Careful, there! Easy, you lump," she scolded an apprentice. She was not at all what Wing had expected. He followed her inside; Harumen and Ndavu grudgingly followed him.

"The people call them links," said Harumen. "Windowcomm is a messenger word."

"I don't get it." Wing gestured at the fixers. "Aren't they corrupted by all this technology?"

Harumen paused just inside the door and held Wing back so that they would not be overheard. "No," she said, "because Teaqua has blessed the links." It was a lame explanation and she acted as if she knew it. "They've become as important as the whispers. The thanksgivings and the gatherings and the truth plays are what bind us all together. These are Chan's machines now, the tools of the god."

Ndavu smirked silently at Harumen's intellectual gymnastics. Meanwhile Kitawog unwrapped and inspected each component as it came out of its crate, rubbing the smooth housings with her thumbs as if she could tell quality from the evenness of the finish.

"Larder for Kunin." She passed the briefcase-sized component to her apprentice, an earnest reborn, who lugged it over to a tub of hot soapy water, plunged it in and scrubbed it like a dirty frying pan.

"Everyone knows that messengers build the links," said Harumen. "So they purify the parts here. Sometimes they wash a new link for days with their strongest soaps to get the messenger stink off. Later the priests come. Then, when it gets to the village, the craftspeople decorate it, maybe with veneers or by embroidering covers. Sometimes they paint or carve figures right onto the housings; it depends on the local skills. They change it from a messenger thing into something they can be proud of, a treasure of their village. When a link breaks, it would be an insult to let messengers tamper with it. Instead the village linkmaster brings it to a place like this."

Wing was still confused. "How do they know. . . ?" Harumen squeezed his arm for silence as Kitawog approached.

"So you want?" She rolled up the sleeves of her tunic.

"Can you show me what you do here?" said Wing.

"At busy time?" She was grumpy. "This one is Phillip Wing, no? Saw on link. Ugly enough." Without waiting for a reply, she grabbed his elbow and steered him toward a workbench. "Poor thing, probably not your fault." She smelled of lye.

Kitawog lifted a housing encrusted with polished stones. The main unit of the broken windowcomm was about the size of the workstation unit in his rolltop. Next to it was a small dish antenna half a meter in diameter. Wing ran a finger along the edge of the dish; it felt more like stone than metal.

"Net," said Kitawog. "Works fine."

"What does it do?"

"Brings ghost to lodge."

"Lodge?"

She snorted impatiently. "Six parts to link." She ticked them off on her fingers. "Larder, eye, net, lodge, host and window. No? All right: when ghost sails through air, net grabs it and brings it to lodge. Then host draws ghost food from larder and feeds ghost which is tired after its long trip and when ghost gets strong enough it comes out window. Most times larder runs out of food and needs filling, but here lodge is busted."

"And what about the eye?"

"Eye sees you and makes you ghost. Then net sends you sailing."

She reached down into the console and withdrew a

rhombohedral prism the size of a football, shot through with copper spikes. Bright nubs of copper protruded from one of the faces. Daisy was restless but still under control as Wing peered inside the windowcomm and saw that it was completely modular. All the fixers had to do was pull the defective part and plug in a new one. "Linkmaster claims when window opens near to stone walls, ghost goes all blurry." Kitawog kept chattering on. "Serves him right for living in stone instead of building with wood like honest folk." She looked at him. "Phillip Wing has no idea what Kita's talking about."

Wing grinned and opened his hands to her. "Just Phillip."

"Touch wand to each part, Just Phillip." She spoke slowly, as if trying to explain the Bernoulli-Euler equation to a toddler. "When Kitawog touches lodge, wand screams. So she sends to base for new one." She nodded at the apprentice busily washing a new prism. "There. Once cleaned, goes in."

"But how does it work?"

"Bright shining Chan!" She threw back her head this time and yowled in frustration. "And here it's Kitawog's busy time." She kept staring at the ceiling as if listening to the god's reply. "Hey, Laquassu," she called to the apprentice, "this one wants to know how link works."

"So tell," said the apprentice.

She rested one hand on Wing's shoulder. "Waves." The other hand cut a sine curve through the air.

Kitawog invited them to stay for thanksgiving. They assembled a working link out of the two broken units and sat down with a humble meal of cold breadroot soup which Wing tried, and dried worms, which he passed. He worked hard not to be revolted by the invertebrates in the local diet. Everywhere he went bugs, worms, snails, slugs, parasites of the fur were on the menu. They had so many domestic animals, it was strange that they seemed to eat no meat and only a little fish.

Wing could not help but notice the fixers' reverence during the thanksgiving broadcast. Unlike the embittered scholars of Kikineas, they behaved as if Teaqua were actually present in the shop and addressing them personally. In fact, they replied aloud to the ghosts of Ammagon and the goddess, calling out their prayers and requests, clapping in time to even the most excruciating musical interludes. Wing had visited the seats of power and had met the goddess herself, but only now, in this rude stall in simple company, did he get a real sense of the power of the thearchy. Teaqua's support ran deep here. She was not some religious icon, remote and uncaring. She was the powerful friend who cared enough to visit every day, and these people, at least, loved her for that. It was a revelation.

As usual at the end of the ceremony, Ammagon led them through the litany of thanksgiving.

"Chan, we thank you for your many gifts. For the light that melts the snow and opens the seeds."

"Look into the sun," replied the fixers.

"For the shriving that takes away our sins."

"Look into the sun."

"For the whispers that comfort us when we are troubled."

"Look into the sun." Wing was surprised to see Harumen mouthing the words; her eyes were shut.

"For Teaqua, who has given us peace."

"Look into the sun."

Only he and Ndavu appeared unmoved by the prayer—and Wing was not at all sure what he felt. The innocent faith of these people struck him like an accusation. What did Phillip Wing believe in? Nothing, not even himself. All his values had been stripped away, his certainties overthrown. He could hardly scorn their religion when he himself was so utterly lost. For an extraordinary moment he tried to pray with them—and was embarrassed that he could not. All he could do was watch as a force that he did not understand worked a healing magic on the faithful. He heard the droning of a parasitical computer; they heard the whisper of a beloved god.

For the first time, Wing envied these people.

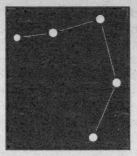

**T**he weathered peaks in the distance reminded Wing of the Presidential Range in New Hampshire. He and Harumen crossed a frozen stream and scrambled up the flank of a long ridge. Crusted snow crunched beneath their boots. They skirted along the timberline, picking their way through the treetops of a forest of scrub evergreens. The afternoon was cold but not bitter; it had the bright chill of a mountain spring. Wing stretched himself, pleased with the stamina of his reshaped body. He needed exercise; for weeks he had felt as if he had been tied up and locked in a box.

He paused by an icefall, a cascade at least twenty meters high. The ice was all the shades of blue; chunks of it glittered like turquoise and sapphire in the afternoon light. Some ice had tiny pink-shelled fossils frozen within them. There was grandeur here; Wing thought he was getting close. Or at least he was enjoying himself. Although he could still sense Daisy fidgeting at the edge of his consciousness, she could not break down his determination to think his own thoughts. As he waited for Harumen to catch up, he savored the exquisite simplicity of life in the mountains. He was glad that the thickets of the world had yet to overrun this elevation.

Just the day before Ndavu had been called away to the messengers' orbital spaceport. A starship had come through the mass exchanger unexpectedly and would make planetfall in three weeks. According to Ndavu, its cargo was revolution.

When sentients were recruited to become messengers, they had to renounce their worlds and the company of their own species. It could hardly be otherwise, since each trip uptime could last decades or even centuries downtime. Messengers became citizens of a new society centered around the mass exchangers. They were, of course, still subject to relativity, but through a combination of cryogenics and the rejuvenation serum, their life spans were extended. In return for their sacrifice, they managed the movement of goods and information through uptime. They did not actually control any single world yet all the worlds of the commonwealth depended on them. The messengers were at once the servants and masters of the interstellar economy.

Now there had been a communications breakthrough: the tachyon transmitter. By using beams of tachyon particles as carriers, data could be sent *anywhen*—even into the past, although the energy requirements were staggering. However, it was quite feasible to send information across the galaxy instantaneously from a downtime perspective. The whole structure of the messengers' relativity-bound society had been undermined. Ndavu claimed that the tachyon transmission would drastically reduce the need for travel between stars. Only a few would have to suffer the pain of irrevocable exile.

The messengers on Aseneshesh were meeting in emergency session, either by windowcomm or in person. Policies had to be rethought, procedures reviewed. Ndavu had refused to speculate about how the news might affect Wing's mission. Of course both Wing and Harumen were itching with curiosity but there was no way to scratch until Ndavu returned to them. Meanwhile, the starship carrying Aseneshesh's first transmitter—and with it the entire commonwealth of messengers—was decelerating toward them.

They hiked the crest of the ridge as it sloped downward through the timberline again. Finally they came upon a ruin: a jumble of basalt slabs perched upon an outcrop with a commanding view of Riverside to the east and, through breaks in the trees, the far edge of Uritammous to the southwest. Harumen did not know the spot.

"Let's look around," said Wing, "then head back."

He wandered away from her. For a time he poked through the rubble but soon his curiosity flagged. He climbed over a snaggle-toothed parapet and found himself outside the ruin. He was confronted once again by an ocean of sand and the green coils of the river snaking to the eastern horizon.

Why not here? They could clear the ruins away—or better—reuse the stone. He would wrap the tomb around a tower, a beacon that would shine day and night. *The eternal flame.* He wondered how high he would have to build so that they could see it from both Riverside and Uritammous. Maybe Teaqua would let him use a messenger light source; she was not shy about borrowing technology when it suited her purposes.

He was sketching on his workslate when a cascade of pebbles clattered behind him. "Harumen?" he said without looking up. The reply was a most uncharacteristic hiss.

A creature hunched on the tumbledown wall. About two meters long from snout to tail, it had a distinctly reptilian face, blunt and scaly-smooth, yet it was covered with tawny feathers. What terrified Wing, though, were fangs the size of a pianist's forefinger.

"Go away!" He gripped the workslate edgewise, like a discus. "Go away before one of us gets hurt." The creature advanced, its tail lashing. He drew himself up, his weapon at the ready. The creature growled a warning. "Nice monster," he said softly. "No offense, take it easy." It paused and cocked its head to one side. "That's right. In a month we'll both be able to laugh about this." Wing crept backward.

"Phillip?" Harumen stepped around the corner. "Are you talking to me?"

The creature pivoted, snarling. Wing hurled the workslate. "Run!" he cried as he jumped five meters from a standstill. He landed in a heap and kicked out again immediately, propelling himself headfirst into an uprooted pillar. Daisy broke through in that moment to inform him that he was confronting a paponay, a carnivore whose diet consisted primarily of birds and lizards. At least he would die knowing what killed him. Then the blackness of basalt swarmed around him as he lost consciousness.

Wing was cold.

He felt a hand on his forehead, opened his eyes and saw Harumen in the twilight. She spoke to him and he shut his eyes quickly, wondering whether, if he died on Aseneshesh, he would go to Chani heaven. If so, he preferred oblivion.

"Phillip!"

Was it possible that he was still alive? "What?" Then he remembered and sat up. His vision turned misty. "Where is it?"

"Gone." She cradled his head to her chest. "You scared it more than it scared you."

"I doubt that." He relaxed in her grasp, listening to her heartbeat. "Getting dark. Got to call for help. Use the slate . . . talk to my workstation."

She shrugged and pointed to the broken workslate. "We'll move when you're ready." She helped him stand. "A close place."

The cellar was narrow and rubble-strewn. She had already begun a makeshift roof. Wing tried to help but the cold confused him. It was getting hard to see and the winds seemed to swirl around his ears and meanwhile Daisy kept buzzing at him; all the queries he had suppressed over the past days were now answered in manic spurts of information: Kitawog had been trained by pedants who had been trained by the messenger Bakure and they could expect a night-time low of −17 degrees Celsius based on seasonal averages and people ate meat only on Kautama's Day and the ruin had been a fort called Chosu, abandoned after Teaqua had become goddess. All Wing cared about was how cold he was, even with isothermals beneath his tunic. Finally he retreated into the shelter. While Harumen wove a lattice of branches over him, he crammed leaves, rocks and frozen clods of dirt into the gaps in the wall. Their present elevation was 5,874 meters above sea level and the creatures in the ice were not fossils but living highland snails which remained in frozen dormancy throughout the winter. Once out of the wind Wing saw reason to hope they might survive the night; by the time Harumen wriggled through the opening he was reasonably comfortable.

"Sorry about the slate," he said. "You all right?"

"C-cold."

He slid closer and put an arm around her shoulder. She embraced him, shivering convulsively. He clasped her tighter and massaged her legs with his free hand.

"We'll be stiffs by morning unless they come looking for us."

She moaned drowsily.

"Stay awake." He shook her. "They *will* come."

Silence.

Her tunic and trousers were tightly woven but thin. Too thin. And she refused to wear messenger isothermals. He clamped his jaws shut and dove out of the shelter. The wind blasted him as he rushed about in the dusk uprooting every scrub he could find. He dragged the needled boughs inside, built them up into a crude bed and rolled her atop it. At least now she was not losing heat to the ground. But her torpor had deepened alarmingly. He shook her again, slapped her, shouted at her but she did not revive. He sniffled in frustration; she might die unless he did something.

He had only one idea and it was reckless at best. Nevertheless, he could not get it out of his head that she had willingly run the risk of hypothermia to save him. Daisy chimed in with the opinion that his plan would probably do Harumen no good and kill him.

Before he knew quite what was happening Wing was arguing with Daisy. I have to do *something*, he thought desperately.

(You won't freeze wearing isothermals. As long as you don't freeze they can track you in the infrared.)

Look at her!

(She can be replaced. You're too important to risk; your mission is too important.)

If she dies, I'm responsible.

Then he realized what was happening. He was actually

confronting an image of Daisy in his mind. She had completely overrun her boundaries and was addressing him directly as a distinct personality. She was no longer even bothering to hide it: she was openly trying to influence his behavior.

(Our behavior.)

"Shut up, *shut up!*" It was a shock to hear words spoken aloud. Wing was as afraid as he had ever been. Maybe he was only hallucinating; there was the numbing cold, the blow to the head. Crisis upon crisis. But his instincts were that if Daisy won now he might never be able to put her back in place. The only way to be sure Daisy did not overwhelm him was to do exactly the opposite of what she wanted. Unless she was right, in which case . . .

He could not afford to think anymore. That was what she wanted.

He slid out of his tunic and spread it on top of the boughs. He stripped off his isothermal jacket and pants and resealed them into a blanket of sorts. His skin pebbled; it felt three sizes too small. He haggled at Harumen's tunic with a sharp-edged rock and then ripped out the seam. Wing snuggled up next to her and spread the improvised bedclothes over the both of them.

He let himself slide into a delirium of sensation. He entwined his legs in Harumen's and hugged her as if to squeeze his own body heat into her. He could feel the friction of fur catching at fur, her stiff guard hairs interpenetrating the denser layer of his undercoat, ruffling the nap. He put his hands on her rump and felt the pads of skin there. Her breath was a whisper on his neck and there was a smell he did not recognize, musky and intoxicating and needle-sharp in the freezing air. It made him dizzy. He brushed his cheek against her mane and spoke her name without quite knowing why.

"Harumen?"

She did not reply but he could sense a quickening within her, vessels swelling, muscles tightening. It was as if he had held her so tightly for so long that they had merged into one body with a single heartbeat. He breathed when she breathed. Her leg twitched and a shock went through him. He had forgotten about the cold.

Wing was not sure exactly when Harumen regained consciousness because she never spoke and it was dark now inside their makeshift shelter. Her hands grasped at the short fur at the base of his spine, resettling his hips closer to hers. He tried to say her name again but the sounds caught in mid-throat and all he could do was growl at her. She seemed to like it. Her claws extended and raked down his side, not hard enough to cut him but hard enough to send the blood surging to the surface. Wing imagined that every hair on his body was as straight as a pin.

When she pushed him over, he was aware of broken branches pointing into his side but he did not care. All sensations had been rerouted through one throbbing spot at the base of his spine and everything now was pleasure. She wrapped the robe and isothermals close around them as she rubbed herself across his abdomen. Someone was wet, him or her—probably both. Her genitals . . . He gasped and for a moment lost all his words. She kept squirming at him and it felt like something was nibbling at his groin. Daisy intruded with an image of a puckered opening like the mouth of a toothless old woman. Wing tried to dismiss it but Daisy made him see. This time she did not translate his Chani sexual responses into human imagery. He licked Harumen's pointed teeth. He could feel drastic and thrilling changes in the fleshy nub between his legs. Once it had been a comfort to think of it as his penis but Wing knew now that was an illusion. He felt as if it were turning inside out, unfolding like a flower from its bud. It struck him as funny that he had an organ shaped like an engorged petunia. He began to twitter and could not stop, unsure whether any of this was real or part of his delirium. All he knew for certain was a blinding delight that seemed to fill the inside of his head and press out against his eyes. When Harumen's tiny cloacal mouth drew his bloom inside her, he thought he might faint. There were a few ecstatic moments of clenching, slipping, aligning. Their mingled scents were overpowering: the heady fragrance of sex. Wing was struck by the thought that this was his first time, he had not known how good it could be, *his first*, maybe he ought to tell her but all he could do now was squeak. She ground against him and there was a sudden release of warmth and Wing felt himself washing away on a wave of ecstasy. He rode the surge all the way to oblivion. For a while he was adrift in Harumen's arms, hot as blood and happy.

"Phillip."

At first he did not recognize his name. He thought she must be talking to someone else. She breathed it once again into his ear. "You took me by surprise," she said.

"You were so cold . . . I didn't know. . . ." He sniffed at the corner of her mouth. "Didn't know what I was missing. You all right?"

She squeezed her legs around him. "Now."

Although he was probably safe for the night, Wing was not exactly comfortable. The covers needed constant readjustment; the slightest jiggle exposed one or another of them. The branches jabbed him, his legs cramped, his head ached but he was as alive as he had ever been. They passed part of the night talking. At first they discussed sharing pleasure and Harumen taught him the words that went with their sensations of bliss. Later she told him more about her relationship with Ndavu than he wanted to know. Finally he had to change the subject. She answered his questions about growing up in the court of the goddess. She told him how she used to play in the preservers' vaults and described some of her adventures traveling with the court.

"You sound sad when you talk about those times," he said.

"I was lonely, the only cub at court. The priests were boring, and the blades weren't supposed to talk to me, although some did. For a long time, Teaqua was the only friend I had. She always told me that it was necessary that I be separate. She said I'd be something new when I grew up." Harumen was silent for a moment, then she hugged him. "She was right about that."

Because they had never spoken quite so intimately before, Wing had not realized that Harumen was in her first cycle and had never been shriven. The goddess had taken Harumen from the temple in order to oversee her spiritual development. She had learned about her world not from scholars or pedants but from the goddess herself. It was an unsettling education. From time to time Teaqua had even allowed Harumen to use her personal windowcomm which could access the messenger net—a privilege that she had otherwise reserved for herself.

"She forced me to be different. So I could serve her in a way no one else could."

"What did she teach you about Chan? The whispers? I had you figured as a skeptic. One of the scholars."

"When Teaqua whispers to me, I hear her." Her voice had an edge. "How am I supposed to know what others hear?" Harumen chose that moment to stroke his belly. Wing licked her lips in response. Then for a while they were too busy to talk.

Afterward, she wanted to know about Earth. He told her about the Glass Cloud and the White Mountains and architecture school and Daisy. The real Daisy. It was easier to talk about her now. He still missed her although he knew she was almost certainly dead. Their world was gone. He had been too busy of late to grieve for all the people and things he had lost. Indeed, as Wing spoke he realized that his memories had begun to fade. Portsmouth seemed less real than Kikineas, Piscataqua House than the scholars' palace. He could not remember what it had felt like to hold the real Daisy as he caressed Harumen's back. It was as if that life had happened to someone else. He thought this must be how these people related to previous cycles after shriving. In which case his *alienation* was nearly complete; he already had the fur and Daisy provided the whispers. Time was shriving him of his humanity. He was going native; tonight was the proof. As he spoke, Wing sifted Harumen's mane through his fingers to keep his arm from falling asleep. That was how he discovered the nodes at the back of her skull.

They were smooth, hard and rounded, about the size of robin's eggs. They were embedded in her flesh.

"Harumen." He touched one gingerly. "What's this?"

"You know." She seemed wary. "Like yours." She did not move. "They displease you?"

"No," he said. It was a lie. "It's just that . . . no one told me."

"I wanted to, but Ndavu said no."

When he wondered why Daisy had not informed him, all he got was the impression that she was too busy for him now, busy processing an enormous backlog of information at peak capacity. She did not have the resources to submit an image for confrontation, although she made it clear that she would have told him about Harumen had he asked. Harumen, meanwhile, explained that originally the messengers had urged Teaqua to have the implant surgery. The goddess had given them Harumen instead. The information in her implant was apparently not as extensive as that in Wing's; it dealt exclusively with Earth and humanity. As she described the implant, her distress came clear. Even though she was serving Teaqua, he could tell that Harumen considered herself a freak.

"I am still Chani," she said, "although I have no people but you."

"And you chose this? Of your own free will?"

"This free will—it's strange. I don't really understand." She was silent for a moment. "Teaqua needed me."

"Who's up here for you?" He brushed her node again with his finger. "Mine makes it seem like there's actually someone who gives me advice."

"Everybody." She touched his chin in the darkness. "Teaqua, Chan, Ndavu, Ipposkenick, even you. I hear many voices."

The night crept by at a glacial pace; eventually conversation lapsed. Wing was drowsing when the roof of their shelter flew off. They both sat up, blinded by a crossfire of light. Someone growled. Someone else called, "We've got them!" The wind flipped Harumen's robe off Wing's leg.

"I hope I am not interrupting," said Ndavu.

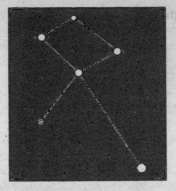

he Goddess
Teaqua, Beloved of Chan, Master of the Twelve Temples, Lord of Scholars and Protector of the Thearchy had fallen asleep in the sanctum of Quaquonikeesak. Her head lolled back on the couch as if her neck had been broken.

She was impossible to ignore. "Should we wake her?" Ndavu stopped talking and settled onto his heels. "Perhaps we should wait until after her nap." He was smirking.

"No." Ammagon was testy. His knees hurt from kneeling on the stone floor and now Teaqua was embarrassing him. This was important news and she was nodding off. "She's been like this lately; she won't sleep long." The prophet was still uneasy in his truce with the messengers but he thought it was time he got used to coping with them on his own. "I want to hear what you have to say."

"You are sure?" Ndavu flagged a pattern of conspiracy. "She might be grumpy when she wakes up."

Actually Ammagon was not at all sure of what he was doing. There was no predicting Teaqua's reaction to anything these days and Ndavu's condescension was beginning to rankle him. Contempt had always come easily to this messenger. Ammagon tried to keep his head still and his anger to himself. He answered with silence.

Ndavu shrugged. "We can guarantee your grain imports for at least the next two seasons. However, it is clear that we will no longer be able to keep up existing reserves using the mass exchanger, especially if you refuse to join the commonwealth. There are going to be cutbacks; we need to divert resources to building the new tachyon network."

"So we starve, is that it?"

"There are alternatives, Ammagon. There always have been."

Ammagon knew what was happening. The messengers were trying to squeeze concessions from him before he took control of the thearchy. They realized that he could not afford to fight a famine while he was consolidating power. "You're threatening me?" His old hostility to the aliens resurfaced.

"Ammagon, I am giving you credit for the intelligence to accept what must be. The old order is passing." Ndavu dipped a shoulder toward the sleeping goddess. "We can no longer afford to be so involved in moving *things* between planets. The costs are too high, both in energy and in lives. The new payloads are going to be information. We are not interested in what you have but in who you are, what you know. Instant communication between worlds will shrink the commonwealth. It is

213

time for your isolation to end, even as Teaqua's reign is ending. Whoever leads your people next must understand—"

Ammagon interrupted. "What do you mean, whoever?" He eased his weight off his aching knees and unfolded his legs; if Teaqua could sleep then he could sit. "Is that another threat?"

"None was intended," Ndavu said smoothly. "However, it is our understanding that the succession has yet to be decided."

"And where did you hear that?"

"It is what we have not heard, Ammagon, that concerns us. Teaqua has been oddly silent on this matter, considering her situation." Again Ndavu leaned toward the goddess; his sly expression returned. "We assume that means that she has not yet made up her mind. Perhaps you have news for us? Can we expect an announcement soon?"

Ammagon flicked a hand open in reply. He believed the messenger was taunting him, throwing his worst fear into his face. It was true; Teaqua had never given her prophet a public commitment. Recently she had been hinting that she might change her mind about who would follow her. Now Ammagon was not only flustered but also alarmed at how easily the alien had put him on the defensive. His instinct was to throw Ndavu out to give himself time to think, but then he would have to explain to Teaqua. He wondered if maybe he ought to wake her up. He did not know what to say . . . he was trapped. The moment overwhelmed him but he was determined not to let Ndavu see just how shaken he was. He shut his eyes and prayed to Chan for help.

All he heard was Teaqua grunting in her sleep.

"Ammagon?" said Ndavu.

*Guide me, shining one.* He ignored the messenger. *Give*

*me strength.* He felt a strange tightness in the muscles around his eyes.

"Are you going to sleep on me too?"

A spectral blue spark flickered; it was as if someone were pressing down on his closed lids.

"Ammagon!"

The spark turned bloodred and began to throb.

"Asleep who?" Another voice: slurred, tired. Teaqua. "What?"

As the spark pulsed Ammagon could just barely hear it ringing like a tiny crystal bell.

"It's Ammagon, he . . ."

Ammagon no longer had to strain to hear the ringing; he understood it perfectly. "Phillip Wing," he said.

"What?" said Teaqua.

"Phillip Wing can't work." Ammagon did not know that he was going to say it until the words came out of his mouth. "He can't see. You changed him too much." He opened his eyes then and saw the messenger's stunned expression. Ammagon knew then that it was true and that Chan had given him a weapon to use against the messengers.

"That is simply not true," said Ndavu. "Wing is fine."

"He needs to see Chan's light. You've blinded him."

"See? What is this, Ammagon?" Teaqua was thoroughly roused now. "Messenger? Tell me!" She sounded shaken.

"It is nonsense," said Ndavu. "I saw Wing today. He is recovering nicely from the accident. There is nothing to worry about. He is working."

"You're trying to turn him away from us. You don't want him to see."

He could feel the heat of Teaqua's stare. Ammagon was so filled with the divine light that he dared turn and meet her gaze. It was a clear breach of custom and propriety yet Ammagon knew immediately that he was right to do it. They were equals, he and Teaqua; it was Chan's will that she acknowledge it.

The goddess seemed to shrink into herself. She looked away quickly as if afraid of what she had seen in the eyes of her prophet.

**W**ing cleared the elevations of the Shwe Dagon in Rangoon from the screen and took a peek at the pagoda of the Horyu-ji Temple in Nara, Japan. Five stories was too short. So far the only tower that had caught his fancy was the minaret of the Great Mosque at Samarra, which reminded him of the Tower of Babel. He thought it was most like what Teaqua wanted: an architecture of hubris.

Wing had studied scholarly re-creations of the Pharos of Alexandria, one of the Seven Wonders of the Ancient World, and structural drawings of the Tour d'Eiffel. He had reviewed the *tenshukaku* of Japanese castles, the freestanding *campanili* of Italian church complexes and a veritable forest of obelisks commemorating personages from Thutmose II to George Washington. He did not much care for obelisks: the phallic overtones would be lost on these people, given their reproductive anatomy. The symbolism was subtle but important. Wing did not want to make the kind of naked proclamation of power embodied by the fortified tower houses of medieval Italy or the glass boxes which had choked the lopsided cities of the twentieth century.

He could tell Harumen was watching over his shoulder; he could smell her grassy scent. Also she kept grooming flealike creatures from his fur and eating them. He had given up asking her to stop. For one thing, it felt good. And it was so ingrained a habit that she did not always realize she was doing it. He had decided that he did not really mind as long as she did not offer the pickings to him.

He kept coming back to pagodas and stupas and dagobas. At least they added a spiritual dimension to the exercise. Although on Earth the many-tiered pagodas served as diagrams of ascending consciousness, Wing thought the various levels could be reinterpreted here as the accretion of past cycles. Each was visibly distinct and yet all comprised but one structure. So his tower would be like a life which pointed to the sun. Not only did Wing want to make a political statement for Teaqua, he wanted to speak to the pilgrims himself. He wanted the shrine to say that he had understood them. Or at least had made the attempt.

Wing had suffered a mild concussion from his encounter with the paponay and Ndavu insisted that he recuperate. Although he had stayed in his room at the scholar's palace for several days now, he was not getting all that much rest. Harumen had moved in with him and they spent many hours engaged in what she innocently called "sharing pleasure." Meanwhile, he was busy with his own research. He had sent the messengers off to Chosu to do photogrammetric and subsurface surveys for him. He had asked for road crews to begin excavating and rebuilding the ancient causeway from Uritammous up to the ruins. Wing had changed. He had stopped watching himself and was, at last, engaging his new life.

"The problem is the short construction season." Wing rubbed his eyes, got up from the desk and stretched. "Got to find a way for them to work year round or this could take forever." His new eyes stung if he looked at a screen too long. He had never had that problem before.

Harumen slipped into his place. "What's your hurry?" She brought up a Tudor mansion, Compton Wynyates. She was fascinated by the splendor of homes stored in the workstation's archives; English manors were her favorites. "Aren't you happy?"

"I was thinking of Teaqua." He wrapped his arms around her. "I've got no place to go."

Wing was not the only one who was busy. He sensed that Daisy was working hard on something. As usual she processed her data subliminally, although from time to time her furious effort crossed over to his consciousness and distracted him, like the ticking of the grandfather clock in the front hall of Piscataqua House. He found it frustrating not to know what was going on inside his own head. However, it was easier to control her if he thought of Daisy as *other*. She was not part of him; she was a trespasser. Ignore her and she seemed to go away. He was glad that she had stopped addressing him directly and no longer appeared on his mental stage; he felt closer to sanity now. Still, she was a link to his humanity; there were odd moments when he missed her. When he wondered if she was jealous of Harumen, she offered no response.

He would have asked Ndavu about her except that he was busy too. On their return from the highlands, he had installed Wing safely in his rooms at the scholars' palace, assured him that the commonwealth's support for their mission had not wavered and encouraged him to pursue his tower design. Immediately after, the messenger had gone up to Quaquonikeesak to brief Ammagon and Teaqua about the tachyon transmitter.

Wing left Harumen to her manor and climbed onto the balcony for some fresh air. Drizzle smudged the view. Kautama's Day was coming: the beginning of Aseneshesh's brief summer. He gazed across the courts of Tetupshem and recalled his panic when he had first seen them. Now he could take in the sights with more equanimity; only a tickle of doubt remained. Somehow he still had to adapt his grasp of structure to the skew of Aseneshesh's lower gravity. There were no indigenous towers to guide him, since these people did not build for height. Even the lookouts of Quaquonikeesak's fortifications were scarcely fifteen meters above grade, if that.

There was a knock at the door. Wing guessed his tower would have to be at least a hundred and fifty, perhaps as much as two hundred meters high to be seen in Riverside.

Harumen let Chiskat in. Wing stepped off the balcony.

"Come on then." Chiskat grabbed his sleeve. "Ammagon wants to see you. Right now." Harumen followed but the pedant barred her way with an open hand. "Alone."


"I made a mistake, Phillip Wing." Ammagon sat crosslegged on a pillow in an empty dormitory room. The door was locked and there was a blade outside. "I should've talked to you long ago." Wing sat facing him. "I didn't really understand what you were doing." The prophet smelled of incense.

Wing was uneasy. "Maybe you could explain it to me." He never knew where to look when he was with these people; he fixed his gaze on Ammagon's hands. "What changed your mind?"

"Whispers." Ammagon picked up a copper pot and poured an effervescing tea into two small ceramic cups. "If only we could've been friends"—he sighed—"but it's too late for that." He offered Wing a cup. "I understand you like strong drink. Try this."

The stuff had a gingery aroma that curled into his nasal slits. Wing waited until the prophet sipped and then took an experimental taste. It had the flavor of caramelizing sugar. "Too late?"

"You've been living with scholars."

"So?"

"And messengers."

"Ndavu, yes."

"Do you trust them?"

He considered. "I listen, but I try to make up my own mind."

"Good for you." Ammagon tapped the floor with his fist. "They've told you I'm the enemy."

He could not deny it. "Theirs maybe." They each took another drink. "No reason why you should be mine." Whatever was in the prophet's tea was pleasantly bracing. He felt unusually bold—as if there were nothing he dared not say. "Is there?"

"The whispers say to help you, Phillip Wing."

"You should call me Phillip."

"Phillip." Ammagon bowed. "You don't hear whispers—yet. But you will." He waved off Wing's protest. "Until then you won't be able to do your work. Meanwhile the messengers will make it hard for you to see what must be done. They'll distract you. You have to look into the sun, Phillip, before you can use the light. Chan has told me this much: Teaqua will rest in the light."

"He told you, did he?" Wing was amused by this clumsy attempt to convert him. "Have you seen final plans?" He did wonder how Ammagon had found out about his beacon tower; only Harumen and Ndavu knew.

"It's for you to see, Phillip. That's your gift. I only hear my whispers. They say you'll serve Chan well."

He could not resist the impulse to tease the prophet. "I thought only Chan's people heard the whispers."

Ammagon gestured at Wing's body. "And what are you?"

"Human." He ignored the twinge of doubt as he said it.

"Not quite." Ammagon drained his cup. "Chiskat tells me you hope to go back someday but the whispers say that you'll never leave. You're becoming one of us. I know you can't accept that because you've never heard the whispers and Ndavu doesn't believe in them and the scholars don't understand them. You all think I'm the enemy. But you'll see the truth soon enough."

The joke did not seem quite so funny anymore. Wing finished what was in his cup; the prophet had not given him very much.

"You don't believe me, Phillip. Then tell me a lie."

"What?"

"Tell me that your fur is blue. That you're sure I'm wrong."

"I think you're crazy." Wing wanted to say something else but his throat tightened around the words. "I do feel something. Strange."

"This potion." Ammagon ran a finger along the rim of his empty cup. "Now neither of us can lie."

"You drugged me?"

"And myself—to make a point. You're not pleased with the way you feel?"

"Yes." Wing *had* been enjoying himself. "No." However, now he was upset. "You had no right. I want to be able to choose."

"Choose silence, if you want. Choose to leave. But at least you know that I've told you the truth."

"As you see it." Wing gathered himself to stand up; he thought maybe he should go.

"I wanted you to trust me." Ammagon seemed disappointed by his response. "I couldn't think of any other way."

Wing's legs were heavy. It took concentration to move them and suddenly everything was fuzzy.

"Phillip, I have a secret for you. Something neither of us is supposed to know. Talk to me and I'll talk to you, yes?"

Wing shrugged as he came to his knees. "Maybe."

"I wish you well. I'll protect you once I'm a god."

"Ruler, you mean. King, chief, number one. Teaqua says she's the last god for a while." He wondered how Ammagon liked hearing the truth.

"What is a god? Someone who the people worship, whose whisper they hear when they're troubled. Does she think that will change once she's in your shrine? If I say I am a god, who will deny me?"

Wing snorted. "That's the secret you wanted to tell me?"

"A starship is coming," Ammagon said. "You know about the transmitter. There's a message for you."

Wing stood. Finally.

"Your mate back on Earth. Her name is Daisy, yes?"

At first he thought it was the tea that left him so lightheaded. Then he heard what Ammagon had just said. *Is.*

"She wants to speak with you."


"But I had to hear it from Ammagon!"

"I was deciding the best way to tell you."

"Try the truth for a change."

"The timing is very bad, Phillip."

"I want to see her. Now."

Ndavu gave him a pained look. "The transmitter is still inbound from the aperture. We could patch through a signal if you want. The quality—"

"You bet I want." What Wing really wanted was to grab the messenger and shake him. "What do you think I want?"

"There are some things I should explain first."

"No."

Ndavu picked a crystal bowl from his collection of glassware, held it to the light momentarily and scrutinized it for dust. He was stalling and Wing knew it. Harumen yawned, showing her incisors. She crouched in a corner of the messenger's room and watched them argue as if she planned to make a meal of the loser.

"I do not understand how Ammagon found out." Ndavu swiped at the bowl with his sleeve, put it back in its place and turned to the windowcomm. "There has been a serious breach of security."

"Maybe Chan told him."

Ndavu flagged scorn. "I believe he is using Teaqua's windowcomm. However, even she should not have had access to this information." He shrugged and Wing realized he had decided. "If you will step out for a moment, I will see what I can do."

It took only a few minutes to span light-years. As he fidgeted outisde Ndavu's door, Wing's anger passed and doubt rushed in to replace it. He did not know what to say to her. What would she look like? He had experienced less than a year of subjective time; how long had it been for her? Harumen watched him. Her scent had the tang of hot iron.

Ndavu opened the door. Daisy was waiting for him.

If he could believe his eyes, she had not changed at all. She was even wearing the blue dress. She smiled at him and even though he knew he was seeing a ghost he stepped forward to hug her.

"Phil." She remained in place.

He let his arms drop. "Oh, Daisy." Wing did not want the others watching. Not now. "I missed you." Nor did he want her to see him as he was: a man trapped in a monster suit. He started to sniffle as all the feelings he had dammed up flooded over him at once. He still loved her. He wanted her back more than anything.

"How are you?" she said.

"Different," he croaked.

She laughed; Wing tried to twitter but he could scarcely breathe.

"This isn't what you really look like." He wanted to speak English but he could not get his mouth around the sounds. He hated his voice. This damned body.

"I can look like anything." She spoke Chani well enough. "If it pleases you."

"You didn't come all this way to please me."

"No. But this isn't what you look like either."

"Hello, Daisy." Ndavu came forward. "I took the liberty of simulating Phillip's appearance as it was when we left Earth. I thought he might be more comfortable that way, at least for your first meeting."

A second window opened and Wing saw what Daisy was seeing. A man in a gray silk Mazzini suit peered out at him. Wing did not recognize himself. There was nothing new written on his simulacrum's face; he had lived what seemed a lifetime since he had last looked like this stranger. It was unsettling and yet he was immediately grateful to Ndavu for arranging it. The messenger had anticipated his reaction very well indeed. Except for one thing.

"We'd like to be alone."

"I am sorry, Phillip, but I cannot yet allow it."

"And this must be Harumen." Daisy bowed. Her ghost

sparkled then and Wing thought she would fade away before he was finished with her. He had to keep reminding himself that she was not really here with him.

Harumen had goggled at Wing's human image right up until the moment Ndavu closed the window. Now she eyed Daisy and flagged disapproval.

"How's the inn?" Wing did not want Daisy wasting time with Ndavu and Harumen. Not when he had so much to say, to ask.

"The commonwealth has owned it for, oh, years. You made Portsmouth famous. They come from all over. To see the Cloud too."

"How long?"

She touched her neck and he imagined she was trying to smooth wrinkles he could not see. "I feel old, Phil." She sighed. "I'm almost as old as I want to be." Daisy glanced around the room. "Can we sit down? Then maybe this won't seem like an interrogation." She settled on the corner of Ndavu's bed, pushed back against the wall, and tucked her legs under her dress. She moved deliberately, as if she were as fragile as one of Ndavu's glass figurines. Wing sat on the edge of the bed.

It was impossible.

"How's your work going?" she asked.

He did not intend to talk so much. He wanted to hear what she had to say. But she was so near—Wing did not care if she was only a ghost. He had given her up for dead and here she was. He knew he had loved her once; now he realized he had never stopped. He rattled on about the local architecture and the tour and how he had found an ideal site. He was surprised to hear himself speaking so confidently about a design he had yet to think through. He even lied to her about having done some preliminary sketches. He was not sure why he said it except that he did not want her to be disappointed in him. It had something to do with the familiar cant of her shoulders when she leaned forward to listen, something about the way her eyes tracked him as if he were the only person in the room. *Eye contact:* he had not realized how much he missed it. He imagined from the way she met his gaze that she knew exactly what he had gone through. No one else understood. He was amazed how easily he slid into the old ways with her.

The others were an annoyance. Harumen smoldered beside the door, her silence thick with suspicion. Ndavu nodded at all the right times and even chimed in with an occasional comment on Wing's progress. Yet he was in a prickly mood. Without ever saying it, Ndavu made it clear that he was under duress; he did not approve of this meeting. The hostility in the room, subtle and overt, only made Wing feel protective of Daisy.

Eventually he ran out of plausible boasts to make about his work and so the conversation turned to her. She was evasive at times, seeming to miss the point of some questions, following odd tangents on others. Often as not she fell silent after he spoke, as if his words were reaching her with a time delay. He thought it must be the transmitter. At first Wing wanted her to tell him everything—just blurt it all out. Yet he realized the need for caution. They were separated by an immense gulf of time and experience. He resolved to go slow and really understand her; he was not going to make the same mistake twice. Besides, he had not exactly rushed to tell her about his imaginary Daisy. There were, however, some questions which could not be avoided.

"I last saw Jim three years ago." Her fingers twined and knotted. "Just before he died. It was hard, very sad. We had been separated for years but I still had strong feelings for him. Very much like what I have for you."

"You'd separated?"

"We were needed in different places. It was necessary."

"And you just left him?"

She nodded—how strange to see her nod! At first Wing thought she was flagging him except that he could not recognize the pattern. "I missed him, still do. He helped me so much. When I started at the mission, I thought I had to deny my emotions. But that's wrong. He showed me how to accept love and hate and anger, control them without letting them control me. Feelings are part of what we are, like bone and blood. That's why the message has been so hard for us."

Wing wanted to ask—shout—what *are* your feelings? Do you love me? Is there anything left for us? He struggled with the impulse because he was not sure he wanted to know. Finally, he gave in. "Did you ever miss me?"

"Of course."

It sounded too easy. "You did not."

She shook her head wearily. "There wasn't a day that went by when I didn't think of you. You don't know—you're important, Phil. That's one reason why I'm here. It's been twenty-three years since you left and only four others have gone uptime. No one has come back. There won't be a fifth until we turn the polls around."

"The polls?"

"Public opinion rules now: the net makes all major decisions. We haven't done well, Phil; the message has stopped spreading. Our negatives are too high. The messengers weren't what people expected and no one has come back from uptime. The isolationists hold power now. That's why we need you. You were first; you're the most important prize of all. Now that we have the transmitter, you can change everything. Tell us we must join the commonwealth."

Harumen flicked a pebble or a bit of plaster at Daisy and it made a glittering scar across her arm. The image wavered and once again seemed on the verge of dissolving. Wing thrust his open hand at Harumen to stop as the ghost stabilized.

"It happened just like you predicted, Ndavu." Daisy did not seem to have noticed. "He became a folk hero, a crazy mix of Columbus and Frank Lloyd Wright. You're remembered as one of the great men of the century, Phil. The polls will believe anything you say."

"How do you know what he will say?" Ndavu asked.

"I don't." She frowned. "Phil?"

"Hadn't thought much about it." He considered. "Maybe the commonwealth isn't for everyone."

"But you survived," she said. "You're happy."

"Am I? I want to come home."

She did not pursue the point. "It was strange, what happened. You were a cult for a while there. They made dozens of biovids; kids still play Phillip Wing in school pageants. Yale named a college after you. They had to build a new maglev from Portsmouth to North Conway just for the tourists. I even sold rights to tissue-culture your rubber plant; twenty thousand clones sold before the fad died out. And through it all I was the sacrificial wife. The one who knew you best, the keeper of the flame. There was no way I could forget you; they wouldn't let me."

"It must've been hard."

"You even wrote a book. Did you know that? Or rather I hired a freelancer and then tinkered with the manuscript. *Design for a New World.* That's how I got to use the transmitter. I stuck in how you wanted me to follow you to the stars someday, go uptime. We'd pledged our undying love but first you wanted me to study the message."

"How do you know it wasn't true?" Her cynicism was just careless enough to sting. "I *am* glad you're here. How do you know I'm not still in love with you?"

"Phil! What a nice thing to say." She seemed surprised

**229**

and touched, as if the possibility had never occurred to her. That hurt too. "But we settled this before you left. Didn't we?"

He was confused. He realized that part of his reaction to her had to do with his relationship with the imaginary Daisy—except that of course he had not loved the interface. He could not love an illusion. "I suppose we did."

"I'm sorry. Maybe I seem a little cold to you. It's just that—I don't know how to say it. I've gotten used to thinking of you as an image, one that I helped create. After you left, all that was important to me was living the message. I did as much as I could. But it wasn't enough."

"And that's why you want me?" He still felt wounded. "So I can do some public relations? All you want is to impress the messengers."

"It's not for them; it's for us, our species. The messengers claim that the polls prove we're not ready to join the commonwealth. They don't care if it takes us one year or a hundred to reach enlightenment. But a century is too long! We have something to offer. It's past time that humans were out and about in the universe."

"Why? What good will it do?"

"He knows nothing of the message, then?" she said.

"No," Ndavu said.

"Does he want to know?"

"No," Ndavu said.

"Yes," said Wing.

Harumen straightened abruptly, making no attempt to conceal her dismay. Daisy smiled.

"He is not ready to make that commitment," said Ndavu quickly.

"No, that's right," said Wing. "I don't want to sign up. I'm just curious."

"Then maybe I can explain." Daisy glowed with righteous sincerity.

"No!" Harumen eased across the room and slid between Wing and Daisy's ghost. "You can't have him. Teaqua comes first." She clamped a hand on Wing as if to claim him. Her claws extended as she looked to Ndavu for support.

"She is right." The messenger stood. "I think this has gone far enough for now, Daisy. Whatever your hopes for Phillip, the project takes precedence. That was our agreement. You are not to interfere with his work."

Wing was annoyed at the way they were fighting over his future: no one asked him. He had one last question. "What I want to know is"—he nudged Harumen aside so he could see Daisy—"are you a messenger?"

She hesitated. "No." Her expression was unreadable.

They said good-bye, promised to visit again as soon as the transmitter reached orbit. For a second, just as her ghost faded, Wing thought she seemed exhausted. He wondered what she really looked like. Something odd she had said stuck with him: ". . . *as old as I want to be.*"

Harumen wanted to go back to the room with him but Wing needed to be alone. She refused to understand. They argued briefly and she went away mad. He could feel their relationship erode but he simply could not cope with her. Not now anyway: she would smother him with attention when he had to think.

In retrospect Wing could separate out the lines of force acting on him. Ndavu, Harumen, Teaqua, Ammagon, now Daisy: people trying to change, fighting change. All wanted something different from him. Teaqua wanted to be remembered. Harumen wanted him to ease her loneliness, Ammagon wanted him to confirm his prophecy. Daisy wanted him to lead humanity to the stars. Ndavu wanted—what? Maybe just to get this job done the way the commonwealth wanted. Whatever that was. Probably he was not above furthering his own career at the same time. And then there was Phillip Wing. What did he want?

That was the real problem. Wing did not really care about Teaqua or the commonwealth. His own kind had become strangers, if Daisy was any example. He did not believe fiercely in anything, not even in himself. Who was he? No longer human, not quite Chani, with no intentions of becoming a messenger. Wing tried to convince himself that he believed in his talent and his work, but his attempts at self-affirmation seemed hollow. At least he could not deceive himself. It was cold consolation. He stretched out on his bed, not exactly thinking, but rather contemplating his confusion. For some reason it bothered him that he could not remember what Daisy smelled like.

He was not sure exactly when it had happened but as he lay in the gathering twilight he realized that the background noise in his head had stopped. The Daisy of the interface had finished her mysterious project. And that was *another* problem, he thought. Now he had to distinguish between the imaginary one and the real one.

(Not necessary.)

Transformed, she stepped out of the shadows into the spotlight of his imagination. He joined her there, astonished and immediately aroused. He thought, Who? and ran his hands along her impossibly long body, breathing in the fragrance of their shared desire.

(Call me Hanu.) His dream lover licked him as he fingered her silky black mane. (Chan sent me to help you.)

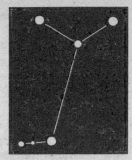

**E**ven Menzere's ghost had stripped down to her blue waistsash. "I am glad you could make it, Phillip." She waved. "Come up."

As he followed her, Wing could not help but notice the small plum-colored pads of skin on her buttocks. But then it was Kautama's Day, which marked not only the solstice but also Hanu's first appearance to Kautama the Upright. The irony was not lost on Wing—or his new interface. Everyone had stopped wearing clothes to celebrate this day of orgiastic renewal. All over the world people were stumbling around in a state of reckless arousal.

Wing's own excesses had left him exhausted. He had practically had to peel Harumen off him before he could get out of their room. Another misunderstanding: it seemed as though he could not breathe these days without worrying her.

He had come to Menzere in part to escape Harumen's relentless passion and his own unsettling appetites, in part because he was curious. Of all the aliens he had met, Menzere alone had never asked anything of him.

Her observatory was cramped and gloomy; it smelled like an indoor swimming pool. Wing groped his way to a bench set against the near wall. Beside him was a low table with a steaming pot and a mug. "Care for an intoxicant?" she said.

"Why not?" The bouquet of hot spiced wine mingled with chlorine stink. Menzere closed her window.

At the same moment a wall faded into transparency. Behind it floated luminous yellow green clouds; beneath them was a glob of pulsing beer-colored jelly with green bits suspended within. It gathered itself and slid forward, leaving in its wake a glistening smear. Trailing it was a device which looked like a bearded dustpan. It scraped up the glob's leavings.

He realized that the glob was Menzere. Hanu informed him that members of this species communicated by ingesting and analyzing each others' exudations. The dustpan's bristles were crammed with receptors which could recognize the chemical messages Menzere left behind; it then translated. Wing drained his mug, coughed and quickly poured another.

"You asked for it." Menzere's voice came from beneath him. "Would you rather I reactivated the ghost?"

"No, no problem." The glob was oozing toward a circle of glassy nubs. "Tell me though, why a female ghost?"

"Femininity is analogous to my reproductive function. After conjugation I collect the zygotes and encyst myself for several—"

"Never mind." The nubs sparked as the messenger passed over them. The glob shivered; needles of gel pricked from its upper surfaces. "What're you doing?"

"I am stunning myself. How is your work going?"

The more Wing described his plans for the tower, the less inspired they seemed. "It'll be tough, no question. The site is all ledge, too cold, and kilometers from nowhere. We'll probably have to blast before we can set foundations. But it is central and you can't beat the view."

"It may be central today. What about tomorrow?"

"What about it?"

"The glaciers are receding. The planet has entered a warming cycle. Overpopulation is becoming a major problem."

"Sure." Wing leaned back against the wall. "If you say so."

"I do. Since we began shipping grain here, each generation of Chani has been longer-lived and more fertile. Thanks to their immunological systems, there is no disease. Nor is there prospect of war. Do you understand? They cannot eat snow."

"The commonwealth feeds them."

"That must end. Land reclamation is the only way—but maybe I should not talk."

"Maybe you're right."

There was a pause while Menzere backed over the studs again. "Can I trust you? You must not tell Harumen or Ndavu."

"Promise." He poured himself another to be sociable.

"I am a scientist, you see, not a diplomat. I could get in trouble . . . but it is criminally shortsighted of her, Teaqua. The Chani crowd onto marginal land here. Meanwhile there are two other continents: millions of hectares along the coasts, ice-free, fertile, teeming with life. The interiors are warming up too. In my opinion the

Chani have only two options: colonization or disaster . . . except that Teaqua wants to keep tight control. Everyone knows why."

"They do?"

"Clearly the thearchy will falter as the Chani spread out. It is a brittle society . . . it cannot stretch. Change will destroy it and change is inevitable."

Wing yawned. The wine was a pleasant weight in his belly.

"Have you considered building on another continent? If you really wanted to help these people, make Teaqua the pioneer god. They will follow her to the new lands. Nothing will be the same afterward."

"They'll still have thanksgivings and the gests. They'll still hear whispers."

"Will they? Well, perhaps this is none of our business, Phillip. I am a scientist, you are an architect. I was just thinking out loud." The glob was oozing up the wall which separated them. He found Menzere at once grotesque and wonderful—certainly a welcome relief from sexual temptation.

"Besides," Wing said, "it's Ammagon's problem."

"Do not trust Ammagon."

"Why not?"

"He believes, Phillip. Change scares him."

"You don't know him," said Wing. "He understands more than you think. At first I didn't like him much either. But at least he's sincere. Besides, he told me about Daisy." He reached for his cup. "Before any messengers did."

"You trust *her*?"

He shrugged; he was not sure he trusted anyone. He could see Menzere's underside now as she reached his eye level. Hundreds of pale yellow nodules flattened against the transparent surface; every few seconds one would swell, burst and smear her end of the conversation onto the wall. Menzere sagged abruptly and fell off the wall. There was a momentary pause as the dustpan scuttled after her. Wing's wine was lukewarm and he considered leaving, even though he had to admit that Menzere was an entertaining drunk. Meanwhile, she flowed over the stunning nubs one last time.

"Maybe I have been here too long," she said at last. "This place is starting to get to me."

Wing could drink to that. "So transfer out."

"My work is almost done. I was going to go uptime and stay there until it was time to choose the next Menzere. Now uptime and downtime are irrelevant. I have been thinking about going home."

"The next Menzere?"

"Ndavu never told you, did he? How typical: we let these new species into the commonwealth and right away they get secretive and so serious . . . I mean, it is serious, the most serious thing there is, but just because we are bound by the message does not mean we must be obsessed by it. I suppose the zeal of the new arrivals carries us all along but the essence does not mind a little fun now and then, some neural stimulation, if you know what I mean."

"Right." He wanted to keep her talking.

"Of course, Ndavu does not mind bending the rules when it comes to his own kind. We all help the home world whenever we can. It is the unwritten rule. You ask them to help a mudder, though, and they will find fourteen reasons not to."

"A mudder. That's me, right?"

"What is it you want to know, Phillip?"

He was suddenly cautious. "I don't want to become a messenger."

There was no reply.

"I thought you were immortal," he said. "How can there be a next Menzere?"

"You have an implant; you have not guessed?"

"I've been busy."

Immortality was simple really, Menzere explained. Essence consisted of viewpoint and structural memory. Viewpoint was each individual's unique style of processing experience; structural memories were those which composed viewpoint. All other memories were trivial, extraneous to essence. So that even if he were to forget his name, for instance, Wing would not stop being himself. He would continue to process experience in a way characteristic of Phillip Wing. The messengers held that most memory was trivial since it did not affect viewpoint. Only structural memory, overwhelmingly the result of genetics and early environment, was essential. For Wing, the thought patterns implicit in English were structural, hard-wired into his viewpoint; fluency in other languages was trivial.

The problem was that essence could be captured in artificial media but would not thrive there. It was the essence of all life forms, including Phillip Wing, to have a body; proprioception was built into structural memory. A purely cybernetic existence would undermine his psychological integrity. Moreover, his viewpoint needed to process experience to maintain his essence; in a static situation it would atrophy. The only way the essence could continue to exist at all after the death of its original organism was in an implant in another organism. It was utterly dependent on its host.

Wing was horrified. "My implant isn't . . ."

"If it were, you would be a messenger. The interface you experience is much less complex than a true essence. It is artificial, a product of your needs. However, your implant could easily carry another's essence. You could become a host tomorrow, if you wanted. Probably not to my essences, we are too dissimilar. However, you could easily be the next Ndavu."

"Forget it."

"I doubt he would choose you. However, you should realize that not everyone is capable of becoming a messenger. Most of those who are eventually do—"

"I said forget it!"

"I am not recruiting you, Phillip. I am explaining the facts."

"Then who is Ndavu?"

"In the same way that the commonwealth is a collective of cooperating species, Ndavu is a collective of symbiotic essences. He is both the host to and a member of the commonwealth of Ndavu, as it were. When he senses the death of his body is near, he will go downtime and recruit a replacement. Or at least he would have before the transmitter."

"Symbiotic or parasitic?" Wing took a deep breath. "So that's the message?"

"Oh, no, the message is something else again. It is the reason why mudders like yourself, who view this arrangement with understandable suspicion, agree to become messengers. However, you asked me not to tell you."

Wing held up both hands, surrendering. "Right." The discussion had sobered him. He tilted the wine pot. Empty. Time to go. He stood and sidled toward the door. "Thanks for the wine."

"You will think about it? I can show you some wonderful places."

"Think about what?"

"You were going to build the shrine on another continent."

"I was not. What about labor?"

"They could found colonies."

"No time." He fumbled at the door in the gloom. "Besides, I thought you were never going to ask me for anything."

Menzere turned the color of sand. "Did I say that?"

"I'm leaving."

"Go then. You are too rigid for your own good."


Wing was doodling rococo balconies onto Frank Lloyd Wright's Johnson's Wax Tower. Daisy was overdue for a visit. He ordered Hanu to tell the messengers he was getting impatient. He wanted to see Daisy; it was important. Hanu paid no attention.

"You heard Menzere. You're nothing but training wheels," he said. "You're here to help me keep my balance."

(I'm the daughter of Chan.)

Wing was not sure what it said about his sanity that his interface had delusions of grandeur. "You're fantasy, a creature of my imagination."

"Who are you talking to?" Harumen woke up.

He pushed back from the workstation. "Hanu," he said, "the daughter of Chan."

"Don't make jokes." She noticed the monstrosity on the screen. "Not working?"

"Thinking." He tapped his forehead.

She came up behind him and ran fingers through his mane.

"Daisy's late," said Wing.

Harumen grabbed a handful of hair and tugged, not quite hard enough to hurt. "So?"

There was a knock at the door. "Phillip?" Ndavu peered hesitantly into the room, as if expecting to find them in bed. "You were expecting Daisy?" When he saw they were up, he closed the door behind him. "We had a problem acquiring her signal."

"Again? Something's wrong."

"One transmitter is simply not enough to handle the traffic. It is almost continually overloaded."

"She's all right though?"

Ndavu shrugged. "We will reschedule as soon as we can." He came up to the workstation and saw Wing's doodle; the messenger let his disappointment show. "I thought you were working."

"He's thinking." Harumen tapped her head.

"Go away and maybe I will," said Wing.

Harumen linked arms with Ndavu and steered him across the room. "I'll keep him busy for you," she called over her shoulder.

Wing contemplated the door long after they had gone. The screen of the workstation went dark. He had wanted Ndavu to leave, not Harumen. Now he wished he knew what they were doing together. No, he was not merely interested; there was an edge to his curiosity. He was jealous. The word took him by surprise because it fit so exactly. *Jealous.* He had been so preoccupied with getting used to Hanu and sorting through his feelings for Daisy that he had not even noticed that something new was happening between Harumen and him. Suddenly it mattered very much that Harumen and Ndavu had once been lovers. He wondered why that should be.

(Maybe you love her.)

The messengers turned in the site surveys Wing had requested. Soil profiles showed that the foundation work would be tricky but at least the area was seismically stable. They had uncovered a spring buried beneath the ruins of the fort, so water was no problem. The road could be repaired although some sections would need regrading. For the most part the reports confirmed his intuition; the site was difficult but promising.

With this information in hand, Wing sketched some of his preliminary concepts—and scrapped them as soon as they were done. It was hard to concentrate. He was worried about Daisy. He found that he could not work when Harumen was around and did not like to work when she was gone. A few days passed before he tried again. Dead end. He could not see the tower in his imagination. The highlanders sent him samples from local quarries; somehow even the rocks looked wrong. He spent a day rearranging his room, obsessively pushing the furniture into every possible configuration. Wing was used to plasteel and permaglass; he had always thought of stone as a finish, never as structural material. How could he trust his design instincts in gravity only seven-tenths that of Earth? But these were merely technical problems, he told himself as he started over once again. Reinforced concrete: the Chani had iron. He drew some rough sketches, erased them and then retired to the balcony to contemplate the stars. He could not find his constellation.

The tower idea was a cartoon because he had never analyzed first principles. Should he imitate the local architecture, reinterpret it from his own perspective or ignore it and use human conventions? As he pondered his options, the days stretched into weeks.

In a sense he knew what was happening to him. He was throwing away his chance. All he had to do was sit down and work. Back home he had been a prodigious worker. He had churned out go-tube racks and ski chalets and office buildings as fast as anyone in New England. But what he had done before did not matter now. Now he was supposed to design a masterpiece, except that he did not know how. Either he was lazy or his nerve had failed. Whichever it was, he was too engrossed in his own weakness to do the work.

Harumen never quite grasped what he was going through. She asked constantly about his progress and took his block as her fault. It came to the point that he dreaded seeing her, knowing that he would have to disappoint her again. When dread turned to resentment, they fought. He did not understand what was happening; just when he thought he was ready to get closer to her, a chasm yawned between them. She said maybe she should move out of his room so he could work and he heard himself say do it. Afterward, he was sorry. He went to her and apologized. He was always cranky at the start of a project, he said, always afraid he would fail. Once he got started he would be himself again. She accepted his apology coolly. She did not offer to come back; he did not ask.

He was often alone now. The scholars had orders not to disturb him. Ndavu tried not to bother him although he also was obviously concerned about Wing's block. Wing was glad the messenger had the good sense to stay away. He was less happy with Daisy's absences. He suspected that she was sick: too many visits canceled at the last moment. He never knew when he would see her; sometimes weeks went by. Even when she managed to come, she might well cut the visit short. Talking too much drained her. Once he asked her if there was something wrong. She had evaded the question.

It was late at night. Wing was sitting in bed with the workslate in his lap when a window opened and Daisy appeared for the first time in a week. She saw the screen before he could cover it with his arm. There was a drawing of an outhouse; underneath it Wing had practiced his signature. Bold and cramped, over and over again: *Phillip Wing, A.I.A.*

"What's the matter, Phil?"

"Nothing." He shut the slate off. "I don't know."

"Everybody's waiting for you."

"Maybe that's it. This shrine has to be everything to everybody." He watched a centipede the size of a string bean scuttle across the floor of his room. "I'm an architect, not a miracle worker."

"Just make it big. They'll take whatever you give them. Get it over with."

He stiffened. "Look, this isn't some warehouse in Manchester. It's my one chance to find out if I have great work in me."

"You have the Cloud."

"No. The Cloud was luck, an accident that I got in the way of. I didn't intend it to be a masterpiece; I was just doodling. A one-shot—look at my other stuff. All ordinary." He draped his legs off the bed. "Maybe that's really why I came here. To put myself in this situation so I would have to *make* a great building happen. No luck involved. Do or die." For a moment the planet seemed to release its pull on him. "So why am I stuck?" He felt almost weightless, as if he might float away. "Maybe I'm not good enough. Maybe Ndavu made a mistake."

"But you've already succeeded, Phil. It doesn't matter what you do here; here on Earth you're already a hero. Somehow you've gotten an overblown idea of this project. Listen to me: if the locals are happy, the messengers will be happy and you should be happy." Her anger was sharp. It gave her a solidity which ghosts normally lacked. "Stop feeling sorry for yourself and build the thing!"

"Maybe you're right." He pushed off the bed. "Maybe it *is* only self-pity. But I've been worried about myself for so long—there were times, Daisy, when I was close to losing myself." He fit the slate into its port in the workstation and sat down. "I know it's selfish. But I don't want to be just another clever technician. I want something more." He idly tapped keys with his forefinger. *Phillip Wing A.I.A.*

"Phil, I can't wait for you to decide if you're an artist. I haven't got time." She hesitated, as if deciding whether to share a secret. "I'm dying. There's a new disease that seems to accelerate aging. We don't understand it yet.

244

Some claim the messengers brought it here. It's what killed Jim McCauley."

He stared through the floor, not sure why he did not feel more. "Is that what you came to tell me?" He had known all along, and yet had somehow managed to keep from acknowledging it to himself.

"I'll tell you exactly why I've come—look at me, will you! Why I have come and what I want from you." Wing would not make eye contact with a ghost but he let Daisy see his face. "I told you I wasn't a messenger. That was true. But I want to be one, the first ever from Earth. I want it very much. If you give up now, you'll ruin everything. You're the key, Phil. We need your success. If I can bring Earth into the commonwealth—"

"We?" It was exactly what Wing had feared all along. Loneliness had kept him from crediting the bitter suspicions. "You sound like Teaqua." She only wanted to use him.

"We, the human race," said Daisy. "Earth needs to be represented in the commonwealth. These are exciting times; we can't wait until some existing messenger decides to recruit a human host. That may never happen; it's a personal choice. So the only way to be sure is for us to create a new messenger. A human messenger, our own. Force our way in."

"And you call me selfish?"

"I want to be a messenger so I can help our world, five billion people. Just like Ndavu and Menzere and all the others help their home worlds."

"I'm glad you explained the difference for me."

"All right, I'll admit it. I don't want to die. I'm only sixty-three. If I can help you, then a messenger, Daisy Goodwin, will live on. But it won't be me, not like I am now. I'll be information—but you know that. You have an implant."

"Sure."

"Look at me, Phil. Look." Her ghost was suddenly transformed and Wing saw Daisy as she really was. She had shrunk into a gray, hairless mummy. "I'm rotting away." Her skin looked like cheap leather; there were tubes coming out of the side of her neck. "I want you to feel the pressure I'm feeling."

"Oh, Daisy." He tried to focus in on her eyes. If he fixed on the eyes he would not have to look at her ruined body. He had loved her.

"Pressure, Phil. Can you feel it yet? If I am going to become a messenger, it has to be soon. And I'm going to have to recruit as soon as I make it."

He recoiled from her.

"Information, Phil. They can send me anywhere. That's the real revolution the transmitter has made. I want you." Like a nightmare, she changed back into the Daisy he remembered. "If that's selfish, all right. I want to be with you forever."

"Daisy, *no!*"

"Ndavu told me who you use for an interface. Phil, you can have the real me!"

He had heard too much.

"You have an implant, Phil. Right now you're the only human I can choose."

"Get away!" He grabbed one of the quarry samples and he threw it at the ghost. It bounced off the wall. He could no longer afford to pretend about her. She was trying to exploit his feelings; he had to give them up. Again—and for good this time. "You all want something. Well, I can't save you. Can't even save myself!" He bolted from his chair; it tipped and fell. "How can I make you understand? I can't cope with this, not any of it. It's too much!" He did not know what possessed him; he made no attempt to analyze it. "You all keep pushing . . ." He put a shoulder to the rolltop. "I just want to stop."

"Phil, don't!"

"Pressure?" The workstation inside was as heavy as a refrigerator but he grunted and it tilted slowly and then crashed, sideways, to the floor. "You don't know pressure." The screen had cracked. Daisy looked as if she might cry. He liked that. He kicked Chair 31 over, pulled vitabulk crates down from the stack and danced on the spilled tubes. "So now you want me?" His own stink made him angry. "You've found another use for me?" He ripped the print of John the Baptist off the wall and threw it at her. "I loved you and you lied to me."

Harumen was pounding on the door. "Phillip, are you all right?"

He flung the door open. Harumen tried to come through but he grabbed her by the shoulders and spun her out of the way. She cracked hard against the wall. "Tell Teaqua she can dig a hole and crawl into it." He twittered wildly, taking pleasure from his rage. Wing lurched blindly through the scholars' palace, running a few steps, slowing to a bristling stride, bounding down stairs. He was ready—eager—to fight anyone who tried to block his escape. However, no opponents presented themselves and he fled the building.

Wing had never been out in Kikineas by himself at night. He kept up a jerky pace, sprinting whenever memory flashed their faces at him. Teaqua, Menzere, Ammagon, Ndavu, Harumen, Daisy. Everybody wanted a piece of him. What would be left? "Get away from me!" he growled at the shadows. The dark streets were empty and he chose his path at random. He wanted to be lost. To lose himself.

By the time he reached the waterfront he was exhausted. The wind blew at his mane and his mouth felt very dry. He trudged to the end of the nearest wharf and perched on the edge. The river lapped at the pilings and Wing realized that Kikineas smelled like Portsmouth.

There were two fishing boats tied up, their bows nodding in the current. He watched the reflected starlight dance across the river's crinkled surface. He imagined how easy it would be to slip into the water. Easier than going back a disgrace, humanity's all-time loser. Or going mad on a strange world. He was so tired. Wing lay down on the deck of the wharf and tried to summon the courage to destroy himself. He looked up at the sky and saw his constellation. What would they call it now? Wing the Suicide. He chittered because he could not weep. All he had to do was roll over and sink into the forgiving depths.

But he stayed on the wharf, alone with his black thoughts. In time he slept. And dreamed. In his dream Hanu, the daughter of Chan, appeared to him in all her blue glory, so that he could not help but believe in her. She licked him with her tongue of fire and, as they shared pleasure, she whispered. The stars fluttered down, clung to his fur like snowflakes and warmed the chill that had grown within him.

He woke with Chan's light in his eyes. The answer was so simple he had to twitter. A fisher was mending nets in one of the boats. "I've got it," he called to her. "I know what to do!"

She eyed him suspiciously. "Good."

It was not what anyone else wanted, it was what he, Phillip Wing, had wanted most of all. He had looked right at it, could have recognized it months ago. And it was certainly better than drowning himself.

"Look into the sun." Wing stood up on his second try. He was as stiff as a log.

"Hear your whispers," she replied.

He stumbled through the city back to the scholars' palace.

"Harumen, wake up!" He knocked, pounded, battered. "Let me in."

She opened the door sullenly.

"I've got it. The tomb!" He took her hands as he entered the room. "I had a dream, a vision from Chan. All I need is your help." He pulled her around in a circle, a celebratory dance to inspiration. "Forgive me. Last night . . . I didn't understand. It's *everything*."

She kept staring at him as if he were not making sense.

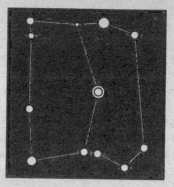

 t first she was
frightened. He had scared her before but never quite like
this. He seemed overjoyed yet there was a crazed edge to
his mood; he was just barely in control of himself. Her
whispers called his behavior manic. All Harumen knew
was that Wing was possessed by something she did not
understand.

He came to her just after dawn, raving about some
dream he had had about Hanu and the stars and Teaqua's tomb. She pressed him about it and he picked her
up and danced her around the room. He put her down
on the bed, bounded over to the door and locked it.
Chittering, he said he could see, finally he could see, and
then he told her that maybe he loved her. When he
asked if she would share pleasure with him, she thought
about saying no for about three seconds. It had been

hard leaving Wing alone; she had wanted him for days but had been too worried to approach him. Ndavu kept saying how fragile he was, how careful they had to be. She had been afraid that she might be the one to break him. Now it was *his* passion that overwhelmed *her*. He lifted her to a new level of arousal and she completely lost herself in sensation. All the troubles and successes, ambitions and fears slid away like their discarded clothing. There was only his embrace, her response— looping back and gathering intensity—then her caress, his trembling reaction. Smells curled into her mouth and she swallowed. They shared each other in a frenzy of pleasure, aligning and realigning their bodies to one purpose, yielding gladly to the wildness. They coupled until both of them shuddered with bliss.

Afterward, as they rested, he stared right into her eyes as if unwilling to pull back into himself. The heat of his gaze warmed her; she stroked the fur on his hip. He shut his eyes for a moment and suddenly he was chittering.

"Are you all right?"

"I was just thinking," he said. "Feeling good about myself actually. You know, they broke up my marriage, lured me into exile, changed me into a alien, made me doubt myself and drove me right to the edge of a nervous breakdown. And I'm lying here asking myself, *that's all?* That's the worst you can do? Come on, I can take all of it and more. I not only survived, I'm *stronger*."

"They? Who?"

"Everybody. Ndavu. Daisy. You. Even me. Sure, I helped make a mess of my life. But now I've got exactly what I want." He reached for her and she hugged him back and soon they were sharing one another again. When they came to themselves this time they both chittered.

Then he told her he had to work. She snuck out to get parchment, ink and pens, and he spent the next few hours sketching. She watched as he muttered to himself, sang snatches of songs she had never heard before, tapped his quill against his forehead while he thought. He seemed absorbed in his drawing; there was a new looseness to the way he held his body. Every so often he glanced up and gave her a playful grin. She was no longer frightened for him.

"Soon." Wing dipped quill into ink and darkened a dimension line.

"It's not a hole, is it?"

"No." Wing twittered. "The opposite of a hole." The ink dried with a soapy fragrance. "Too bad it's so messy."

"Vellum made from the skin of hatchlings." Harumen chided him with mock outrage. "And you're just sketching like it was paper." She wanted to see what he was doing. "*You* wrecked the workstation." He would not let her look.

"I know." He squinted, using his eye to scale the drawing. "Seemed like a good idea at the time."

"Why can't I see?"

"Because." Wing blotted a spill. "Because my dear, you'd offer an opinion, and my mind is already made up. The only one I have to convince now is Teaqua and a little whisper tells me that she's going to love it. And because having a secret is a kind of power, and if you don't mind I intend to keep this one as long as I can."

"Phillip!"

"You'll just have to trust me. Or rather, trust Hanu. It's her idea."

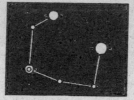

"O r rather, trust Hanu. It's her idea."

"Don't make a joke of it." Harumen rubbed up against the wall like a fidgety cat.

Wing hoped it was a joke. He could not tell whether the idea had come from within or without, although either way he thought it was inspired. He had needed a bit of meteorological luck to see the Glass Cloud; maybe a goddess's tomb needed some divine spark. He was not going to worry about it now. For the first time since he had come to Aseneshesh, he was at peace with himself. He refused to fall into the trap of wondering why.

As he roughed in a final sketch, he wondered whether inspiration might be biochemically similar to falling in love.

(Yes!)

Just drawing a simple roof truss had made him inde-scribably happy. Admiring this last elevation was like gazing into the eyes of his beloved. He glanced at Harumen, who was watching him from the bed. He de-bated moving from one pleasure to another.

The air in the middle of the room condensed into a window. "Phillip!" Ndavu was grim. "Are you all right? I have been . . . what are you doing?"

"Not doing." Wing rolled up the vellum before he could see.

"Here he is." Menzere's ghost floated near the ceiling.

Yet another window opened and Daisy's ghost mate-rialized on the bed. She looked exhausted. "Oh, Phil, it's all my fault. I've been so worried." Harumen's room was too small for all its occupants, real and projected.

"I'm done." Wing tied the sheets of vellum together with a string. "I'm going to see Teaqua."

Then the ghosts were arguing with each other—and him. "His workstation will take days to fix."

"You told him!"

"But what's he got?"

"I don't know," Harumen said calmly.

"You cannot quit like this, Phillip. Too much depends on you."

"Not quitting, Ndavu." Wing was enjoying the com-motion. "Finished. Now we sell it to the client."

"You did this." Ndavu turned to Daisy. "You spoke without authorization."

"Phil, please . . ." She was aghast.

"Would you listen?" Wing waved the sketches at them. "It works. Everybody's going to be happy." He sa-luted them with the roll. "Including me."

"You really have something?" said Menzere. "Show us."

"You'll get a turn." Wing drew back. "After Teaqua."

"I'm coming down to Kikineas." Ndavu seemed the

most upset by Wing's behavior, the least ready to hear what he was saying. "You wait there for me."

"You don't understand." Wing could not resist teasing. "I've heard whispers—it's a miracle."

The commotion escalated to uproar. When the window boundaries touched there was a flash, like sunlight flaring off mirrorglass. Ndavu was ten centimeters above the floor and brushing up against Menzere. Daisy tried to bump past Ndavu. The room smelled of ozone. Wing had to look away from the ghosts and he saw Harumen observing silently. She believed in him. He flagged confidently and pumped his fist for her.

"Shut up! Ndavu, you just wait there at the temple." Wing waved off the messenger's objections. "I'm on my way up. Tell Teaqua."

"Phillip, you are jeopardizing everything—"

Harumen stood and faced down the ghosts. "Whatever he has," she said, "Teaqua wants to see it."

"You're right," Daisy said. "She's right. He decides, Ndavu." She sounded as if she were changing her mind as she spoke. "He's the architect."

Wing was taken aback that she would come to his defense. It had to be some kind of ploy.

"You have no say in this." Ndavu was bitter. "You interfered and now he is crazy, blithering about miracles."

"I'm not blithering."

Daisy stiffened. "If you don't believe in him, why is he here? Give him a chance."

Maybe it was not an act; he believed she might actually be sincere. Nice try, Daisy, Wing thought. But too little and way too late.

"Enough talk." Harumen grabbed Wing and pulled him toward the door. "He's going to see the goddess." Sparks crackled in Wing's fur as they plowed through the ghosts.

Daisy haunted the wagon as Harumen drove Wing up to Quaquonikeesak. However, she was so listless that after a while he wondered aloud whether she ought to break contact and rest for a while.

"I do believe in you, Phil," she murmured. "Always have."

"Sure." He wished she would go away. He did not want her begging for his help—at least not in front of Harumen. So he chattered to keep her from talking. "You won't be disappointed, Daisy." It made no difference to him whether she was sincere or not; he had already let her go. "No one will. It's better than the Cloud. Means more. They'll be handing out promotions for everybody, just you watch. They'll put your statue in Prescott Park, right next to old Uncle Josiah's oak." However, he knew then that what happened on Earth did not matter to him; it was no longer his world. He would not grieve for her passing; she was a stranger.

"Cocky, aren't you?"

"I feel different today. Like I can do no wrong." He considered. "Maybe I'm getting used to this."

The wagon clattered across the Wensbridge and climbed Chemish Hill. The pilgrims along the road goggled and fell back in horror. From Daisy. She was a monster; he was one of them.

(Of us.)

"I was wondering," Daisy said, "if you had thought about it."

Wing knew what she meant. "It's not the kind of offer you forget." He had no intention of becoming a messenger. Even if he did, he was certain that he did not want her with him; he thought he deserved better. "But I don't really need to think about it. I'm just not interested. I'm happy the way I . . ."

Before he could finish, the window closed and Daisy was gone.

By the time they reached the temple, Ndavu had calmed down. He did, however, meet the wagon a couple of hundred meters from the gate and swung aboard while it was still moving.

"The goddess is ready," he said, "to discuss your plan." He made it sound as if it were his idea. "However, I really think you should try it out on me first."

"No." At first the secrecy had been a whim; now he realized its necessity. "Look, if you approve ahead of time, then I'll always wonder whether it's really mine. You tampered with my memory. You could have implanted the idea back then." He rubbed a finger around the top of the sketches. "Maybe that sounds crazy, but I know myself: I find ways to doubt. And if you don't like my idea, well, I'm not going to argue. Something is driving me to pitch it to Teaqua now. I'll never be able to explain it as well again." They passed into the courtyard of the temple. "Maybe that's selfish or paranoid, but there it is. I have to prove something to myself."

Harumen reined in the surunashes. Chiskat and two grooms strode across the temple courtyard toward them.

"You worry me, Phillip." Ndavu was being stubborn. "You are not yourself."

"Not myself?" Wing patted the fur on his chest. "Or myself at last?"

Harumen turned the reins over to a groom and hopped down from the wagon. "Are you coming?"

"Let's go." Wing clapped Ndavu on the back. "I've never felt better in my life." Yet even as he said it he knew his moment would pass. He could not feel inspired forever, any more than he could continually be falling in love. Ndavu was right in a sense: eventually he would have to settle down. However, that was tomorrow's problem.

As usual, two blades stood guard by the stairwell of the innermost court of Temple Quaquonikeesak. Ammagon was chatting with them as Wing's party approached. The door to the vault was open.

"So you've seen something." Ammagon made the sign of supplication to Wing. "Now you believe me."

"I'm impressed," Wing said, "and scared. Did your god do this or did I?"

Ammagon gave him a sly, John-the-Baptist look. "Both."

Ndavu grunted in disgust.

Wing ignored him. "I'm not ready to believe yet." He tilted the sketches toward the prophet. "You don't know what's on these?"

"No."

"Well, you guessed right, or rather the whispers did. How can that be? It's the light, like you said. She'll rest in the light. But even so, it's what I wanted. My work."

Harumen yelped in astonishment and dropped to hands and knees, pressing her forehead to the pavement. Wing turned to see Teaqua floating up out of the stairwell like a bit of milkweed fluff. She did not appear as an idealized ghost but rather showed her true age.

"We've waited so long," said the goddess.

The blades prostrated themselves; they betrayed no shock at seeing a wizened ancient wearing the golden waistsash and cape of blue feathers. When Wing wondered who knew what she really looked like, Hanu informed him that everybody did. The bright deity of the thanksgivings and this declining elder were but avatars created by the divine Teaqua. Chiskat and Ammagon knelt and Wing was about to do the same when Ndavu caught him by the waistsash. Instead they bowed together.

"Come with me." Teaqua's voice was as sharp as two rocks being struck together. She beckoned to Wing, who had been expecting a private audience. He was surprised when Ammagon, Harumen, and Ndavu were allowed to follow him back into the vault.

As she led them to the reception room, Wing realized that this was Teaqua herself, not a ghost. He remembered her scent: that attic smell, dry and papery. Although her feet did not touch the ground, some of her feathers dragged, rustling against the spiral ramp. She glided quickly down to the hall of dolls where she had first received Wing.

As he threaded between the figurines, Wing noticed some differences in Teaqua's congregation of stone. Dust had settled thickly on many of the statues arrayed in the miniature rooms which formed the walls. All of these older works represented Chani. The overflow ranks on the floor were mostly alien. Clearly Teaqua had underestimated the numbers and kinds of creatures who would someday bow to her.

She settled on her couch with a pained grunt and adjusted her regalia. Four pillows from her own couch were positioned between her throne and the rows of statues; she bade her visitors kneel.

Wing was already imagining the reactions of his audience as he took his place. Teaqua would embrace the plan with weary gratitude. The symbolism would appeal to Harumen; Ammagon would see the hand of his god. From Ndavu Wing expected not only approval but respect. At last. Wing could barely resist hugging himself in anticipation. He wanted to blurt it all out—*now*. Teaqua, however, had a different agenda.

"Hanu visited us last night," she said. "We spoke of many things, of Chan's will and the world. She said she'd licked Phillip Wing's eyes so that he could see what he had to do."

Wing shivered, then steadied himself.

"You've brought us the shrine our sister promised?"

"Yes." Hanu must have had a busy night. "That is, I've drawn plans." The dreamy inevitability of her mysticism disturbed him. "But they're mine!" He was not going to let anyone tell him that he was a slave of the whispers. He still believed in free will. "No one else could've done this for you." Flustered, he offered her the sketches.

She ignored them. "Then you've bowed to Chan." She gestured at the statues which surrounded them. "As we all must." She turned to address the other three then, as if she did not care to see what he had done. He could not help but remember Daisy's advice: they'll take whatever you give them. He felt foolish holding out the roll of sketches; he wanted to throw it at her.

"Hanu says that soon we can put our burden down. She revealed the god's plan for our people and we saw that it was right and just. When we go back to Chan, the thearchy must end. The time has come for a new order."

"Teaqua, no!" Ammagon came off his pillow. "The people aren't ready—you'll shake the faith." He glanced desperately about for support. Ndavu was beaming, Harumen looked wary. Wing was too frustrated to care about local politics. "It was a false vision," said the prophet.

"Chan and Teaqua," she said. "One and the same one." Her expression turned hard as ice. "You don't want to hear our bequest."

He sank back into place, seething. "I'll listen."

She spoke as if reading a proclamation. "To our prophet we give the northern coastlands, the mountains and all of Riverside. We leave you the past, Ammagon, the greatest part of our legacy. It's for you to keep and preserve the old ways. Look into the sun and hear your whispers."

Ammagon twitched as if his pillow were burning him but said nothing.

"To Harumen—"

"No." She flagged embarrassment. "I'm tired of all the rivalries. This isn't what I want anymore, Teaqua. They've changed me, Phillip, the messengers. Pick someone else, Ipposkenick or Arinash—anyone. I'm not—"

"You're our cub, Harumen," Teaqua said harshly. "You're bound to us. You'll rule the city of scholars and the southern coast. To you we leave the present, the world with all its problems. In Riverside life is easy and the whispers are clear. Kikineas is a misty, difficult place; its people have learned to think for themselves. You say you're changing? Good. Find a way to live with it; many will be coming to change with you. Let the messengers help. They say there are lands across the sea. These also we give to you; take them back in our name. Chan's light can warm both the new and the old."

The longer she talked the more Wing's design seemed an instrument of her new policy. He could see how they fit together as if both were parts of a master plan.

Ammagon still did not like it. "One god, Teaqua," he said. "One people."

"The whispers aren't the only way to know the god," she replied. "Those who are locked in silence need another way to look into the sun. They'll never follow you, Ammagon."

He bristled.

"To you, Ndavu, we leave our blessing: teach our people. Their bellies may be full but their minds are starving and so the Hunger War drags on. It's time to make a true peace. Help them understand the commonwealth and its worlds. Turn them gently toward the future, so that someday they can carry word of Chan to the stars."

Something went out of Teaqua after she finished this last speech; the shift in her mood was subtle but unmistakable. Her shoulders dipped, the light in her eyes dimmed. Before, she might have been an actor giving a rehearsed speech; now she sagged out of character and was her old spent self again.

"It just won't work," said Ammagon. "People won't understand. I don't understand."

"You have the whispers to guide you," said Teaqua.

"But as you say, not everyone hears the whispers." Harumen seemed uneasy to be taking Ammagon's side. "And I'm not sure I trust the messengers."

Wing glanced over at Ndavu, expecting him to object. The messenger stared back at Wing, as if challenging *him* to speak up.

Meanwhile Teaqua was in retreat, her certainty crumbling. "Nothing will be the same," the goddess agreed vaguely. "It's so; the whispers will pass." She paused, drawing her feathered cloak around her. "Chan sees far and our sight is failing." She gazed across the ranks of her stone worshipers, as if taking comfort from their eternal and unthinking homage. "There are unholy times coming."

She seemed so confused that Wing wondered whether she disagreed with her own bequest. The division of Aseneshesh struck him as creative but very risky statecraft. He had always thought Teaqua a conservative; suddenly she was acting like a visionary. Maybe Hanu had not come to her in the night to consult but rather to inspire. That was what Ndavu had claimed from the first. The goddess was herself subject to whispers. And who could resist a true inspiration? Certainly Wing had not.

Yet he could not believe that a sun had intervened in his life. It was absurd. He knew himself and his work and this design was certainly his: done in his hand, shaped by his imagination, sprung from the same place as the Glass Cloud. They were trying to diminish him with their superstitions. They had made him angry.

"So it's all settled then?" He untied the sketches.

"Chan wins again. You know, Hanu came to me too. Anyone want to see what she left?"

"Yes." Teaqua cocked her head in suspicion and it occurred to Wing that he could still wreck everything if he tried. "Show us." He could still prove he had free will, but only at the expense of his masterpiece.

"Be careful, Phillip." Ndavu shifted a little closer to get a peek at the drawings. "This is important."

"You asked for a shrine that your people could build. Here's what I recommend."

Teaqua finally took her sketches. Some would probably need explanation, the floor plans and framing diagrams, but he had also drawn a rendering that anyone could understand. She unrolled them. The vellum trembled in her hands. She flagged outrage.

"What is this?" Wing had a glimpse of how fearsome she must have been at the height of her powers. "What?" Her voice cracked.

Ndavu reached for the roll of sketches. "If it displeases you, he can still—"

Teaqua was not listening. She struggled out of her nest of pillows and stood, holding the rendering at arm's length. "You cheated Hanu." She released it. "Go, all of you. Leave us." It fluttered to the floor.

Ammagon and Ndavu pounced at the same moment. What they saw were sketches for the construction of a timber-framed, post-and-truss building, approximately twenty by thirty meters. Wing had adapted the structural system from the highland cottages he had visited. The main posts propped up tie beams which supported the roof trusses; it was a simple variation on the box frame. It rose eighteen meters from bottom plate to ridgepole. The foundation of the shrine was a raftlike assemblage of logs, rough-cut clapboards covered the exterior walls and it was roofed with timber shakes. It had one door; Wing had intended to let Teaqua decide about windows. It could have been the lone building on a hardscrabble farm in Netasu, sheltering farmers, beasts and crops under one roof. It might have been a warehouse in Uritammous or a barn on Nish. It would not even have been out of place in colonial Portsmouth—perhaps the first home of the prospering Dr. Nathaniel Goodwin, before he could afford to build Piscataqua House.

"This," said Ammagon, shaking the plan triumphantly, "is an insult." If he could topple Wing, perhaps Teaqua's radical bequest would fall as well.

"I trusted you." Ndavu was wounded. "I took you where you wanted to go. You must have seen something."

Wing chittered, enjoying himself. "This."

"*Leave.*" Teaqua swayed in her anger; clearly Hanu had not prepared her for this. Wing's confidence leapt. He imagined her whispers rising to a shriek.

He could no longer kneel. It was his turn now. "All structural members are hardwood; some may have to be reinforced with iron rods. And although I haven't shown it on the plans, all exterior surfaces must be sheathed with polished gold leaf."

"He's mocking you." Ammagon was not about to let Teaqua be mollified. "Trying to mask his scorn for us with gold. Is this a building people will remember the way they remember your palace at Nur, or Temple Quaquonikeesak, or the Eye at Harean?"

"Ammagon is ready to speak in your name." Wing was close enough to touch the goddess; she did not shrink from him. "Eager. But I'd rather hear it from you. Something's wrong?"

"More." The goddess batted at the vellum rendering and Ammagon obligingly let it drop once again. "We want more than a house that any farmer can build." She pushed the sketches toward him with her foot.

264

"But no one, farmer, scholar or priest, would ever think of putting your house where I'll put it."

"Where?"

"Where all the people can see." Wing raised his arm and pointed straight up. He realized he looked like Da Vinci's Baptist. "In the sky."

It was the first time he had said it aloud but it had exactly the effect he had imagined. It was as if he had uttered some arcane spell which had brought everyone in the room under his sway. He thought that Ndavu must have understood at once; Wing knew he had the others' attention.

"I've done not only what you asked but also what you left unsaid. The people will see your shrine racing across the night sky, a golden star shining for all time in Chan's light. They'll know you are with them, yet you'll also be with Chan as no one has ever been. It's the only shrine worthy of a goddess."

At first he worried that the goddess had snapped. Her head twitched slightly, her eyes were empty. Lost in her whispers?

"How can a house get into the sky?" Ammagon, meanwhile, was desperate.

"Teaqua knows," said Wing. "She already has satellites of her own. She's always borrowed from the messengers when it suited her purposes. This building has approximately the same mass as a loaded grain pod. Someone will have to help me calculate the stresses of boosting it to low orbit, but that shouldn't be a major problem. Teaqua, you said you want your people to keep faith with Chan and at the same time take their place in the commonwealth. Show them how. Let the messengers help you join Chan. If you trust the messengers, the people will too. You'll be leaving behind an everlasting sign of peace and cooperation. They'll remember you every night, for as long as your people look into the sky.

Your shrine will be more powerful than the whispers. If you really want them to go to the stars someday, lead them yourself."

A tremor shot through Teaqua. She stared at him as if he were an apparition, bowed and made the sign of supplication—to him. Then she turned away and stooped, pushing at the pillows on her throne.

Harumen took his hand and squeezed it. She flagged awe—of him. However, Wing did not know what to make of Teaqua's behavior until Ndavu squeezed his arm. "I picked well," said the messenger.

"Chan is great," said Teaqua as she produced a new statue from behind a cushion. Trembling, she offered it to Wing, indicating that he was to place it in the front row of her worshipers.

Somehow they had gotten a picture of Wing before he had been reshaped. Even so the proportions were all wrong; the sculptor had elongated his body to Chani size. The stone eyes were half-lidded and he was smiling as if amused by some private joke. Wing stooped to set the piece in the place of honor. When he straightened, his face mirrored the sculptor's conceit.

At that moment he felt an odd shifting inside his head, as if something had finally settled into place.

(I'm leaving now. You don't need me anymore.)

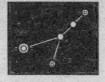

**C**han was making Wing crazy. He shielded his eyes but the midday glare still scorched his optic nerves and blazed inside his head. He was sure that if he actually looked into the sun he might explode. It was his own fault. Last night he had drunk enough wine to flood Riverside; now he owed a staggering debt to pain. Wing would have come drunk to the ceremony if Menzere had given him the chance.

"How come I have to be here live and you get to send a ghost?" Wing said.

"It is not easy projecting a ghost," said Menzere. "Sometimes it is more trouble than it is worth."

The light was merciless. It pounded colors flat and seethed across the river. Thought faded in such light; curiosity withered. He thought Riverside was the perfect place for Ammagon's conservative regime.

"Here they come," said Menzere. The procession had marched completely around Mateag island; Wing thought some of them must be blinded by now. A cohort of blades swept through the crowds toward the shrine. Behind them strode Harumen and Ammagon. Next came Teaqua's litter and then Ndavu, walking alone, nobody within twenty meters of him. A hundred or so bell ringers followed, setting the pace with their solemn polyphony. Trailing in their wake was half the population of Riverside, from the looks of it.

Wing had never had much use for dedications. They were nothing but rituals to force architects to hand over their work to people who did not understand it. Everyone was calling his shrine the godstar. Wing hated the name. People told him it was a miracle, a direct intervention by Chan, the ultimate expression of Teaqua's divinity. Wing was already a footnote, and he had no doubt that he would soon be forgotten.

However, that had always been the fate of architects. His inspiration belonged to them now; let them name it what they wanted. All they expected of Wing was that he watch the launch and look pleased and not throw up, at least until after the ceremony. He thought he could handle it, if only they would hurry.

"I'm thirsty," Wing said.

"It will not be much longer." Menzere, at least, was sympathetic. Wing appreciated that. It helped him cope, even if it did not make his decision any easier. After today his work here would be done. The messengers had held the ship that had brought the tachyon transmitter. It was going uptime soon. If he left with it, he could return home. But where was home? Did he want really to start his life all over again? He had no interest in taking part in Earth's politics—or its epidemics. Sometimes he wished he still had Hanu to consult; he could use some inspiration.

He had been thinking a lot about his father lately. The binges, the silences, the tears had always made Wing feel guilty, as if the father's sadness had been the son's fault. Now he realized that the old man had lost his wife, his country, part of himself; he had good reason to seek the comforts of oblivion. Wing knew exactly how it must have been. He himself could not say that any single moment of loss was too awful to bear. Rather it was the accumulation of minute upon minute, day after day with no relief. Part of him was gone and would not be replaced. The sense of dismemberment was inescapable—unless he escaped himself altogether. It was as if his hand had been amputated. No, he thought, that wasn't right. He clapped hands to eyes, closing out the searing light. It was as if he had gone blind. Someone had said it to him once. Look into the sun and go blind.

But his father had never found anyone in the new country to ease the aching solitude, the grinding sense of loss. His father had never dared to belong again, not even to his son. Wing had Harumen to heal him. Or rather he could have her, if only he could commit himself. He had already made the transition; if he left now he would have to make another, perhaps many more. He saw himself changing again and again, always becoming but never quite being. Harumen wanted him. What did he want?

"Phillip," said Menzere. Wing uncovered his face.

The shrine was draped in a tarpaulin, an enormous patchwork in shades of blue, staked to the ground. All of Aseneshesh had contributed to the shrine's construction so that the project had been finished in a matter of months. The wood had come from virgin stands along the north coast; it had been milled in Kunish, shipped halfway around the continent to Cosh and barged up the Chowhesu. The structural iron and most of the gold leaf had been dug from highland mines, although every temple on Aseneshesh had contributed some small golden treasure: icons, goblets, candlesticks. It had all come to Mateag, where master carpenters and gilders and black-smiths assembled the shrine on the launch platform pro-vided by the messengers.

The procession arrived at the shrine. Blades fanned out and pushed the throng back from the immediate launch area. Several helped Teaqua descend from her litter. She wore her glass crown and prism torque and a golden robe which gleamed in the sunlight. As she hobbled up the stairs, Wing thought the brilliant regalia too large for her: she looked like a child dressed in her mother's clothes. The reflections made her hard to watch for long, but from the stoop of her shoulders and her labored gait, he realized that she was making her farewell in her true form. She reached the entrance to the shrine, turned and gestured for her two successors to follow. Wing could scarcely comprehend, much less accept, what Teaqua was about to do. The final act of her long reign would be a ghastly one. The godstar had no life-support systems.

It was the custom, when shriving no longer brought relief, to make a final pilgrimage to Firstlight, Hanu's mountain. No ancient ever returned from Firstlight. Wing could not imagine marching calmly to die of ex-posure as countless pilgrims had done. As Teaqua would soon do. He wondered if she realized how she would die: alone, gasping in the thin and finally unbreathable air, scrabbling across the floor as she coughed crystals of blood into the cruel and frigid vacuum of space.

Wing felt queasy.

Her people would never know. They would see only a brilliant apotheosis. The messengers were putting on a show for the entire world. In most cities and towns there were enormous windows open, large enough to project a full-sized ghost of the shrine. Everyone could watch as if it were happening before their eyes. In Kikineas the shrine would take off from Quaquonikeesak; in Uritammous it would emerge from the Skywater and in Hunnakay it would rise over the Chowhesu. Big as life.

All over but the crying, thought Wing. Do they still say that? Except I can't cry. Can't laugh either.

Ammagon and Harumen knelt before Teaqua. She went to each, spit on her hand, rubbed it into their manes. Ndavu looked up from the stairway leading to the launch platform. The goddess proclaimed her bequest in public then, a more elaborate recapitulation of what she had said in the vault. The crowd rippled with religious fervor. Then she turned and pushed through the opening in the shroud. She did not wave or say good-bye or bless anyone. She did not hesitate at all.

The new rulers of Aseneshesh came down off the platform. For a time there was no sound but the wind. The ropes which held the tarpaulin down went taut and began to sing. Wing saw the ridgeline of the roof knife slowly upward, its edge clear beneath the fabric. Seams split, lines snapped and the shrine burst free of its shroud. It looked like a place where the sky had caught fire. Then everyone was shouting, pointing, dancing, waving their arms, hugging one another. Chan's light flared off the gold leaf and a new sun climbed into the sky. It was probably the greatest moment in the history of these people—and in Wing's career. He watched them, wondering why they were so happy. He could not possibly understand them; it was wrong to pretend that he did. When he finally glanced up, the shrine was a spark lost in the ethereal blue. Then it was gone.

"Congratulations," said Menzere. "It was almost enough to make a believer of me."

It was time to start a new project, Wing thought. A renovation. He was going to have to rebuild his life.

Wing had reason to believe that he was the only sober person in Harean that night. He was surprised that he did not feel like drinking. He was in a strange mood, indeed. His enthusiasm for the shrine had cooled and he blamed Teaqua. Not that it would have made any difference, but he realized now that he objected to what she had done. He would never be able to think of the shrine again without imagining her last spasms of beatific agony. He was still fiercely proud of the idea of the orbiting tomb but somehow she had taken its reality away from him. At the price of her life, Teaqua had made the god-star her own.

Long after midnight, there came a knock. When he answered it, Harumen pushed him back into the room, kicked the door shut and embraced him with a boozy vigor that bent his ribs.

"We watched her pass over," she said. "About an hour ago. It was beautiful."

"Sorry I missed it." He grimaced. "I was busy."

"She was very brave at the end, don't you think?" The fragrance of incense clung to her mane. "I couldn't have done it."

He hugged her. "Good." When he wrapped his arms around Harumen, everything was simple. He loved her; he wanted to be with her. It did not matter that he was not part of her world.

She dragged him over to the bed and they shared pleasure. Wing was surprised at how much he wanted her. Their entwining lacked the surprised abandon of their early days. Yet for all its deliberateness, Wing found it more satisfying. Together they had done something remarkable; this was the best way to reaffirm their unlikely bond. Two beings separated by a vast abyss of nature and nurture had come to respect and trust and love one another. The sheer improbability of these feelings made their relationship a kind of miracle. The best kind. But miracles are fleeting. Afterward Wing felt the distance stretching between them.

"This can't go on," he said.

"Not if you're leaving, no." She groomed the fur on his chest. "So don't."

For a time neither of them spoke. Wing broke the silence. "I think I have to."

"You know what I think?" Her breath smelled of wine. "You're afraid to stay. Afraid you might be happy."

"Happy?" He scowled. "What would I do here?"

"Whatever you want."

"I don't know what I want. That's always been my problem."

"And I don't want to rule." Harumen ran a fingertip around his lips. "But I have to."

He liked it when she touched him. "The people need you. Teaqua chose well."

"I never wanted it. You know; you're my witness." She sighed and snuggled up to him. "What will you tell them about us? If you go back?"

Wing had not thought about it. "I don't know." He licked her finger. "You're a mystery."

"You don't like mysteries. They worry you."

"I suppose." He reached behind his neck and slapped at the nodes at the back of his skull. "Most of what I know about you comes from here. That's not me. How can I keep the implant—much less this body—and be myself?"

"You're always wading against the current." She rolled away from him and stood up, flagging her annoyance. "Flow with life, don't fight it. We change, Phillip. My implant has become part of me, part of what I am." She slithered into her tunic. "You are what you are *now*, not what you were or what you might be someday. I don't say it's easy to accept." She stooped to pick up her waistsash; it was made of spun gold. "Sometimes you have to be able to hold true and false in your mind at the same time. You have to believe in both Chan and the messengers. And if it doesn't always make sense, so what?"

He reached for her but she batted his hand and turned away.

"I want you to stay with me, Phillip Wing." She stopped at the door. "But I can let you go if I have to." Then she left him.

On the night before Wing was to leave Aseneshesh, Ndavu threw a huge party for him in the commons of the scholars' palace. Wing's expectations for the evening were low. It was not that he minded the company of the scholars; he liked Arinash and Chenock and especially cranky Ipposkenick. He was glad for the chance to say good-bye to Menzere. Ndavu, however, had invited priests and pedants from every temple in Kikineas and the local keeper chief and her deputies and various other minor functionaries whom the messenger was cultivating. Teaqua had announced the design for a new political structure, now Ndavu was determined to see it built. Wing, however, did not care about sewers or the beggar situation or temple gossip and he thought it poor taste for the messenger to use the occasion for public relations.

So when Chenock waved a wine pot at him, Wing passed his mug without hesitation, ending weeks of abstinence on a moment's whim. He told himself that a judicious application of alcohol would help him get through the evening and indeed, he felt more convivial after indulging. However, no amount of wine could mask the fact that Harumen had yet to arrive.

In order to give the neophyte party-goers something to do, Ndavu had provided a banquet. The variety was extensive, if somewhat inappropriate for the evening meal. Mush was not on the menu. There were platters of boiled breadroot garnished with baby's mane, several kinds of fish, loaves of wheat and rye breads, still warm from the oven, the typically repulsive assortment of arthropods and annelids, some of them cooked, many still squirming, baskets of fresh fruit and flowers. Wing was offered a platter of pizza-flavored vitabulk, but he chose from the common table instead, knowing that he would get more than his fill of bulk during the trip back to Earth. The meal was served, consumed with gusto and cleared away and still Harumen had not put in an appearance. The wine continued to flow during the evening's entertainment. There were acrobats who raised tumbling to an art form, a quartet who played droning stringed instruments and finally a chorus who sang songs about sharing pleasure and the shortness of summer. The weather had already begun to turn here in Kikineas. There was a chill in the air. Yet another reason to be going; Wing was working hard to come up with them.

Eventually Ndavu passed behind his chair, reached around and picked up Wing's mug.

"Let us share this wine to honor Phillip Wing, who is leaving." He held the mug high, for all to see. "You may all join in." The assemblage was agreeable if somewhat befuddled. Some quickly exchanged mugs with their neighbors, others hoisted what was in front of them. "This world will honor his name as long as the godstar shines."

Wing took back the mug and proposed his own toast. "I honor you, the people of Aseneshesh. Tonight I feel almost as if I were one of you." He drank and everyone followed. He did not mind at all that several priests looked insulted as they lifted their mugs.

Ndavu smiled for his audience and thrust his right arm toward Wing. Wing drew back, momentarily confused. He did not recognize this sign at first, then he realized that the messenger wanted to shake hands. It had been a long time. Ndavu said, "I will miss you, Phillip." A few of the guests turned to one another and politely shook hands without having any idea what they were doing. Ndavu clapped Wing on the back and went to work the crowd.

Ipposkenick swerved across the room to him, obviously under the influence of wine and strong emotion. "I'm sorry to see you go, Phillip Wing."

"You've been a friend, Ippo. I appreciated your help."

"Just wanted to say . . ." The scholar leaned across the table to confide in Wing; he could smell Ipposkenick's sour breath. Wing believed he was about to be subjected to a heartfelt and embarrassing farewell. ". . . have to tell you. Didn't like it." He grabbed at Wing's arm to keep from falling over. "The godstar, you know. Clever maybe, but not what I would've done."

Wing caught a glimpse of Menzere's ghost over the scholar's shoulder. The eavesdropping messenger flagged sympathy. "That's all right, my friend," said Wing. "You just keep thinking for yourself." Wing patted Ipposkenick's arm. "That's what Harumen needs her scholars for."

Time seemed to meander as the wine flowed. Wing was just getting up to relieve himself when a window opened beside his table. Ammagon appeared and the good-natured din of the party quieted abruptly. Projecting his ghost into Harumen's territory could easily be considered a provocation. It was no secret that Ammagon was unhappy with the division of the thearchy. Already relations between the temple, which Ammagon now controlled, and Harumen's new government of scholars had been strained.

"Phillip." Ammagon made the sign of supplication. Wing sat back down and crossed his legs.

Ammagon faced the room. "You people." The loyalists in the room squirmed. "Why are you here?"

"This is Phillip's last night." Ndavu hurried up to Ammagon. He did not seem at all upset to have this uninvited guest. "He is leaving tomorrow."

Ammagon gave the messenger a look of pity and contempt. "No." He gestured across the table at Wing. "No, you're not finished here, Phillip. If Harumen can't find anything for you to do, I can."

"I don't think I can stay." Wing was trying to be polite but he was annoyed that Ammagon talked to him and played to the crowd at the same time.

"Is that what your whispers tell you?"

"I don't hear whispers," he said harshly, hoping maybe Ammagon would take offense and disappear. He wondered why Ndavu did not do something. He wished Harumen were here.

A ripple passed through the crowd. Some people shifted uncomfortably in their places, others repeated his admission to those out of earshot. Although Wing knew that many in the room did not hear the god, there was something brazen about a public admission, even by an alien.

"Then look inward, Phillip," said Ammagon. "Keep looking for what they don't want you to see. I told you before that Chan has shown me the new world. You're part of it." He was in full voice now; it was as if he were hosting the daily thanksgiving. "I say to you all, go home now. You've gathered here for no good reason." He bowed to Wing and his window closed.

Wing expected Ndavu to be more flustered. Instead the messenger meekly accepted the intrusion. "Perhaps it *is* time to end this. Phillip, you have done well. Have a safe journey." He turned, gave Wing and the assembled guests an airy wave and strode from the room. Wing sat frozen at his table, watching numbly as people began to follow the messenger out. In silence. It was the most bizarre ending to a party that Wing had ever witnessed, although probably most of the guests thought this was some quirk of human etiquette. A few scholars came up to murmur last good-byes. Wing recrossed his legs.

He would have suspected some kind of collusion between Ammagon and the messenger—except that he could not imagine why they would bother. When he finally got up to leave, he felt edgy. Suspicious. What else could they want from him?

All he wanted was to see Harumen.


Just as Wing entered his room, Daisy's ghost appeared. "I need to talk to you, Phil. Please? I can't stay long; I had to call in a lot of favors to get transmitter time. It's costing us a great deal."

"Us?" Wing sighed and shut the door. "We're talking."

"I'm glad you're coming back, Phil. Really. You've already made a difference in the polls. We understand the commonwealth is pleased with your work. We're all so proud—I'm proud of you. I knew you could do it. But it would mean so much more if you could just send a ghost, explain exactly what you've done. Tell us more about the commonwealth."

"You still want the sales pitch."

"The truth, Phil. That's all."

He snorted. "I don't know what the truth is."

"How long would it take? A few hours. You can do it on the way to the exchange aperture. We'll make the arrangements. But once you go uptime, the opportunity is lost. The transmitter won't—"

"Why, Daisy? Why should I do this?"

"For your world."

"Don't have one."

"Then why are you coming back?"

Wing could not think of a reply.

"What can I say to you, Phil? What do you want to hear?"

"From you, nothing." Her ghost appeared as usual: a handsome woman in her mid-thirties wearing a blue dress. But it was a lie, a clever tool she had contrived to manipulate fossil feelings. Seeing her ghost only made Wing mad. "You know, I feel sorry for you, Daisy. You've given yourself over to this cause, this *message*, but I can't see that it's done much for you. You've always been so hard. Maybe it's good to be hardheaded, but you've still got a heart like a stone. Otherwise you'd know better than to keep—"

Harumen did not bother to knock. She opened the door and froze. For a moment she and Daisy stared at each other.

"You're busy." Harumen began to pull the door shut again.

Wing caught it. "Go away, Daisy."

"Please, Phil."

"I'll think about it. But go away. Now!" He swiped his arm back and forth through her image as if to clear his way through a puff of smoke. Static crackled in his fur.

When she was gone, Wing drew Harumen into the room and they embraced. "I missed you." He rubbed his cheek against the velvet fur on her forehead.

"I came to say I love you," Harumen whispered. "I want you to know what that means."

He was lying next to Harumen, his belly pressed against the curve of her spine. Her fragrance seemed to bloom inside his head. There was something different about it; he realized he was smelling himself as well. He liked the way their scents mingled.

The sky was turning the blue of smoke and through the open shutters he could just see the rim of the sun over the rooftops of Kikineas. 82 Eridani. Spectral class G5. Expected lifespan, 12.65892 billion years. Yet it was also Chan. The god of the Chani. Gods never die. What had she said to him? Sometimes you have to be able to hold true and false in your mind at the same time. In a little while Ndavu would come by to take him to the messenger base. If he wanted.

He looked into the sun. There was no revelation, only the seashore whisper of his lover's breath. He looked inward then and saw that the interface had changed again. He saw inside of himself and there was Phillip Wing at rest. Happy. At peace as a Chani.

(If we love her, why are we going?) he said to himself.

Wing shivered. This was going to take some getting used to. He woke Harumen up to tell her the news.

# ACKNOWLEDGMENTS

I'd like to thank the following people for their help and support: Patrick Delahunt, Gardner Dozois, Barbara Flynn, James Frenkel, Sue Hall, Beth Meacham, Lucius Shepard, Dori Stratton and the Philfordians.

A special thanks to my family and to John Kessel, Sheila Williams and Connie Willis for listening.

# THE BEST IN SCIENCE FICTION

# THE TOR DOUBLES

Two complete short science fiction novels in one volume!

---

# THERE WILL BE WAR

Created by J. E. Pournelle
John F. Carr, Associate Editor

---

# THE SAGA CONTINUES...